"*Your grandfather has given me permission to court you,*"

Nikolai said. "If you agree, we can be married right after New Year's."

For a moment, Katya imagined she was hearing things. "But that's absolute craziness! We don't even *know* each other, Nikolai," she gasped.

"I admit what I'm proposing is a drastic solution," he confessed. "But I'm afraid it's your only chance. You'll have to be a consummate actress."

What in God's name was he talking about?

"As my wife—in name only, of course," he continued, "it will be your job to convince the authorities you've had a change of heart, that you want to remain here because of me. Eventually you may be allowed to travel with me. Then I can arrange for your escape." He paused a moment. "But we can only succeed if you can make them believe that we married for love."

Dear Reader,

When two people fall in love, the world is suddenly new and exciting, and it's that same excitement we bring to you in Silhouette Intimate Moments. These are stories with scope and grandeur. The characters lead lives we all dream of, and everything they do reflects the wonder of being in love.

Longer and more sensuous than most romances, Silhouette Intimate Moments novels take you away from everyday life and let you share the magic of love. Adventure, glamour, drama, even suspense—these are the passwords that let you into a world where love has a power beyond the ordinary, where the best authors in the field today create stories of love and commitment that will stay with you always.

In coming months look for novels by your favorite authors: Kathleen Creighton, Heather Graham Pozzessere, Nora Roberts and Marilyn Pappano, to name just a few. And whenever you buy books, look for all the Silhouette Intimate Moments, love stories *for* today's woman *by* today's woman.

Leslie J. Wainger
Senior Editor and Editorial Coordinator

Never Say Goodbye

SUZANNE CAREY

Silhouette Intimate Moments

Published by Silhouette Books New York

America's Publisher of Contemporary Romance

SILHOUETTE BOOKS
300 East 42nd St., New York, N.Y. 10017

ISBN: 0-373-07330-5

First Silhouette Books printing April 1990

Printed in the U.S.A.

SUZANNE CAREY

is a former reporter and magazine editor who prefers to write romance novels because they add to the sum total of love in the world.

For William Palmer Matson,
my best friend and beloved husband

PART ONE

Chapter 1

As fine and grainy as soap powder, the first snow of the coming winter blew sharply against the windowpanes. Hugging her sweater more closely around her shoulders and pulling down the misshapen wool skirt she'd bought last week at GUM, the huge state-run department store, Katya Dane pretended to be reading the book in her lap. In reality she was listening to the low rumble of voices. Half a world away from everything that was familiar to her, she was trying to catch what snatches of conversation she could.

Tonight, as usual, the two men who leaned toward each other over the small, old-fashioned table turned on the radio as soon as they finished their chess game. Military music all but drowned out what they were saying. Katya, seated just a few paces from them, could distinguish only a word of two despite her proficiency in Russian. Naturally she knew that the electronic listening device—assuming one had been planted in the small, shabby apartment—would be similarly thwarted.

As they spoke, the men sipped hot, sweetened tea from plain glass tumblers. Their deep regard for each other was evident in every look, every gesture. Nonetheless, their friendship puzzled her deeply. It wasn't just the disparity in their ages that made it seem so unlikely to her. Their philosophical differences were also great. How could two men be such good friends and yet have completely divergent ways of looking at the world?

Briefly she focused on the elder of the two, who was also her grandfather. Bearded and bent with thinning hair, a nose like an eagle's beak and eyes that gleamed as lively as any teenager's behind thick glasses, seventy-year-old Lev Petrovsky still worked part-time as an English instructor at Moscow University, where he was the only Jew on the faculty. Long since widowed, he'd never sought safe passage to the West. To Katya, his willingness to remain in the Soviet Union was inexplicable since his only child, her mother, lived in faraway Wisconsin.

Since arriving in the Soviet Union a month and a half before, she'd asked her grandfather a thousand questions. He'd responded to them all with deceptively offhand answers and the same ironic smile. Of course he was opposed to totalitarian rule, just as her parents were. Whenever he could in his teaching at the university, he hinted at concepts such as freedom and self-determination. And he liked to think it made a difference. But that didn't happen often. He had to admit that sometimes he got discouraged and lonely and wanted his family near him again.

"Then why haven't you applied to emigrate, Grandfather?" she'd asked with all the straightforward logic of her youth. "It wouldn't mean the end of your career. I'm sure you could teach in the United States."

His response had been a simple one, so simple she hadn't fully understood it. "Ah, but that's easy, dear child," he'd told her softly. "Russia is my home."

It was because of Lev that she'd come to Moscow in the first place, flying in the face of her parents' most urgent counsel. Without their knowledge, she'd changed tour groups and applied for a Soviet visa in Berlin. She'd had no way of knowing then that such visas usually took at least a month to get. Hers hadn't. The bland, bespectacled clerk at the Intourist office had been exceptionally helpful. In retrospect she guessed that he or one of his superiors had recognized her as the daughter of Alex and Petra Dane. It was her theory that they'd wanted to get her into Russia, then find a way of keeping her there.

A premonition of trouble had prickled her awareness as she'd boarded her flight. And she'd ignored that, too. My grandfather's getting old, she'd reasoned. We've never met, and if I don't go now it may be too late. There may never be another chance. She'd also wanted very much to see the country of her heritage, view firsthand the monolithic and sometimes contradictory country she'd studied while acquiring her international studies degree.

On some deeper level, she supposed, she'd pictured herself standing nervously in the tired and disgruntled queue of tourists at Sheremetyevo Airport. Even though she'd been braced for the sudden stab of fear she'd felt when a grimly triumphant official had held up the slender book of contraband poems she'd tucked in her suitcase beneath her underwear, she hadn't expected things to turn out like *this*.

She didn't know very much about Nikolai Dvorov, the man who was so deeply engrossed in conversation with Lev. From Lev she'd learned that Nikolai was the son of Dmitri Dvorov, a high party official. No doubt because of his father's position and influence, thirty-four-year-old Nikolai held an important cultural affairs post with the Soviet government.

Nikolai's job, her grandfather had confided, sometimes required extended business trips to London and other cities outside the Soviet bloc, particularly in the Scandinavian countries. Despite increased cultural exchanges in these days of *glasnost*, it placed Nikolai in a small, elite group of Soviet citizens—those regularly permitted to travel abroad.

She was certain that her father's dark-haired, goodlooking friend was also an officer in the KGB, the Russian counterpart of the United States' Central Intelligence Agency. Without exception, all Soviet cultural ministers were spies—or so her parents claimed.

Because of her questionable status as an American citizen whose passport had been confiscated by the authorities, she kept a low profile whenever Nikolai was in the apartment. It had occurred to her that he might be stopping by from time to time especially to check on her. She wondered if he monitored her comings and goings on other occasions as well.

Without a purpose of that kind, his friendship with her grandfather simply didn't make sense. What common bond could a rising star in Soviet officialdom possibly have with an elderly Jew whose main interests were literary and religious? Surely their friendship wasn't based solely on a shared passion for chess. Chess had been played since the tenth century in Russia. Accomplished chess partners weren't that difficult to come by.

Yet Lev would never help the KGB spy on her; she'd bet her life on that. The camaraderie between the two men had to be real. Their casual gestures and the trust they displayed toward each other seemed too genuine to be part of an elaborate charade. What could they be talking about that was best kept from listening ears?

From her own point of view, she was forced to admit that Nikolai's presence failed to set off the instinctive alarms she might have expected someone in his position to evoke. His quick smile and warm hello whenever she let him into the apartment seemed completely without artifice.

Not once had he questioned her about her parents' literary guerrilla tactics or mentioned the foundation they'd set up on their farm near Hayward, Wisconsin, to translate forbidden books into Russian and smuggle them into the motherland. Unlike his probable colleagues at KGB headquarters, where she'd been transferred from the airport for questioning, he didn't keep asking for a list of her parents' contacts or insist that she plead with them to cease their efforts.

Yet he almost certainly knew about their activities and frowned on them. From time to time during his visits, he'd glance in her direction, a quizzical look in his dark-brown eyes. Lev would follow his gaze, and she'd wonder if they'd been discussing her. But they never included her in their conversations or gave her the slightest hint of what they were talking about.

What a good-looking man Nikolai is, she thought, covertly studying his blunt, dark brows and firmly sculpted features, the deep laugh lines that framed his mouth. His thick, neatly trimmed dark hair looked as if it would be wiry yet luxurious as sable to the touch. His tall, well-built physique was relaxed and powerful. Even his hands, strong, beautifully groomed and expressive, added to the air of mastery he wore as comfortably as an old sweater.

If Nikolai was a spy, a highly placed strategist in the espionage war between his country and the West, he was also a poet, at least in a figurative sense. The sensitivity, irony and humor that gleamed in his luminous eyes were difficult to miss.

At times he made her think of Omar Sharif playing the role of Dr. Zhivago, or the character of Prince Andrei in *War and Peace*. I wonder if he's married, she asked herself... or if he's ever killed anyone.

More than once, the precautions he took to make sure he and Lev weren't overheard during their conversations had made her speculate he might be a double agent. But, wishful thinking notwithstanding, she doubted it very much. He'd hardly spy for the West, given his family connections.

Just then, there was a break in the music. Over the announcer's voice, she managed to pick up a few words. "I think it's time," Nikolai was saying.

Her grandfather nodded. "Katya," he said. "Please join us at the table."

A chill of apprehension feathered over her skin as she laid her book aside. Here it comes, she thought. The interrogation I've been expecting. But she didn't quite believe that's what she was facing, thanks to her grandfather's reassuring look.

How lovely she is, Nikolai said to himself, noting her softly parted lips and gleaming mane of naturally wavy, light-brown hair. And how American, with that fierce, naive independence. Yet something tells me she has the melancholy spirit, the exuberance and pragmatism of a true Russian. I almost wish what I'm about to say to her could be the literal truth.

He waited until another stirring march blared over the airwaves before beginning to speak. "No doubt you've been curious, Katarina Danilova," he said, using the original Russian version of her name. "Probably you've been wondering what your grandfather and I have been talking about these many evenings. Simply put, it's this: he's given me his permission to court you. If you agree, we'll begin going out in public next Saturday. We can be married after New Year's without displaying undue haste."

For a moment, Katya imagined she was hearing things. She cast a startled, almost frightened look at her grandfather.

"What Nikolai said is true, *drushenka*," Lev confirmed. But he didn't explain further. Apparently he was willing to let his erstwhile chess partner do most of the talking.

"But that's absolute craziness!"

Forgetful of wiretaps or Nikolai's highly placed connections, Katya let her voice spiral out of control as she turned back to him. "We don't even *know* each other, Nikolai Dmitrievich," she gasped. "I'm here simply as a tourist. And I'll be leaving . . . just as soon as the misunderstanding over that silly book can be straightened out!"

His expression very serious, Nikolai laid one finger against his lips. "If you'll be patient, my dear young lady," he answered, "I'll try to explain. First let me say your passport won't be returned to you. Despite somewhat improved relations between our two countries, officials have decided to make an example of you. Your parents, who wage cultural warfare against the Soviet Union, left this country illegally. You were born while your father was on a concert tour of the eastern republics. The birth occurred aboard a Trans-Siberian train, several days before your parents reached Vladivostok and the fishing boat that spirited them away to Hong Kong. Hence, you're a Soviet citizen.''

Katya caught her breath. ''I'll *never* be that!'' she vowed even as a cold, sick feeling took possession of her. Yet this time she spoke in a whisper. ''The United States government won't permit this.''

Sadly Nikolai shook his head. ''America can't protect you here,'' he reminded. ''It isn't as if you were granted a visa, then entrapped the moment you set foot on Russian soil. The crime in question is smuggling. It's a very serious one. For the time being, the charges against you have been dropped. But I'm sorry to add that they'll be reinstated if your claim of American citizenship is honored. In that event there will be prison time, not this lenient demand that you cease protesting and become a useful member of society. By the time you return to the United States, you'll be middle-aged.''

She was twenty-three. For a moment, all the fight went out of her. It was painfully clear that on one pretext or another Soviet authorities planned to keep her in Russia. And through her own foolishness she'd given them the political leverage to do just that. It hardly mattered whether officials wanted to punish her parents or just to put a damper on their activities. Either she pretended to see things their way or she went to prison—it was as simple as that.

From the moment she'd been detained and questioned by customs authorities, Katya had known she was in serious trouble. Yet she'd refused to acknowledge the magnitude of the situation. The Soviet bureaucracy moved slowly, that was all. Eventually its dour commissars would listen to reason. They would let her go. It had taken the quiet, reasoned words of Nikolai Dvorov to make her realize the true gravity of her plight.

By now, Katya thoroughly regretted tucking the slender volume of banned poetry in her suitcase as a present for her grandfather. Written in the U.S. by a former dissident, the poems attacked the Soviet system with a vengeance. Bitterly they focused on a multitude of human rights violations.

With the advent of *glasnost*, she'd told herself, they'll probably confiscate the book if they find it and I'll get a stern-faced lecture. However, I might be able to sneak it through.

That thinking, she realized now, was typically American; it had scant application to the way business was conducted half a world away. With the perspective she'd gained, she realized her actions had been tantamount to signing a warrant for her own arrest.

For the first time it struck her that she might never see her parents again. Never pursue her dream of a State Department career specializing in Soviet affairs. Never fly home to the family farm for Christmas. Never attend another of her father's concerts or taste her mother's incomparable Eastern European cooking. Never pick up an uncensored American newspaper or express an opinion openly without worrying about who might hear.

The Katya Dane, as she was known at home, who'd lived most of her life as a privileged American in a world full of less fortunate people would cease to exist. I'll never give in, Katya vowed defiantly. Not if I have to fight them with my last breath.

"Why should I believe you?" she asked Nikolai at last, her tawny eyes glittering at him in the lamplight. "And anyway, how could marriage to you make a difference? As your wife, I'd find myself even more helplessly caught in this waking nightmare. You tell him, Grandfather. If appeals through regular channels fail, I can always take refuge in the American embassy."

Gently Lev laid a hand on her arm. "Katya, my darling," he urged, "please calm yourself and listen to what Nikolai is saying."

Realizing she was outnumbered, Katya held her tongue. Almost instantly she'd regretted giving away her secret intentions. Of course Nikolai would report them to his superiors, and she'd probably be arrested again. At the very least she'd be more closely watched. She felt like a cornered rabbit beneath his steady gaze.

"So far, the American ambassador has been unable to help you, isn't that so?" he pointed out when he was certain he had her full attention. "Despite all the talk these days about human rights, neither side wants an incident. Maybe you can tell me why you haven't tried to barricade yourself in the embassy before today."

"Because..." Katya hesitated. All too well she remembered the KGB colonel's warning that she confer with U.S. representatives only at police headquarters or by telephone. "You're being released in your grandfather's custody," he'd announced with a cold glint in his eye. "If you attempt to visit the embassy in person, he will be held responsible."

She couldn't see how they could blame Lev for her actions if he didn't participate in them. Perhaps if she took a subway train while he was at work, threw herself on the mercy of one of the Marine guards at the gate...

It was as if Nikolai could read her thoughts. "Don't even think of approaching the embassy unless you're eager to go to prison and cause your grandfather a great deal of trouble," he warned. "It's only because of my long-standing friendship with him that you haven't spent the last month in jail."

"I have every right..."

Firmly he clapped one hand over her mouth. It was their first physical contact, and Katya felt his warmth like an electric shock despite her fury and dismay at the preemptive gesture. In the space of a few moments they went from friendly but wary strangers to adversaries with a burning physical awareness of each other. A frightening and seemingly inexplicable proposal of marriage was on the table. Yet all she could think about was the firm pressure of his hand over her mouth and the sensation of liquid fire it evoked in her blood. Heat and vulnerability spread to her innermost places in lightning-quick response to the powerful essence of the man.

Only his eyes gave away the fact that Nikolai had been similarly affected. "Promise me you'll speak softly," he said, "or I'll gag you to make you listen. I have no intention of letting you compromise everybody in this room."

Her eyes huge, Katya didn't respond for a moment. But her grandfather was on his side. Mutely she conveyed her willingness to cooperate.

"All right, then." Nikolai slowly withdrew his hand. "I admit what I'm proposing is a drastic solution," he said. "It will probably take a year or more before we can get you out of the country this way. But I'm afraid it's your only chance. You'll have to be a consummate actress...."

What in God's name was he talking about? Though she still breathed fire, Katya was swamped in puzzlement.

"As my wife...in name only, of course...it will be your job to convince authorities you've had a change of heart," he explained. "If you can make them believe we married for love, that you want to remain in the Soviet Union because of me, eventually you may be allowed to travel with me. Once we're in London together, I can arrange for your escape."

"If I ever make it to London," Katya replied with asperity, "I won't need your help."

Nikolai and her grandfather exchanged a look.

"Ah, but you're wrong, my beloved child," Lev told her patiently. "Especially in London, the danger will be great. To Nikolai as well as to yourself. Soviet citizens who travel abroad are closely watched. Even if all goes smoothly, your defection will involve a personal sacrifice for him, maybe even a major setback to his career...."

She let his assessment of the risks involved sink in for a moment. "What about you, Grandfather?" she asked. "Won't you be in danger as well?"

An ironic smile played about the corners of his mouth. "Who knows?" he shrugged. "Maybe they'll ask me to retire. I have a feeling it won't be long, anyway."

If Lev was joking, Katya failed to get the point. Meanwhile the word defection was still ringing in her ears. So her world had become as cockeyed as that.

Staring at Lev and then at Nikolai, Katya shook her head. They were serious; she could see that. It wasn't difficult to understand why her grandfather wanted to help her. But Nikolai was a stranger to her. Why should he risk everything for her sake?

The dark-haired man who had called forth such riveting physical awareness from her was watching her face. "For our plan to succeed, everyone must believe you've accepted Marxist-Leninist doctrine," he continued calmly, as if she hadn't interrupted him. "You must appear to turn your back on the American way of life. Eventually that will mean denouncing your parents and disparaging their activities. Above all, you must show deference to Soviet ideals. Volunteer to take a job, any job, whether it be sweeping the streets or working as a translator."

"They'll have to believe you love your husband dearly, that you'd never leave him," her grandfather interposed.

For several moments, the stirring music that poured forth from the radio was the only sound in the room. Katya's head was swimming. The idea of marrying Nikolai Dvorov under any circumstances conjured up feelings she didn't dare examine too closely.

Self-consciously she folded her hands.

"Why should a man I scarcely know make this kind of sacrifice for me?" she asked. "Put his career in jeopardy for someone who means nothing to him? As close as Nikolai's friendship with you is, Grandfather, I can't believe it's worth that much."

The two men exchanged another look. "Perhaps more," Nikolai responded. "I agree, Katya. We don't know each other. My willingness to do this favor for you must seem very puzzling. But if it weren't for your grandfather, I wouldn't exist."

At this curious pronouncement, Lev bowed his head. "Perhaps we should get out the vodka before you tell her the whole story, Nikky," he said.

Nobody spoke as the elderly professor of English language and literature rinsed out the tea glasses, took another off the shelf and poured a generous portion of colorless, fiery liquid into each. Returning to the table, he handed one of the drinks to Katya, another to Nikolai. Heartsick at the mess she'd made of things, Katya didn't join in the silent toast.

Tossing back his vodka, Nikolai fixed her with his steady gaze. "Many years before you were born, during the Nazi invasion of Russia in World War II, your grandfather was a young teacher of literature at a military academy in Minsk," he began. "When the Germans came, there was destruction everywhere. The academy was shelled by tanks and largely destroyed.

"By the time that had happened, of course, most of the young cadets and their teachers had long since fled. Only one boy, a very sick boy who happened to be the son of a Soviet general, remained behind as the enemy advanced. One teacher, a Jew, stayed with him, though it meant risking deportation to one of the death camps."

Involuntarily glancing at her grandfather, Katya saw that his eyes were glazed with tears.

"That boy was my father," Nikolai went on in his deep, resonant voice. "And the Jewish instructor was Lev Petrovsky, a person of great daring and compassion for his fellowman. Somehow, hiding in a boarded-up cellar and foraging for food and water at night, he managed to nurse young Dmitri Dvorov back to health. Carrying my father on his back, he made his way east through fields and forests, penetrating the German lines outside Moscow just as the city seemed about to fall. There he took Dmitri to stay with relatives. Though there was barely enough food to keep anyone alive, Lev shared his meager portion with my father. Dmitri was thin but well when my grandmother returned to the city after the Nazi retreat."

Nobody spoke for several moments as Katya absorbed the tale. Only the radio announcer's voice and the strident beat of his next selection filled the room.

In her mind's eye she could see the terrifying drama unfold. Her heart went out to the sick child trying not to cry out at the sound of shelling, even more to the recklessly brave young man whose blood she carried in her own veins. If he'd failed—if he'd gotten caught and been shipped to the Nazi ovens—Petra Dane wouldn't have existed, either. Or Katya herself.

"Oy vey," Lev sighed at last, as if he'd been having similar thoughts. "So many years ago. And it's like yesterday. Thanks be to God we survived."

Though he was surely an atheist, Nikolai didn't flinch at the prayerful reference. "Do you understand now?" he asked, watching Katya's face.

"Maybe. I don't know." She looked at her grandfather and then back at him. "Are you telling me it's a point of honor with you? I didn't realize avowed communists—"

"Believed in anything like that?"

His wry smile made her feel foolish and even more defensive. "Does your father know what you plan to do?" she demanded. "It's his debt after all. Why doesn't *he* pay it?"

Something closed in Nikolai's face. Clearly she had trespassed into an area he intended to keep rigorously private. "I don't choose to discuss my father with you," he answered shortly. "Well? What do you think? Are you willing to gamble on what I'm suggesting?"

Without realizing what she was doing, Katya got to her feet. "I think you're certifiable," she said after a moment. "An absolute loony, if you want to know the truth!"

Though he didn't smile, a hint of amusement returned to Nikolai's eyes. Deep down, he was laughing at her and perhaps at himself as well. With what was probably a masterful command of the English language, he'd understood her American slang all too well.

As if on some kind of signal, the two men pushed back their chairs. "That's no way to talk to an honored guest, Granddaughter," Lev reproved her. "Nikolai has offered to help you. It's late and he's leaving now. As a courtesy to me, you will walk him to his car."

Her grandfather's request left her with little choice. This was Russia, after all—not America. And he was an elderly Jew, still head of the family in his own eyes. He was entitled to her respect.

"While we finish our vodka," Lev added, "you can put on your coat."

Her cheeks flushed with stifled rebellion, Katya disappeared into the sleeping alcove her grandfather had curtained off for her in his small bedroom. As she put on the scratchy but warm wool coat a neighbor had lent her, she wanted to cry.

For some reason, a favorite piano nocturne of her father's drifted into her mind. She could almost hear the fire crackling in her parents' fieldstone fireplace. Smell the *piroshki* baking in her mother's oven.

Never, she thought, drawing on her mittens. I'm never going to see my home again.

Her eyes were suspiciously bright as she accompanied Nikolai downstairs. Lev Petrovsky's apartment was on the fifth floor, and the building didn't have an elevator. Neither she nor Nikolai said a word as they descended the poorly lit stairwell, their shoulders brushing in the narrow space.

It was snowing hard as they stepped out onto the sidewalk. Nikolai's car, a sleek black Volga that had probably cost the earth in terms of Soviet wages, was parked illegally at the curb. Because he was KGB, he could get by with that. Yet she didn't begrudge him the privilege. What he'd proposed to do for her was very generous.

She lifted her face to his. "Mr. Dvorov—"

"Nikolai."

Their breath smoked and mingled in the air.

"All right, Nikolai," she amended. "I want to say that I appreciate your offer. I just think it's, well, a bit extreme."

He didn't answer for a moment. The snowflakes had grown very large now, like perfectly formed lace medallions. They were sticking to her lashes, and he found himself wanting to kiss her. She looked extraordinarily appealing in her old scarf and coat.

"Katya," he said, impulsively taking hold of her hands, "I know it is. But it may be your only chance, *sweetheart*."

Interrupting the flow of Russian, the English endearment sounded strangely exotic to her ears. But it didn't startle her half as much as the warm, sweet pressure of his mouth. Descending on hers without warning, it had taken complete possession. Freezing cold though it was there in the snowy dark, Katya suddenly felt overheated and breathless. Effortlessly turning up the considerable heat of his complex personality, Nikolai Dvorov had set her soul ablaze.

Chapter 2

The sensible part of her wanted to resist. Nikolai might be her grandfather's friend, but he was also part of Soviet officialdom. As such, he symbolized the enemy. If she gave in to him, she'd be lost.

His warmth, his spirit, the fierce yet tender onslaught of his kiss, argued otherwise. His hands, strong and capable in their leather gloves, gripped her firmly but effortlessly, molding her to him as if the furnace blast of their interchange could create an alloy of their separate selves. She could feel her bones go soft with desire.

With a sigh of capitulation, Katya wrapped her arms about his neck. Invading her mouth, his tongue was piratical, delicious. It asked nothing and demanded everything—the utmost possession of all she had to give. She felt plumbed, robbed of every treasure. Yet conversely she knew herself to be enriched and deeply nurtured. Whatever this man took, she knew, he would give back a hundredfold.

Through the heavy clothing that separated them, she could feel the sinewy strength of his body. Rock hard, it pressed against her, thoroughly aroused and quintessentially male, threatening the sanity of a woman who wanted to escape to her own world without a web of entanglements.

Never had she felt anything approaching such splendor. Never burned to lose herself in a man that way. It was as if kerosene had been thrown on a fire, causing it to shoot up in a roaring chimney of flame. The resulting conflagration threatened to consume them both.

Katya shook when he finally drew back a little to study her face. He was still very near, his dark eyes burning into hers like live coals. The warmth of his breath trailed like an invitation across her mouth. Clean and tantalizing, his skin-scent filled her nostrils.

"You shouldn't have done that, Nikolai Dmitrievich," she protested when she finally found her voice. "You've made it more difficult for me to reject your proposal."

His mouth curved in tribute to her honesty. She had an American's candor. Or perhaps a Russian's startling but casual straightforwardness. "Then don't," he said. "Sleep on it awhile. Maybe you'll change your mind."

For what seemed an eternity, his eyes continued to hold hers in intimate communication, though his hands only loosely encircled her waist. Then he released her and got into his car. The big Volga purred to life, its headlights raking the curtain of snowflakes.

He lowered the window on the passenger side to speak to her. "Keep out of trouble," he advised. "My power to fix things isn't unlimited, you know."

Then he was gone. Feeling oddly bereft Katya watched the big black car's taillights disappear. The street, with its pale, towering flat blocks, seemed suddenly empty, a stage set without substance, or the looming backdrop of an uneasy dream. He's KGB, she warned herself, fighting back the depression that threatened to blanket her thoughts. You can't afford to get emotionally involved with him. Not if you want to see your home again.

Lev was reading his Torah when she reentered the apartment. He had placed his yarmulke on his head and drawn his prayer shawl about his shoulders. Quietly he appraised her as she threw off her coat and chafed her hands over the radiator coils.

"It's getting colder out," she complained, hoping he wouldn't question the brilliance of her eyes or the rosy flush that must still stain her cheeks. "The snow's coming down like crazy and everything feels damp."

Lev shook his head. "Patience, Granddaughter. What will you do when winter comes?"

If I have my way, she thought, I'll be back in America by then. Yet after Nikolai's pitiless assessment of her situation, any assertion of that sort would have seemed an empty boast. "As far as I'm concerned, it's already winter," she said.

Her grandfather didn't answer for a moment. Then, "Despite what you may think of his connections, Nikolai's a good man," he replied. "You can trust him, child."

Twenty-three years of being her parents' daughter, of hearing about the evils of communism at the family dinner table, stood in the way of her doing that. "How can you be so sure?" she asked.

Lev seemed about to launch into a lengthy explanation. Then he apparently thought better of it. "I am, that's all," he replied.

Katya knew his trust in Dmitri Dvorov's tall, good-looking son had been nourished over a lifetime. But to her, despite the kiss still imprinted on her mouth, Nikolai was a stranger. His plan to help her, if that's what it truly was, seemed highly impractical and doomed to failure. Even if he could get her out, it might take years. He'd said so himself. She didn't want to wait that long. The more likely outcome would be a lifetime spent in Russia as the wife of a Communist Party member.

Her grandfather seemed to have no such qualms. Resting one arthritic hand on the page he'd been reading, he regarded her with mixed exasperation and affection. "You'd be wise to consider Nikolai's offer," he said. "You're not likely to get another. A great many lives have been spent in this country trying to outwait changes of policy. Or should I say changes of heart?"

Stubbornly Katya held her tongue. Wouldn't the U.S. government come to her rescue? Nikolai's words to the contrary rang in her ears.

"I know what you're thinking," Lev ventured when she didn't speak. "Nikolai is a member of the Soviet elite, part of the inner circle. Why should he flout the authority that has given him every advantage? Risk losing everything for the sake of an old man who once saved his father?"

Why indeed? Katya thought. Despite Nikolai's indication to the contrary, communists don't have principles like that.

"The answer is loyalty," her grandfather said when she didn't speak. "In his heart of hearts, the true Russian is supremely loyal. Not to the Party...that's just an abstract entity, a flimsy superstructure imposed on more than a thousand years of history. Instead, he owes his fealty to the land of his birth and the people he cares about. Why do you think I wasn't punished when your mother and father defected and why I was still allowed to teach at a university where Jews weren't even admitted until a few years ago?''

The question was clearly a rhetorical one. In response, Katya could merely shrug. The concept of loyalty and debt binding two unrelated families across the generations was utterly foreign to her. Even if she subscribed to it, she found it difficult to believe that hardheaded, atheistic communists would do the same. For the second time she asked herself if Dmitri had any idea what his son was proposing.

Resolutely she tried to thrust Nikolai from her mind. Her best bet was to concentrate on getting out of the Soviet Union under her own steam, not tie herself to a marriage of convenience that might unwittingly become permanent. She didn't even want to think about what it would be like to live under Nikolai's roof even if they didn't sleep together.

She went to bed soon after that, with the quilts pulled up to her chin and her sweater over her nightgown. Though she hoped she'd be lulled to sleep by the comforting drone of her grandfather's prayers, it was not to be. Long after Lev was snoring comfortably on his side of the curtain, Katya lay awake and restless in the chilly dark. As if he were standing there before her in the cramped sleeping alcove, she could see Nikolai's emphatic brows and large, dark eyes, the bluntly chiseled features of his face. With a little shiver of excitement, she imagined the firm pressure of his capable hands laying claim to her physical self. The clean, spicy skin scent that so powerfully telegraphed his masculinity hovered just out of reach.

There was no denying it—his kiss had caused her defenses to topple as if they were made of matchsticks. She felt vulnerable now, like a fortress with its gates standing open to the enemy.

Her deepest instincts argued he could never be anything of the kind. Despite the alien philosophy he must surely profess, there was something so decent, so nurturing about Nikolai that she couldn't help but respond to it. She sensed humor in him, too; he liked to laugh, even when the joke was at his own expense. The way he'd smiled at her, with one corner of his mouth turning up slightly, made her want to know his every thought.

Balancing the restraint and honor he projected was the emotional fire she'd experienced firsthand. Before succumbing to his embrace, she'd never been kissed with real passion by any man. Perhaps that's because he is a man, not a boy, she decided. *He knows who he is and where he's going in the world. Until now, all your male friends have been boys, confused and callow in their emotions.*

Abruptly she realized she'd categorized him as a friend. In her precarious position she couldn't afford the luxury. *The man's a KGB officer,* she told herself. *His father serves on the Central Committee. You can't possibly get involved.*

Though she half expected Nikolai to stop by for her answer a few days later, she didn't see him for several weeks. No doubt he was busy, weaving together the strands of some espionage coup or arranging for an incident that would embarrass the West. She had to concede that, even if he wanted to, he couldn't call. Like most Muscovites, her grandfather didn't have a telephone.

Without a job or friends other than Lev and with very little of her traveling money left, Katya found the days drab and empty. Though she didn't want to rely on her grandfather for the basics of life, that would soon become an economic necessity.

It was a safe bet that none of the notes she'd mailed to the U.S. embassy had ever made it there. Each time she went to the local police prefecture to call the ambassador, there was something wrong with the telephones and she couldn't get through. Confined to books, long walks in the plummeting cold and endless shopping in miserably understocked state stores for the raw materials of her grandfather's supper, she felt buried alive—a forgotten and thoroughly insignificant pawn in the struggle for supremacy between East and West.

She'd embarked on one of the interminable shopping trips necessary to provision even the simplest meal when she spotted the *Pravda* headline on one of the official bulletin boards. Quickly she hurried over for a closer look, almost dropping her parcels in the process. Shoulder to shoulder with other passersby who gleaned their daily diet of news that way, she scanned the heavy Cyrillic characters. To her joy and amazement, she read that the U.S. vice president would be visiting Moscow the following week. During his three-day stay, the article said, he would visit Lenin's tomb.

Excitement and renewed hope coursed through Katya's veins. The vice president here! And approachable in a public place! If only she could get to him, attach herself to his party somehow, it would cause an incident. Red-faced, the commissars who had insisted on detaining her would likely mumble something about a misunderstanding. But they'd be forced to let her go.

Covertly she began to plan.

On the morning of the vice president's scheduled visit to Red Square, she fixed her grandfather a sumptuous breakfast by Soviet standards and poured him an extra glass of tea. Obviously bemused by her nervous energy and the subtle tension he could read on her face, he gave her several inquiring looks.

"Have you thought any more about Nikolai Dvorov's offer, my darling?" he asked. "As much as I love your company, Moscow isn't the place for you. It would be so much better if you could return to your own life."

"Yes, I agree, though I would miss you, too. And I am thinking about it," Katya replied. Her voice quavered a little on the words. She didn't expect to see him again after that morning, and she was trying to memorize his face.

Careful not to arouse his suspicions, she hugged and kissed Lev as he was about to leave for work. Squeezed in the fervor of her embrace, his shoulders felt bony, even frail. I'll never see him again, she thought, fighting back tears. But I'll always have my memories.

At one o'clock she put on her coat and mittens and fastened the ugly wool scarf she hated so much around her head. Her eyes shone damp and bright as she looked around her grandfather's shabby but genteel living space. Mama will want to know everything, she realized. She'll be hungry for the smallest detail.

Her father had left the Soviet Union for artistic freedom, and to Katya's knowledge, he didn't even go back in his thoughts. But for people like her mother, the enforced separation was a bitter one. What kind of world is this, she asked herself, where you must choose between your country and the people you love? If there was any justice, you could have them both.

Weighed down by her sadness, yet half incredulous too
at her own daring, she stepped out of the small apartment and descended the narrow stairwell with its lingering cooking smells. Outside, it was a dark, snowy
afternoon. In the weeks since Nikolai had last visited
them, it had snowed all too frequently. They would have
an early winter, a radio commentator had remarked. As
Katya walked to the Metro station, thickset, muffled
bodies moved stolidly through a white blur of snowflakes. Buses were lined up at the curbs, their headlights
piercing the early gloom.

Puddles of slush had been tracked into the marble
mausoleum of their neighborhood subway station.
Merging with a sea of humanity, Katya got aboard one of
the underground trains. At each stop, more huddled
passengers waited. Their bodies seemed compact, solidified against the cold.

She got off at Ploschad Revolutsii, the station nearest
the Kremlin. Since arriving in the Soviet Union she'd
taken in the sights, passing through that particular station a dozen times. Yet perhaps because of her stranded
condition and the resentment it evoked, she'd always
done so hurriedly. Now that she was about to leave, she
found herself really looking at the station's grandiose yet
somehow simplistic architecture. The huge bronze figures of collective farm girls, Young Pioneers and border
guards with their rifles and trusty canine companions,
nestled in pairs beneath the station's arches, seemed
crudely idealized, almost featureless. They bore little re-
semblance to the passionate and melancholy icons of an
earlier age.

She felt guilty and highly conspicuous when she
emerged on the sidewalk, and she wondered if she'd ac-
quired a Soviet consciousness. I'm not disobeying any-

one's orders. I'm not going to the embassy, or trying to call the ambassador from a public phone booth, she thought. I'm just behaving like any curious Russian does when foreigners appear.

As she approached Red Square, she saw that a larger-than-usual crowd had gathered outside the Lenin Mausoleum. In their somber winter wear, the patient Muscovites looked like a flock of crows. Police had cordoned off a route for the vice president's motorcade, and a number of official cars were patrolling the area, which was usually closed to vehicular traffic. Television cameras and reporters were already in place.

After nearly two months in Moscow, Katya hadn't expected to be followed anymore. In fact, on her most recent trips to the government-run meat and produce stalls, there hadn't been a shadowy, discreet figure hovering in her wake. Thus it came as a shock when she realized someone *was* tailing her as she stepped out into the square's vast paved area.

The man in question was short and stocky with horn-rimmed glasses and an anonymous look. He wore a Persian lamb hat over his close-cropped graying hair and a brown wool coat with a fur collar. She remembered seeing him get on the subway near her grandfather's apartment, though she hadn't noticed him since.

Suddenly her plan seemed foolhardy, even doomed. What in God's name am I supposed to do now, she thought? Turn around and face him? He won't believe I'm sightseeing with the vice president due to arrive at any moment.

Confrontation was an acceptable tactic for a free country, but it wouldn't work here. At best, she'd find herself embroiled in a lengthy contretemps, unable to take advantage of the moment. Not daring to glance over her shoulder again, she quickened her footsteps. The man in the brown coat adjusted his pace accordingly. She broke into a run just as a black Volga moved into her peripheral vision. A moment later, Nikolai was taking her into his arms.

"Katya, my darling," he said, kissing her warmly on the cheek. "I hope you haven't been waiting for me too long."

"You!" The single word was more accusation than greeting. She tried to twist free of his grasp. "What are you doing here?" she demanded.

"Shhhh." He drew her closer. "The man who's been following you is KGB."

The cold stung her eyes, making them water. At the same time she wanted to weep in frustration. "So are you!" she whispered furiously. "So are you!"

He didn't confirm or deny the statement. Instead, he took her by the arm, his manner forbidding any argument. "Come on," he said, making sure his voice would carry. "You wanted to see St. Basil's. It's a good day for it, with everyone trying to get a look at the Amerikanski politician."

Katya discovered Nikolai had been using a chauffeur when he turned around and instructed the driver of the Volga to park it at Dzerzhinsky Square. Four blocks to the north, the square was home to a large children's store—and KGB headquarters. She gave him a withering look.

"Come on," he repeated softly, urging her over the slippery gray cobblestones. "Try to look as if you don't hate me, at least. Maybe Boris or whatever his name is will take the hint and disappear."

You know what his name is, Katya wanted to scream at him. He probably works for you! But she didn't put her thoughts into words. Despite her best intentions, she hadn't been able to get Nikolai out of her mind. His gloved hand on her coat sleeve was sending prickles of excitement up her arm. Meanwhile, any chance she might have to seek the help of her country's second-highest official was rapidly slipping away.

"Please," she begged, deciding to throw herself on his mercy. "If you owe my grandfather anything at all, let me go back there. I can slip into the crowd unnoticed, get away from them. Once I've gained the vice president's protection, they'll have to concoct some kind of story about a mix-up and let me go."

Ahead of them, that most Russian of all cathedrals brooded over the godless heart of the Soviet state. Its gaudy bouquet of swirling domes and intricately detailed towers seemed strangely austere in the wintry light.

"Don't be a fool." Pausing just outside the cathedral entrance beside the monument to Minin and Pozharsky, Nikolai framed her face with his hands. "The American is running an hour behind schedule," he told her. "Even if you could elude the men assigned to follow you that long, they'd close in the moment you tried to make contact. I assure you the charge wouldn't be smuggling this time. What would you say to 'attempted assassination' instead?"

Katya wasn't carrying a weapon of any kind. Yet her heart sank as if it were made of lead. "You can't be serious," she protested.

"Ah, but I'm very serious," he said. "Legend has it that Ivan the Terrible, who built this place, had the architects' eyes put out after they completed it. I don't know if the story's true. But it could be. This can be a brutal country. Don't say you haven't been forewarned."

Overcome by a feeling of helplessness, she let the tension drain from her body. Reluctantly she realized Nikolai was telling the truth. They wouldn't need to find a weapon in her possession to lock her up in the Lubyanka and throw away the key.

"Well?" he prodded. "Are you coming with me? The choice is up to you."

Avoiding his eyes, Katya let him lead her inside. It didn't surprise her that St. Basil's had been converted into a historical museum. As they stamped the snow off their boots, she saw that the first room contained exhibits about the building's history. Possibly there would be some mention of the blinded architects, but she wasn't in the mood to check out Nikolai's story. Though he kept up a running commentary as they passed the rows of glass display cases, she scarcely listened or even looked at them.

I'm like a rat in a trap, she thought as they went on to view the murals and collection of icons in the other rooms. The sad-faced Byzantine figures from a bygone era seemed to concur in her despair. Marriage to Nikolai may be a desperate gamble, she thought. But perhaps it's the only one I have left. If I become his wife, at least his colleagues might not follow me around so much.

She was thoughtful as they walked back to his car. If his estimate and her watch were correct, her country's number-two executive would be arriving at Lenin's tomb at that very moment. No doubt he would turn toward the crowd for a goodwill round of handshaking. Meanwhile, though she was only a few blocks away, she might as well have been in Siberia. In a transparent attempt to forestall any further foolishness on her part, Nikolai had chosen a route that led behind GUM, circumventing Red Square altogether.

As she'd expected, the Volga was parked in a numbered space outside the KGB's massive headquarters. Producing a set of keys, Nikolai unlocked the doors. Staring down at them from the huge building's facade was a four-story-high portrait of Lenin. At least we needn't concern ourselves any longer with the fiction that you're an innocent cultural minister, Katya thought unhappily, brushing past him as she got into the passenger seat.

He'd take her back to her grandfather's apartment, she supposed, to drop her off with a stern lecture and a warning not to try any more crazy stunts. When he turned south instead, toward the Moskva River, she shot him a questioning look.

"I have the rest of the day off," he said, smiling at her with the unexpected brilliance of the winter sun when it breaks through a bank of clouds. "I hope you know how to skate, *drushenka*. Because you're going to get the chance."

She'd been on the verge of causing an incident that would have embarrassed him greatly with his superiors. And he was taking her skating as a result? For a moment she stared at him in astonishment. Then she melted, unable to maintain such a severe expression when he looked at her that way.

"Is the pope Catholic?" she teased, a dimple flashing beside her mouth. "Or the general secretary a communist? I grew up in Wisconsin, you know."

"Yes, I did know that," Nikolai replied.

Gorky Park looked like a frosted wedding cake beneath its mantle of snow. Drifts of trees sheltered it from the city's relentless geometry. Its iced-over ponds and flooded, frozen walkways were thoughtfully provided with warming huts and refreshment stands. Bundled to

their ears, the usually taciturn Muscovites were laughing
and skating, chatting boisterously with one another as
they lined up for the carnival rides.

Unlike their American counterparts, Katya realized,
Russian amusement parks stayed open during at least
part of the winter. Because of the leaden skies, the Ferris
wheel and hydra-headed Tilt-a-whirl had been lit early in
a fairy-tale mass of colors. A Viennese waltz blared from
loudspeakers atop tall poles.

"What size skates do you wear?" Nikolai inquired as
they approached the rental booth.

When she gave him her American size, he translated it
to its Russian equivalent. "Here, try these on," he said
as they strolled over to one of the benches. "I hope the
socks you're wearing are thick enough."

She'd left her leather handbag in the car. Standing up
and doing a little pirouette on the ice, Katya felt light and
free for the first time since she'd been detained by customs officials. "What a marvelous idea this was!" she
exclaimed, her natural exuberance asserting itself. "You
don't waltz by any chance?"

Nikolai got to his feet. He looked curiously formal in
his sable hat and dark, British-made topcoat. Yet he was
the kind of man who would draw the attention of women
anywhere. "Try me," he answered, holding out his
hands.

When she placed her mittened hands in his she couldn't
help feeling as if the gesture was prophetic. For the space
of a heartbeat they stood very close, their breath mingling
as it had on the night they'd kissed. She could feel his
power and warmth like a tangible thing, pulling her to
him like a magnet.

Then he put one hand on her waist and they were off,
picking up the beat of the music as their blades hissed and

scraped over the ice. The sensation was one of delirium, one of flying. They anticipated each other's every movement, as if they'd waltzed together a thousand times. This is how it would be if we ever made love, Katya thought. We'd burn out of control, yet be aware of every nuance, every miniscule delight. Without her meaning it to happen, she realized, something wonderful but dangerous had clicked into place.

Nikolai's dark eyes glowed with the satisfaction he felt. Katya seemed nearly weightless in his arms. She was all woman, far too inviting when she forgot her unfortunate circumstances and became her bubbly, natural self. She had an innate sense of rhythm that prompted erotic speculation.

If only we'd met in London, he thought. I could have courted her with flowers and beautiful jewelry, made love to her at her hotel. There wouldn't have been this crushing need to honor an obligation.

And then what? Mockingly his inner self posed the question. He'd known from the beginning they didn't have a future together. He was Russian to the soles of his feet, and she unquenchably American despite her heritage. If they learned to care for each other, to *need* each other, they'd be trapped, stranded on an ice floe of politics between two rival continents.

Yet he wanted her so much that he dreamed of it at night. There was something indefinable about her he found difficult to resist.

As they took a turn beneath one of the tall floodlights that ringed the pond, Katya saw a shadow cross his face. "What's the matter?" she asked at once. "Aren't you enjoying yourself?"

"More than you can guess."

Probably she'd be surprised to hear it, but it had been several years since he'd skated there. When he was home in Moscow, he didn't have much time for frivolity. *The only thing to do, he decided, is to carry out my mission to the best of my ability and take what pleasure I can from that, short of compromising her. All too soon, I'll have to face them with an explanation.*

He'd be blamed, of course, though the degree of culpability he'd have to admit was open to question. Ultimately it would depend on his father's political weight. In the current scheme of things, Dmitri was a very powerful man. And that power could be used to blunt official sanctions, provided it was done behind the scenes. If he could make a charge of a CIA kidnapping in London stick, he might not have to give up his KGB career—he'd just cool his heels at a desk in Moscow for a while. The idea that Katya might truly fall in love with him and actually want to remain in Russia didn't even bear thinking about.

"How about some hot cider?" he asked. "We need to keep the inner fires stoked."

"That sounds lovely," Katya replied.

A few moments later they were standing side by side, sipping at their steaming mugs and watching the other skaters. Above and beyond the dark copse that ringed the pond, Katya spied a church steeple topped by the ubiquitous red star. *I'm really here, in Moscow,* she reminded herself, stunned at the unreality of it all. Yet with Nikolai she felt less abandoned, less alone. As they'd glided over the frozen pond, she'd imagined they could be anywhere: Rockefeller Plaza in New York City or Round Lake behind her parents' vacation cottage. All notion of time and place had disappeared.

Just then, one of the skating rink attendants changed the musical tape. Admittedly tame in comparison with the original, a Soviet version of American rock music rang out on the frosty air.

"Come, Nikolai," she urged, brushing aside the slight melancholy she felt. "I'll teach you to skate American-style."

With a smile, he let her draw him out on the ice. Though he was eleven years older than she, Nikolai regularly danced to much more radical music in the London clubs. But if she thought she was showing him something new, he'd let her have her fun.

Katya had dressed that morning in a bulky sweater and narrow, faded jeans. Her legs flashed long and slender beneath her heavy coat as she skated backward, gyrating provocatively to the music and inviting him to do the same. Gradually her heavy scarf slipped off, allowing her light brown hair to tumble around her shoulders. For the first time since they'd met, her amber eyes sparkled. Her cheeks were pink with exertion and delight.

Indulgently Nikolai mimicked her movements, though with less exaggeration than she employed. He felt rather than saw the other skaters make way for them. "Foreigner," he heard some whisper. But the mood of the other skaters was generally amiable as they took in the show.

"All right, that's enough!" Laughingly Nikolai caught hold of her as the rock number ended. Without thinking he pulled her into his arms.

"Oh, no, you don't...."

They were at the edge of the pond, and giving him a playful shove, Katya tottered up the bank in her unfamiliar skates. A swift look over her shoulder dared him to follow. In response, he scooped up a handful of snow.

Forming it into a ball, he aimed it at the seat of her pants. It hit the target with a satisfying thunk.

"How dare you?" she shrieked, turning around and letting fly with a snowball of her own.

Within moments they were pelting each other with loose snow as he chased her up the hill. When he caught her just past the crest, they fell into a snowbank, struggling to stuff more of the cold, wet stuff down each other's necks.

Seconds later they'd gone deadly serious in each other's arms. The weight of his body pressing her into the snow, Nikolai held her with his gaze as if he could see the bonfire in his eyes reflected there. With a little gesture of inevitability he lowered his mouth to hers.

No, she thought. No. You mustn't. He's a spy, a communist, the sworn enemy of everything you hold dear. Yet she couldn't fight him. Helpless, she was prey to the tumult of emotions that had overwhelmed her outside her grandfather's apartment block.

This time they knew the secret pathways to each other's vulnerabilities and desires. As his mouth nuzzled hers, owning it and plumbing the heat of its depth, need burst in Katya like an explosion of fireworks. Sharp and insistent, it cried out for the release only he could give her. Desperately she wanted to hold him, surround him, merge with the blazing passion of his hard, tall body.

It might be madness, even a death blow to her freedom. Yet there in the trackless wilderness of the Russian winter, she wanted to burn to ashes with his kiss.

"Stop that behavior at once!"

Coming up for air, Katya and Nikolai found themselves facing a gruff young military officer in a blue uniform with scarlet facings. His stern policeman's visage was chapped and red with cold. Quickly brushing themselves off, they got to their feet.

"Hooliganism isn't allowed in the park," the police officer lectured them in a menacing tone. "I should arrest you both for setting a bad example. Let me see your papers."

Chapter 3

Swiftly they met each other's eyes. Nikolai could see the fear in hers. She hadn't grown up with such restrictions on her conduct, and she didn't understand them. She was also afraid because of her uncertain status. She probably thought she'd end up in jail.

She didn't realize yet that he'd be her protection. Reaching into the inside pocket of his coat, he withdrew his identification badge.

"KGB," he announced, knowing she'd guessed it anyway.

Briefly the police officer clung to his authoritarian stance. But he was clearly out of his depth.

"Yes, of course. Forgive me, Comrade Major," he stammered, his face even redder than before. "I assume...the young lady isn't giving you any trouble?"

More than any woman ever has before, Nikolai said to himself. And not because of her need to escape to the West. His response didn't reflect his thoughts. "You assume correctly," he answered, his tone annoyed and a little clipped.

The young officer fidgeted nervously for a moment. Clearly Nikolai's impatience was a reproach to him. "Well, then," he said as if he were speaking to himself. "I'll be about my business."

As he turned away, Nikolai slipped an arm around Katya's shoulders. She didn't shrug it off this time. But it was as if their kiss had never happened. All the lovely, spontaneous light had gone out of her face.

"Sorry about that," he murmured, giving her a little squeeze. "I should have seen it coming. What do you say we turn in our skates and get something to eat?"

Katya glanced at her watch and saw it was after four o'clock. While they'd been skating and wrestling in the snow, the afternoon had resolved itself into twilight. Now it was almost dark.

"Won't Lev worry if he comes home and finds me gone?" she asked.

Try to imagine how he'd feel if there were state security people hammering at his door, Nikolai thought. But he kept his recriminations to himself. "He's probably still at the university," he said. "If you like, we can phone him there."

There wasn't a phone book in the public booth. Only fifty thousand or so had been printed for a city of nearly ten million people. Nikolai retrieved the correct number by ringing information. They had to wait a long time while someone called Katya's grandfather to the phone.

To her relief, Nikolai didn't mention the day's misadventure. "Katya's with me," he told his old friend simply. "We happened to bump into each other near St. Basil's, and we've been skating. I'd like to take her out for a meal."

Lev gave his permission readily enough. "You know I
trust you, Nikolai Dmitrievich," he said. "The door to
the apartment will be unlocked." Naturally he didn't re-
fer to their proposed arrangement. "Let me speak to
Katya."

She took the phone and they spoke briefly. Her
grandfather's voice, so filled with affection for her, made
her realize all over again how much she would have
missed him if she'd succeeded in her quest that afternoon. She told Lev goodbye, and then she and Nikolai
took their skates back to the rental booth and walked to
the car.

What a catch Nikolai must be in the eyes of young Soviet womanhood, Katya speculated as they drove back
across the river, turning northwest onto Kropotkinskaya
Street. He's handsome, sexy and well-to-do by Russian
standards. He drives a Volga, and he carries an identification card that can stop overzealous policemen in their
tracks. It made her sad to think that, even if she married
him, their relationship would be a temporary one.
Though he could kiss like an angel, Nikolai Dvorov
wasn't for her.

"I'm taking you to a place that's only been in business several years," he said, breaking into her thoughts.
"It's very popular...an experiment in the new Soviet free
enterprise. As a Yankee capitalist, you should feel right
at home."

A long line of prospective patrons waited outside the
elegant green-and-cream-painted nineteenth-century
building. After he had parked the car, Nikolai walked her
past the others. The doorman recognized him with a
smile.

"Good evening, Major Dvorov," he said. "And the same to the beautiful young lady. We just happen to have a table...."

Already familiar with Moscow's grandiose public monuments and shabby service sector, Katya was amazed at the restaurant's damask wallpaper and turn of the century decor, which blended beautifully with its stunning collection of modern paintings. Two bearded musicians, one with a guitar and one with a violin, were playing Moldavian folk songs as the waiter held out her chair. She was enough of a Yankee that she didn't feel out of place in her jeans.

"Everything's good here," Nikolai told her across their immaculately laid table. "The manager used to direct the restaurant at the Metropol. You can even order wine now. Before you had to settle for fruit juice or bring your own."

Carefully studying the menu, Katya selected the most American-sounding dish she could find—pork chops glazed with orange peel. Nikolai ordered liver, a delicacy to Muscovites who found it in chronically short supply. It arrived fried with cucumbers. She pronounced it delicious when he offered her a bite.

First, however, they were presented with an array of appetizers: cold sturgeon, miniature *piroshki* almost as good as those Katya's mother made and home-pickled vegetables, Russian-style. The wine was from Soviet Georgia, a dry and very passable white.

Seated across from Nikolai in such civilized and pleasant surroundings, Katya wondered if the whole thing was a dream. Her anguish in Red Square and the incident with the police officer in Gorky Park were fading. Meanwhile, the memory of Nikolai's kiss was burning a brand into her consciousness.

Lying in the snow with the hard bulk of his body pressing against hers and his alluring warmth flooding her senses, she'd wanted to offer him complete surrender.

He deserves more than the passion of a moment, though I'm aching to share even that with him, she thought. A man like Nikolai deserves love and commitment. If she spent very much time in his arms, she knew, she'd be moved to give him those things. And that would be a terrible mistake.

Quietly noting the firmly sculpted line of his cheek and the long, thick lashes that shuttered his beautiful eyes, she tried to picture herself married to him. She found it wasn't very hard to do. The difficult part would come in observing the terms of our agreement, she thought.

When we touch, it's as if a hot current of electricity is passing between us, fraying what's left of our common sense and making us want to explode in a hail of sparks. If we were legally joined, it would be like trying to walk a tightrope blindfolded for us to stay out of bed.

Yet they'd have to do just that if his plan were to work at all. Its ultimate object was for them to part, not spend a lifetime together. As much as she treasured her Russian heritage, she didn't want to fall for him and stay in Moscow. That was simply out of the question.

Following their meal, a waiter brought brandy. Nikolai raised his glass in a toast. *"Na zdarovy,"* he said, clinking the balloon-shaped snifter against hers. "I hate to introduce a topic like this at such a mellow moment. But it's been several weeks since we talked at your grandfather's kitchen table. Have you given the matter we discussed that evening any further thought?"

The alcohol, fiery and a little sweet, made Katya's eyes water and burned her throat. For a moment she wasn't sure how to answer him. But she couldn't deny the truth. She had been thinking about his proposal, especially since her aborted attempt to contact the vice president that afternoon.

"I...I'm not sure it would work," she said at last. "In the beginning, I'll admit, I wasn't exactly inclined to trust you."

"And now?" He crooked one brow slightly as he awaited her answer.

"Now I think you're for real."

A small silence lay between them, warm and intimate. In it, their mutual liking and trust seemed to expand like the relaxed glow of the brandy that was spreading in Katya's bloodstream. As if drawn by a powerful magnet, her thoughts returned to the way they'd kissed that afternoon before the police officer came. What might we have said or done, she wondered, if we hadn't been interrupted that way? Perhaps fortunately for both of them, Gorky Park was a very public place.

Nikolai's eyes held a hint of the same speculation. Smiling at her, he swirled the remaining amber liquid in his glass so that it was scattered as it caught the light.

"Just the same, I worry," Katya continued after a moment.

"About what?"

She shrugged. "About you. And my grandfather. Lev's getting on in years, and he's almost ready to retire. If you say he won't be...affected beyond giving up his job, then I'll believe you. But your career is just beginning, Nikolai. I couldn't let you make such an enormous sacrifice."

It was the first time she'd expressed any concern for him. He wasn't maudlin or overly sentimental, but the idea that she cared what happened to him once she was home safe in America touched his heart. Without stopping to consider what effect it might have, he reached across the table and took her hand.

Her physical response was immediate, leaping like a flame to the source of oxygen there in the fashionably dim restaurant. Yet she declined to pull her hand away. So expressive of the inner man, Nikolai's dark eyes were gleaming at her. Her candlelit image was reflected in their onyx depths.

"It's very kind of you to think of my welfare, Katarina Danilova," he said. "But any ill effects on my career can be kept to a minimum, I think. I may be temporarily demoted to a desk job in Moscow. If that happens, don't forget that my father is a very powerful man. Eventually he'll be able to put things right."

Her hand resting in his, Katya wondered if he was making light of the situation. If so, she knew he wouldn't admit it. Despite her qualms, the prospect of accepting his help didn't daunt her the way it had just a few hours before.

"So," he said, watching her. "I see you're considering my offer, at least. Shall we court a little while you make up your mind?"

That night, as she lay waiting for sleep in the curtained-off alcove at her grandfather's apartment, Katya half regretted giving Nikolai a qualified *yes*. Agreeing to go along with his scheme, even provisionally, signaled the end of her independence. For his sake as well as her own, there could be no more attempts on her part to contact the American embassy, and no more pleas to Soviet authorities, begging them to relent.

It also meant they'd be spending a great deal of time together. Emotionally speaking at least, that might be difficult. Like it or not, they were on opposite sides of the greatest power struggle of the twentieth century. They couldn't afford to pursue the attraction they both felt.

Nikolai's idea of courtship, she discovered, was to show her the sights. Theirs was a very public affair—staged, no doubt, for the benefit of his colleagues and the rest of Soviet officialdom. There were no more private kisses, though they held hands often and exchanged hugs on several occasions when he brought her home.

No longer drab, Katya's life evolved into a whirlwind round of visits to the Tretyakov Art Gallery and Pushkin Museum and to performances by folk singers and dancers at the Tchaikovsky Concert Hall, followed by vodka and *blini* with sour cream at the hard currency bar patronized by foreigners and top party officials in the National Hotel.

Several times they attended the Bolshoi Theater, watching a superb Russian ballet from one of the tiered red-and-gold balconies. There was even a trip to the circus to see the skating bears.

Then loneliness threatened to rear its ugly head.

"I have to return to London in a few days," Nikolai informed her casually one evening as they sat over drinks at the National bar. They'd just come from a jam-packed reading by one of Moscow's favorite poets.

Katya turned to him in surprise. "Must you?"

"I'm afraid so, *drushenka*." He gave her his curving, half-secretive smile. "As it happens, I won't be back in Moscow until the end of December. Meantime, you must notify the authorities of your willingness to remain in the Soviet Union. Sign up for a class in Marxist-Leninist theory. And apply for work." He paused. "That is, if you want to proceed with our agreement."

She was silent a moment, absorbing the news. "You'll be gone for Christmas," she said, instinctively focusing on what had upset her the most.

An emotion she couldn't define flickered on his face. "I realize that," he said. "Don't forget this is an atheistic country, my angel. Christmas isn't a holiday here."

During their time together, Nikolai had adopted a whole series of pet names for her that made Katya squirm a little, though privately she dwelt on them with delight. In addition to being sophisticated, intelligent and often humorous company, he was also one-hundred-percent male—good-looking, sexy and far too adept at paying subtle compliments that made her feel feminine to the core.

She knew that it wasn't wise to let him color the fabric of her days and nights that way. If she got lucky and managed to escape, she'd find herself missing him too much. But she couldn't seem to help herself. Without him, she knew, Christmas would be a grim occasion— one more empty square on the calendar, another bead on the abacus to count.

Intently Nikolai observed the play of emotions over her face. She was looking festive in the black wool sheath, suede pumps and sheer, dark stockings that were part of her travel wardrobe. He wanted to make her expression match her dress.

"Don't look so sad, topaz eyes," he coaxed. "We'll be together on the first day of the new year. You'll meet my parents then."

With Nikolai gone, Katya wasn't sure which she missed the most—his company or her life in America. Though the pretense galled her, she dutifully carried out her part of the bargain.

The commissar to whom she unveiled her purported change of heart was polite but skeptical. "What brought this on, if I may ask?" he queried, folding his hands.

She fought off the urge to shrug and give him a flip reply. "I suppose you could say I've seen things from another perspective," she lied, keeping her voice expressionless. "My parents neglected to explain the merits of the Soviet system—the equality women enjoy, for instance. The absence of crime and unemployment. Besides, I've begun seeing a Russian man."

Katya let the implication dangle, hinting that politics meant nothing to her, that she'd do anything for love. She hated herself for sounding like such an airhead, such a turncoat. But perhaps the official had taken the bait. The slight flicker in his gaze revealed that her involvement with Nikolai came as no surprise.

For several moments, he simply stared at her as if in a crude attempt to read her thoughts. "Wait here, Miss Danilova," he said heavily, getting to his feet.

She had to sit a long time, but the wait proved worthwhile.

"Very well," the commissar said abruptly as he returned to his desk. "Temporary citizenship papers will be issued in your name. You will be allowed to register at the university. A job will be found for you in due course, if you keep out of trouble and demonstrate your commitment to socialist ideals."

With one beefy hand, he pushed some forms across his desk, asking that she fill them out listing her training and qualifications. Though she hadn't made up her mind completely about marrying Nikolai, it seemed that one by one her bridges to any other solution were being burned.

* * *

It was a bleak, sub-zero day when he returned, unannounced and bearing gifts. Katya was stirring cabbage soup on the tiny stove in her grandfather's kitchen.

"Nikolai!" she exclaimed, her face flushed and her hair curling from the steam as she wiped her hands on her apron. She had to fight back the urge to throw her arms around him.

"Come see what I've got for you," he said, including both her and Lev in his smile.

For Katya's grandfather, Nikolai had brought shaving supplies, British toiletries and a warm cashmere sweater. He presented Katya with a red wool coat and shiny leather boots.

Giddy with the delight of seeing him again, she twirled about in her new possessions. "But I . . . *we* don't have anything for you," she protested.

Nikolai smiled. "Your pleasure is recompense enough. Besides, you haven't been shopping in London the way I have," he reminded her. "On New Year's Day, you and Lev are invited to my parents' dacha. It's one of the few with indoor plumbing and decent insulation."

Katya wasn't sure what to expect as they set forth from Moscow on an overcast New Year's morning, heading east toward the Dvorovs' country house. She was nervous about meeting his family, nervous about their whole plan now that it was going forward again.

What will Nikolai's parents think of me? she asked herself, glancing at him as he drove. They know Lev, of course, though they seldom see him. But do they realize what their son has in mind? If not, how will they react to a prospective daughter-in-law who's American with Jewish ancestry on her mother's side? A tourist with a smuggling charge hanging over her head?

At the moment, there didn't seem to be any answers. Gradually they left the city's suburban flat blocks and factory districts behind. Military checkpoints for motorists became fewer. At last the sweeping, primitive countryside surrounded them.

Here and there, frozen streams dotted with ice fishermen wound under low bridges. Somber stands of pines and birches bracketed the road. The occasional village with its onion-domed spires seemed to be dreaming in the snow.

Most of the country cottages they passed were ramshackle wooden affairs. Clustered near the rail lines for the convenience of the city-dwellers who owned them, they had separate outhouses and icicles crowding their eaves. To Katya they looked cold and inhospitable in the wintry weather. She shivered in her bright new coat.

By contrast, the Dvorovs' dacha wore a prosperous look, which proclaimed the family's rarefied political status. They entered its winding drive and soon saw the picturesque two-story wooden house that obviously predated the revolution. It was painted a cheerful yellow with white trim. A Victorian-style cupola adorned one corner. Intriguingly erratic in shape, it boasted an odd assortment of glassed-in porches. Surrounding the house was a dense thicket of bushes and trees.

Several cars, one of them another shiny black Volga, were already parked at the foot of the dacha's rambling steps.

"The rest of my family...brothers, sisters, in-laws and various children...is already here," Nikolai explained. "Everyone will be very interested to meet you. I've brought along salmon, caviar and some wine."

I should have thought of contributing something, Katya chided herself. Uneasily she let him lead her up the steps. Lev followed behind them at his somewhat slower pace. She was absurdly grateful for his calm, steadying presence.

Someone had seen them coming. The door opened and arms enveloped them, reaching out to hug Nikolai, shake her hand, take Lev's coat.

"Hello, hello, hello!" a babel of Russian voices proclaimed. "So you've finally made it!" "Oh, *syomga*! And caviar! How nice!" "So happy to meet you. Would you like a drink?"

Katya knew she wasn't imagining the added warmth and friendship she saw in Dmitri's eyes as he shook her grandfather's hand.

In quick succession, she was introduced to Nikolai's parents—Dmitri with his heavy brows; plump, outgoing Yelena—and the seemingly endless complement of brothers, sisters, in-laws and other relatives he'd warned her about. Names like Drosha, Vasily, Aleksandra and Sergei were all mixed up in her head. "I'll never keep everyone straight," she admitted with a smile.

Nikolai's relatives beamed at one another in pleased surprise. The Amerikanskaya's Russian was excellent, with scarcely the trace of an accent.

Katya felt particularly drawn to Natasha, Nikolai's sister, who was about her own age. "You seem chilly, Katarina Danilova," Natasha remarked, linking arms with Katya. "Come into the sitting room. The warmth of the stove and a glass of vodka will put things right."

Smiling encouragement, Nikolai disappeared into a small study with his father. Lev settled down contentedly with a tumbler of vodka and Nikolai's uncle, a fellow professor of literature who was visiting from Novgorod. She had no choice but to accept Natasha's smiling invitation.

Though she felt something of an intruder in their midst, Katya found the company of the Dvorov siblings and their spouses surprisingly comfortable. As if they'd been warned of the pitfalls beforehand, they didn't ask any awkward or embarrassing questions. Had she seen this or that monument, cathedral, museum? they asked instead. Was she looking forward to her class at the university next term?

Basking in the warmth from an imposing blue-and-white tile stove and the rapidly spreading glow of the vodka, she couldn't help thinking what a warm, mutually supportive family group they made. Even in a society like this, she realized, it's possible to grow up feeling safe and loved. Nikolai's a product of that kind of environment. It's part of what's made him the person he is.

In the study, the dark-haired man who was on Katya's mind so much these days sat down in a window seat beside his father.

"Well, my son," Dmitri said, regarding him affectionately as he leaned back against the cushions. "She's quite charming. And she speaks excellent Russian. Are you sure you want to go through with this?"

Nikolai was silent a moment. "It's what you *want*, isn't it, Father?" he asked.

The older man shrugged. "Yes and no. Though I wish it were otherwise, there's nothing I myself can do for her. Yet I'm obliged by the very fact of my existence to help. If it weren't for Lev, I wouldn't be here today, helping the general secretary reform our communist system and our glorious Party. The mantle of savior, if anyone is to wear it, must fall on your shoulders."

Dmitri paused. "Of all my sons, you're the only one with the means to do this thing. And sufficient courage..."

"Then I'll do it gladly." A sense of pride and quiet determination pervaded Nikolai's words.

Regretfully Dmitri shook his head. "I don't like putting your career in jeopardy, my son. I'll do all I can to minimize the damage, of course. Pull whatever strings are available to me when the moment comes. But there's still considerable risk."

"I'm very well aware of that. Lev put his life and possibly his sanity on the line for you."

"Yes," said Dmitri. "Yes, I know."

Neither spoke for a moment as each thought about what could have happened so long ago.

"You're my pride and joy, the apple of my eye, though you aren't my firstborn," Dmitri said at last. "Has she agreed to marry you yet?"

Nikolai's dark eyes were glowing with the compliment. "I plan to ask her again today."

Something about the way he answered made his father take a second look. "Don't fall in love with her," Dmitri warned. "That would be a mistake."

Seated close to the stove in a white wool sweater and skirt that had been part of her tourist wardrobe, Katya rapidly became overheated, even flushed. Or maybe it was the vodka. Somebody kept refilling her glass. When the conversation veered away from her after a few minutes, she wandered out onto one of the porches. Beyond the fantastic scenes etched by frost on the windows, the low, wintry sun had broken through a dense layer of clouds. The tall pines that surrounded the dacha were suddenly illumined with color. Long, blue shadows splashed across the snow.

How beautiful it is here, she thought. We're not that far from the rabbit warren of Moscow, yet this house seems light-years distant. Close to rivers and trees, the smell of a garden. You get a sense of old Russia, the country my great-grandparents knew and loved.

"Katya," said Nikolai behind her.

Her head buzzing a little, she turned to face him. She liked the relaxed, informal way he looked in his gray sweater and pleated trousers.

"What are you doing out here?" he asked.

"Looking at the frost pictures. Your family is wonderful. I think they gave me too much vodka, though."

"Then you need something to eat."

But he didn't try to lead her back into the sitting room. Instead, he continued to look at her with a difficult-to-read expression.

"Tell me what's wrong," she said finally, feeling consumed by his gaze.

"Nothing's wrong." He took a step toward her and then another. A moment later his hands were settling about her waist. "You're so lovely today," he whispered. "Like a Russian princess of the old Romanov order. My brother Yuri is single. He's burning to get better acquainted."

Nikolai was single, too. Her cheeks grew pinker still with his praise. "I don't know which one is Yuri," she said.

"When we came in, he was playing the guitar."

Katya didn't answer, and their conversation seemed to continue in silence. "It's a new year," Nikolai said at last. "A fortunate time for new undertakings. Once again, I'm asking you to marry me. Let me help you to escape."

They were alone on the little porch—in truth, alone in the world when it came to carrying off the kind of enterprise he was suggesting. A man and a woman, strongly attracted to each other, but rooted in vastly differing cultures. They could never share anything permanent. But it was the vision of that kind of permanence he caused to dance in Katya's head.

Don't fall in love with her, his father had advised. And Nikolai knew the caveat was just. He couldn't leave his country, and she longed to return to hers. From the standpoint of anything personal between them, it was an impossible situation.

If I relax my guard for an instant, Katya admitted to herself, I'll be lost. It would be so easy to care for him. "All right, Nikolai Dmitrievich," she replied, making up her mind. "I place my fate in your hands."

A powerful current crackled between them, as it had in their relationship from the outset. But Nikolai didn't take advantage of it. Lightly, as if she were made of porcelain, he brushed her lips with his.

Perversely his restraint made her want more, much more. Resting her hands against the hard wall of his chest, she could feel the strong beating of his heart. Her nostrils were filled with his clean, spicy skin-scent. Through her white wool skirt she could feel the delicious presence of his long, muscular thighs.

If this were real, I'd want him to make love to me now, Katya thought. We'd find a private place to take each other with heat and promises—perhaps an ice-frosted summerhouse, huddled beneath the blankets of our coats.

By great effort of will she managed to step back from him, causing their lips to part. She was astonished a moment later when he produced an engagement ring. A garnet winked in its old-fashioned setting.

"I found it in a London antique shop," he said, slipping it on her finger. "Come, let's tell everyone the news."

Dmitri had rejoined the group in the sitting room by the time they went inside. He shook his son's hand and embraced Katya with what was surely a Russian bear hug when Nikolai made the announcement. Enthusiastically Yelena kissed them both. "It's time my son was married," she whispered in Katya's ear. "I'd begun to think it would never happen. You'll make beautiful children together."

How can I deceive such good people? Katya asked herself. Luckily they'd attribute the flush that spread over her cheeks to happiness.

"I wish to thank Katya's grandfather, Lev Petrovsky, for granting his permission," Nikolai said as fresh bottles of vodka were brought out for the toasts.

"Yes," added Dmitri, clapping Lev on the shoulder. "I'm very happy our two families are to be united, old friend."

More vodka flowed as the couple was inundated with congratulations. "You must wear my wedding dress, sister," Natasha offered. "It was frightfully expensive, and good fabric is sometimes difficult to come by. I think we're about the same size."

Smiling, her arm linked with Nikolai's, Katya thought her heart would break. I don't want to take advantage of Nikolai or hurt his family, she cried in the depths of her soul. But I can't stay in Russia, not even as a part of the warm and obviously loving Dvorov clan.

Despite his kisses, Nikolai didn't intend that, either. She'd have to find the courage to leave him—and her grandfather—when the time came.

Chapter 4

The following morning, Nikolai requested an appointment with his superior, Colonel Mikhail Gagarin, a second cousin of the famous astronaut who was buried with the Soviet Union's most honored dead in the Kremlin wall. While he was waiting in the colonel's outer office, Vanya Kutzov, an operative who sometimes worked with him in London, poked his head in the door.

"I hear you've gotten yourself engaged, old man," Vanya said.

News always traveled fast in KGB circles. But then Nikolai hadn't told his family to keep quiet about his plans. In fact, quite the opposite. "That's right," he admitted freely. "It happened yesterday."

Vanya gave him a knowing grin. "The secretaries around here are going to be inconsolable," he predicted. "When's the happy date?"

Nikolai shrugged. "Next week, if it can be arranged. I'm here this morning to get Comrade Gagarin's permission. I have to fly back to London on the twenty-first."

"So soon?" His colleague's forehead puckered in a slight frown. "She isn't pregnant, by any chance?"

"No, she isn't. You realize I'd knock out anyone else's front teeth for even suggesting that."

"No offense." Vanya hesitated, glancing at the colonel's door. "Do you think it's wise . . ." he began.

Quickly Nikolai silenced him, laying one finger against his lips. "My fiancée is sincere in rejecting the capitalist-imperialist way of life," he said in his most overbearing tone. "I know what her background is, but that's all finished now. She's Russian and she belongs here. What's more, she knows it. We love each other very much."

Propagandizing of any kind wasn't typical of Nikolai at all, and Vanya gave him a puzzled look. "Well, Nikky," he said philosophically as the door to the colonel's inner sanctum opened, "I wish you all the luck in the world. That's what it takes for a successful marriage, I suppose."

Colonel Gagarin was heavy-set, with fading red hair and almost colorless lashes that gave his pale blue eyes a falsely innocent look. The lines in his face, etched during the past half century, hadn't recorded many smiles, and he wasn't smiling now. Instead he'd drawn his brows together as if he couldn't quite suppress his disapproval. It went without saying that, as a highly placed cog in the Soviet Union's most efficient intelligence-gathering machine, he already knew the reason for Nikolai's visit, right down to the last detail.

The colonel's first remark proved Nikolai's assumption right. "So, Major Dvorov," the older man said without preamble. "You've fallen in love and you wish to marry the Danilova woman. Perhaps you've forgotten...the Committee frowns on unions between its operatives and foreigners of any kind."

Nikolai knew the committee to which his superior was referring wasn't the exalted Central Committee but rather the agency that employed them both, the Komitet Gossudarstvennoi Bezopasnosti—Committee for State Security—or KGB. Nikolai knew its rules as well as anyone. Unobtrusively he dug in his heels.

"Naturally I know that, sir," he said. "But my fiancée *isn't* a foreigner, as you're well aware. I'm sure her file states that she was born here in Russia, *before* her parents defected. Since her return several months ago, she's been officially declared a Soviet citizen."

Mikhail Gagarin didn't answer immediately. Without question, Katya's entire case, including the record of her arrest for smuggling and her initial pleas to leave the country, lay somewhere in the pile of manila folders on his desk.

From long practice, Nikolai could almost read his thoughts. Despite the technicality he'd seized upon, his marriage to Katya would seem strongly inadvisable from the KGB's point of view. Her parents were enemies of the state, and presumably she still cared for them. In addition, her grandfather was a Jew with mildly liberal leanings. The ink on her application for permanent citizenship and a job hadn't even dried yet.

Nobody, himself included, could guarantee she wasn't a new variety of "mole," an American agent who'd come to Russia for the express purpose of infiltrating the KGB—maybe even discrediting him and his father. He'd considered that possibility himself at the outset and discarded it. But Colonel Gagarin and others didn't know

Katya and her grandfather as he did. And they wouldn't be ruled by his instincts in that regard.

His chance of getting permission for them to marry was better if the drawbacks weren't directly stated, Nikolai knew. Once he'd received a *nyet*, he'd have to move heaven and earth to change bureaucratic minds.

"With all due respect," he added, playing his trump card a bit more hastily than he'd intended, "my father approves of her. He sends you his unqualified recommendation."

An awareness of Dmitri Dvorov's position flickered momentarily on Mikhail Gagarin's bland face. "Of course I respect Comrade Dvorov's judgment," he acknowledged, signaling that their meeting was at an end. "Perhaps I'll take the opportunity to discuss this matter with him. You'll have my decision in a few days."

To Nikolai's amazement, the requested permission was signed, sealed and delivered to his in basket by the end of the week. Braced for greater difficulty, he began to worry about the implications of a too-easy success. Yet despite his nagging sense that something was amiss, he didn't waste any time arranging for a license and a wedding reception at the Ararat Restaurant.

On the appointed day, Katya prepared for her nuptials with tears in her eyes. Since accepting Nikolai's proposal, she'd been overwhelmed with misgivings of her own. It wasn't that she didn't like him or have faith in him. Hadn't she placed her destiny in his hands, after all? In truth, she was strongly attracted to her dark-eyed betrothed, though she knew it would be a profound mistake to fall in love with him.

No, the tears were for her parents and the life in America she'd so carelessly jeopardized. Tears rolled down her cheeks even more copiously when she thought of Nikolai's family and her grandfather. Last but not least she found she was crying for Nikolai himself.

If his plan didn't work, she'd be trapped in the Soviet Union and obliged to offer Nikolai a divorce. If it did, she'd never see him or her grandfather again. Either way, the Dvorovs—so kind and welcoming—would be disillusioned by her treachery. Worse still, the consequences of helping her might turn out to be much more severe than Nikolai or Lev expected, even if their role in her escape couldn't be documented.

She couldn't bring herself to share her second thoughts with anyone. They'd gone too far to retreat, in her opinion. She wasn't free any longer to change her mind.

I'm damned if I go ahead with this thing and damned if I don't, she admitted to herself in frustration. It made her sad that, from that day forward, she couldn't stay in her grandfather's apartment anymore. Her bags were already packed, waiting to be stowed in the trunk of Nikolai's Volga. After the ceremony, she would go to live with him at his apartment in the Sistev Vrazhek district—even share his bed, though they'd vowed not to have marital relations.

The news that they'd have to sleep together had come as something of a shock. Yet not to do so might arouse suspicion, he'd warned. Someone was sure to search the apartment while they were out, perhaps on a regular basis. There were ways of determining whether or not two people used the same bedcovers.

Drying off from her bath with a thin, harsh towel, Katya put on her best underwear and her last run-free pair of Western-style nylon stockings. With a sigh she took Natasha's wedding gown off its padded hanger. Fashioned by a Moscow dressmaker from imported white silk satin, it came with a veil and matching headpiece of satin petals. True to Natasha's prediction, it fit her perfectly. But even after she'd slipped the gown over her head, brushed out her wavy, light-brown tresses and fastened the headpiece in place, she didn't feel like a bride.

The essential radiance was missing from her eyes. How different all this might be if there was no ideology, no rivalry between nations to build walls between people, she thought. *Nikolai and I might truly be on the verge of promising to love and honor each other for a lifetime.* As things stood, she couldn't imagine herself continuing to live with him in Russia, any more than she could picture him defecting to the United States.

She had just finished dressing when he arrived, punctual to a fault in his sober, dark suit with a carnation in his buttonhole. For once, his smile and friendly "hello" seemed a little forced. With a quiet formality that unnerved her, he shook her grandfather's hand and presented her with a small bouquet.

"Thank you, Nikolai Dmitrievich," she said in a small voice.

"It's my pleasure, Katarina Danilova," he replied.

A small silence fell between them as she, Nikolai and her grandfather stood in the flat's cramped living area, simply looking at one another. *They both feel as I do,* Katya guessed. *The whole context of what we're doing seems unreal. As for the tangle of emotions it evokes, words won't suffice.*

"If you're ready, I'll carry your things downstairs," Nikolai said at last, his voice strangely without expression. "No sense hiring a taxi or limousine when I can drive, even though it flies in the face of tradition."

There's no need to honor tradition in our case, Katya thought as he settled them in his shiny black automobile. Yet she realized he hadn't neglected it altogether. There was the bouquet, for one thing; the midwinter luxury of its sweetly scented white roses and delicate stephanotis had surely cost him a fortune, even at one of the special stores that served the Soviet elite. He'd also tied a bride doll, which signified a newly married couple, to the Volga's front bumper.

Still, such embellishments were probably just part of the show. She'd have to become adept at acting her part in a torrid romance and perfect husband-wife relationship.

Nikolai's parents and several of his brothers and sisters, including Natasha and her husband, were waiting for them at the Palace of Weddings Nikolai had selected. The large, fairly plain room in one of the government buildings contained a desk and several tidy rows of chairs for guests. Shyly she greeted them, feeling her own duplicity like a wound.

"Don't be nervous!" Natasha soothed, squeezing Katya's arm. "It's a very simple ceremony, really. It'll be over before you can think about it twice."

That's what I'm afraid of, Katya thought. Once we're married, I'm committed. I should never have agreed to do such a crazy thing.

The utilitarian atmosphere of the wedding palace did nothing to lighten her mood. Its only adornments were the inevitable portrait of Lenin and a pressed-glass vase containing two chrysanthemums. The magistrate who would marry them turned out to be a woman. Unsmiling and squat of build, she wore a boxy gray suit and sensible shoes. She had a no-nonsense air and didn't look as if she'd ever been in love.

Like their surroundings, the socialist rite of marriage turned out to be incredibly bleak. All too quickly, the Dvorovs and Lev were taking their seats as Nikolai led Katya to the front of the room. Hand in hand, they stated their names and addresses and produced the mandatory papers. Though Katya's voice shook a little, Nikolai's was firm and steady. His earlier reticence seemed to have evaporated; she could feel his strength and reassurance flowing into her through the warm pressure of his fingertips.

Somehow she managed to sign her name beside his in the marriage register in an extremely shaky Cyrillic script. Next, their dry, somewhat pedantic vows were read. Staring straight ahead without really focusing on the magistrate's stern countenance, Katya mouthed the required phrases. Only the trembling of her hand hinted at her tangle of emotions as Nikolai slipped a plain gold band onto the finger that already bore his antique garnet.

Her ears were ringing, and she felt as if her legs might not hold her while the matronly official read a seemingly interminable homily on commitment to one's spouse, one's family and socialist ideals. I hope to God I don't disgrace Nikolai by collapsing at his feet, Katya thought. Try to pretend you're only dreaming. Any minute now, you'll wake up in your grandfather's apartment, find yourself sleeping alone in your narrow little bed.

Finally it was over. The magistrate pronounced them man and wife, and the hushed expectancy in the room told Katya it was time for the nuptial kiss. Reality set in with a little rush as Nikolai turned to her. This stranger, she reminded herself—a KGB operative and member in good standing of the Communist Party—is now my husband. The trouble is, I'm half in love with him.

They were only a breath apart. With a proprietary air, Nikolai gripped her waist through the slippery satin of Natasha's dress and drew her tightly against him. Her hands resting against his chest, she could feel the strong, steady rhythm of his heartbeat. Make believe we're mad about each other, his dark eyes instructed as he lowered his mouth to hers.

For Katya, there wasn't any need to pretend. Instant pandemonium raged in her blood even as confusion and desire spread in shock waves through her body. Prepared for a chaste ceremonial brush of the lips, she hadn't counted on reliving their first kiss—that private, wildly passionate tumbling into ecstasy conducted inside a maelstrom of snowflakes that still haunted her dreams. The resulting urge to surrender, to grant him the most profound liberties she'd ever tendered anyone, nearly swept her away.

Though at first he tasted her gently, his restraint itself was like an aphrodisiac. She knew instinctively that it couldn't last. As if he could read her thoughts, his kiss deepened. Parting her lips, his tongue plumbed moist depths, rewarding fear and anticipation.

Nikolai, she thought. Oh, Nikolai . . .

Time fluttered to a halt as they stood pressed together. The room and everyone in it disappeared.

They were locked in an unexpected foretaste of the kind of communion they could share. Totally consumed yet feeling almost worshipped, Katya yielded up the depths of her being. Willingly she gave the man she'd just married her permission to ravage and protect.

A rustle of indulgent whispers brought them back to the everyday world. Embarrassed, Katya stepped back from his embrace. She saw her grandfather and Yelena had tears in their eyes. Yet like everyone else they were beaming. Only on Dmitri's part could she sense any reservation.

Quickly she and Nikolai were engulfed in a flood of bear hugs, kisses and congratulations. At Yelena's urging, Natasha's husband, Vasily, snapped a series of wedding photographs. Even the dour magistrate unbent a little at so much good will. "Good health and many children, comrades," she told them, offering them businesslike handshakes.

By then another couple was awaiting its turn. Careful not to overstay the allotted time, the Dvorov clan filed out. Still branded by the emotional onslaught of Nikolai's kiss, Katya was shy with him as they ducked into the Volga's back seat. But she didn't draw back when he took her hand in his.

In yet another bow to tradition, she learned, Vasily would be their chauffeur for a tour of city landmarks. With a little bow, he got in behind the wheel while a smiling Natasha slid in beside him. To their rear, the rest of the wedding party was piling into a series of cars. We'll form a kind of caravan, Katya thought. Everyone will be staring at us. But she was most apprehensive about the scrutiny of those closest to them. Would Nikolai's mother and father, or Vasily and Natasha perhaps, expect additional displays of affection?

Nikolai seemed to think they would. Chatting expansively with his sister and brother-in-law, he whispered simultaneous endearments in Katya's ear, pausing occasionally to kiss her neck, her earlobes, her fingertips. The familiar sights of the Kremlin, St. Basil's and the classic facade of the Bolshoi Theater passed in a nerve-rackingly sensual haze.

At last they drew to a halt at the north entrance of Alexander Garden where, in observance of modern Soviet custom, Katya would place her bouquet at the Tomb of the Unknown Soldier. Vasily and Natasha got out to accompany them, while the rest of their motorcade waited.

Hand in hand, Katya and Nikolai walked toward the low red-and-black granite monument, their steps leaving parallel footprints in the snow. Katya's veil blew over her face as the tomb's eternal flame hissed and sputtered in a brisk wind. The honor guard remained impassive as she laid her bridal flowers beside the massively sculpted helmet that decorated the bier. No doubt the flowers would freeze in half an hour. Soberly Nikolai read the snow-dusted inscription, which honored Russian casualties of the World War II defense of Moscow.

"Is it true," Natasha asked, partially dispelling the solemnity of the moment, "that in Western countries the bride throws her bouquet to the wedding guests?"

Katya nodded. "But only to single women. The one who catches it is supposed to marry next."

Her sister-in-law laughed and shook her head. "That seems a frivolous custom," she said, "although a rather charming one. Luckily I'm already married to my darling Vasily. Since I wouldn't be allowed to catch your flowers, I'm not missing out on anything!"

Giving his wife a fond look, Vasily posed the newlyweds for more pictures. As he fussed with the apparatus of his camera, Katya began to shiver with cold.

Nikolai noticed it at once. "Come, it's getting raw out here, and my new wife is hardly a polar bear," he remarked, drawing Katya into the shelter of his arm. "Time for supper and a toast."

Old-fashioned and gracious despite its enormous size, the Ararat Restaurant was a favorite for wedding recep-

tions. The smooth-tongued maître d' assured them a
ringside table had been reserved for their party.

To Katya's surprise, the place turned out to be something of a nightclub. It boasted a large dance floor that
Nikolai said did double duty as a stage for various acts.
The cuisine was Armenian. It featured stuffed vine
leaves, *cheboureki*, a sort of meat pie resembling a
Cornish pastry, and grilled *shashlik* with rice pilaf. Caviar and vodka were plentiful. They were also offered a
somewhat cloying vintage of Russian champagne.

The toasting began the minute everyone was seated at
the table. "To many happy years!" Dmitri proposed,
raising his glass to the newlyweds.

"To many happy years!" everyone echoed enthusiastically, draining shotglass-sized portions of vodka. Would
it were so, Katya thought, feeling the pull of Nikolai's
presence beside her as she grimaced and did likewise. But
you can't give in to such thoughts. More good wishes
followed, interrupted only by the refilling of their glasses.

With a promptness that reflected Dmitri Dvorov's
status as a high government official, the *zakuski*, or traditional Russian hors d'oeuvres, arrived. By then, Katya's nervousness had abated. She felt light-headed and
slightly helpless, swept along by events and afloat on a
tide of more alcohol than she usually consumed.

"Thank heaven for some food!" she whispered to Nikolai as she filled her plate. "I haven't eaten a thing all
day, and my head is buzzing."

It appeared the vodka had relaxed him, too. "Better
thank Lenin instead, like a good communist," he teased,
putting one arm around her. "In old Russia, vodka was
drunk from cups that were round on the bottom, like
thimbles. It had to be dispatched in a single gulp. And
most people still drink it that way today. However, as a

bride, you're not expected to carry the custom forward, sweetheart. No groom in his right mind wants to lead his wife away drunk from the wedding feast.''

Just then, Natasha claimed their attention, and Katya didn't have time to do more than wonder about her groom's intentions. Dessert turned out to be crepes suzette and ice cream. Following the meal, it was time for the floor show. Katya gazed benevolently if a trifle hazily at a parade of singers, dancers and hat tumblers. There was also a magician and a man who performed tricks with a rope.

When the show ended, a sixteen-piece orchestra began to play. But nobody stepped out on the dance floor. ''You and Nikolai must have the first dance together,'' Yelena prompted. ''It's your prerogative as newlyweds.''

A bit unsteady on her feet, Katya let her husband draw her out onto the vast expanse of parquet. Yet, unorthodox as their situation might be, it felt like coming home when he took her in his arms. The music was a traditional waltz, and she found herself following his lead instinctively, much as she had on the skating pond in Gorky Park.

Our marriage may not be real in the sense that it isn't intended to last, she told herself, drowning in the expressive pools of his beautiful dark eyes. But our attraction to each other is all too genuine. How long will it be before we go back on that vow that wasn't part of the wedding ceremony... and make love to each other?

The toasting, it appeared, would go on all night. But custom dictated she and Nikolai could leave early. Availing themselves of the opportunity, they drove to his apartment. Expecting to spend the night there, Katya was surprised to learn they'd be stopping for only a few min-

utes—just long enough to change into casual clothing and
pick up his suitcase.

Exercising his KGB privilege of parking in a loading
zone, Nikolai ushered her inside his yellow-brick apartment building. Politely he introduced her to the *dezhur-
naya*, or duty person, who kept watch beside the cage-
style elevator. The old woman's gaze sharpened as she
appeared to memorize Katya's features. "Congratulations, Comrade Dvorov," she said, nodding over her
knitting again.

Katya didn't have much chance to look around. She
formed a hasty impression of heavy drapes, antique furniture and a priceless collection of samovars before
shutting herself up in the bathroom to don slacks, a heavy
sweater and boots. Carefully she hung Natasha's wedding gown in an armoire beside Nikolai's bed and
shrugged on her red wool coat.

"Where are we going?" she asked breathlessly as they
went downstairs again.

Decidedly mellow but still sober despite all the vodka
he'd drunk, Nikolai gave her a pleased look. "I have a
few days off before I have to return to England," he said.
"My parents have loaned us the dacha for the duration."

Katya fought back a wave of disappointment. So he'd
be leaving again almost immediately, for God only knew
how long this time. Meanwhile, she'd be living in a
strange apartment, coping alone with the demands of an
alien life.

Yet as they left the city, abandoning its lights for an
inky black expanse of fields and woods, it was the immediate future that claimed her thoughts. For the
"duration," as he'd said, they'd be hidden away together, sheltered from prying eyes in a house where she

could picture them raising a family. Anything might happen if they let down their guard.

By the time they arrived at their destination, it was quite late and icy cold. The dacha was dark and silent. No cars were parked in its driveway. No laughing tribe of Dvorovs rushed to greet them at the door.

Unlocking the front door, Nikolai thrust their cases into the unlit entryway and swept Katya off her feet. "For luck," he explained, carrying her over the threshold. "We're going to need all we can muster, you and I."

When he put her down, they were standing as close as they had at the Wedding Palace that afternoon. But the price of indulging themselves in soul-rending kisses was higher in that isolated setting, and they both realized it. "Come," said Nikolai, leading her into the cluttered but charmingly decorated sitting room where just a few weeks earlier they'd announced their engagement. "It's as cold as Siberia in here. You'd better get warm under one of these fur throws while I build us a fire."

With a skill that bespoke long practice, he kindled a crackling blaze inside the blue-and-white tile stove. As its heat gradually permeated the room, Katya let herself relax a little. Nothing will happen, she promised herself. We can't afford to let it. Yet she knew that her own feelings would make it a difficult promise to keep.

She didn't demur when he piled pillows, quilts and another fur throw on the thick rug before the fire and invited her to lean her back against the couch and join him. They were both completely sober and very tired now, though still keyed up from the day's events. From somewhere he produced a small bottle of brandy and two glasses.

"Drink this . . . it'll warm you," he said, offering her a modest portion. "I'd toast the success of our venture, sweetheart. But we've had more than enough toasts today."

It was past midnight, their wedding day already history. Accepting the brandy, Katya took a sip. She found that it heated and revived her even as it relaxed her again. Cuddling closer to Nikolai for warmth, she stared into the fire as if the patterns created by its flickering light could somehow predict the future. Would they be parting in London a year hence as planned, she wondered? Or would their separation come about in a Soviet divorce court, after all hope of her escape to America had died?

She didn't dare think about the possibility of having him for the rest of her life. To entertain it at all was inviting heartache. Ironically she'd never met a man who so completely monopolized her thoughts.

Part of the unseen force that drew her to Nikolai, of course, was pure physical attraction. She couldn't stop gazing dreamily into his eyes or feeling the wry tenderness of his lopsided grin. She wondered if he knew how frequently she noticed the powerful span of his shoulders, his lean midsection and trim buttocks, those long, muscular legs.

But her fascination with him was more profound than mere physical desire. There was a depth in him, a resonance that called out to her very soul. It made her want to know his every thought, share each of his smiles and sorrows. She wanted to be the woman who brings him joy, she thought. The one he comes to for emotional refuge.

She knew she'd be lost if she continued to allow herself to think that way. But she didn't pull away when he sighed, stretched and drew her closer. This moment was far too precious to hurry its end.

Though Katya couldn't know it, Nikolai was also lost in bittersweet imaginings. How lovely she looked this afternoon, he thought, dressed in Natasha's white gown. He'd seen the hesitance and bravado warring in her tawny eyes. He remembered how passionately she returned his kiss in front of the wedding guests.

A woman like that—soft, feminine, yet alight with enough determination and daring to go after what she wanted—had long been missing from his life. He wanted to make love to her, taste her every secret. But he knew she wouldn't let him. And she'd be right to refuse. They didn't have a future together, and she wasn't the type to indulge in casual sex, like so many young women he'd known.

Perhaps it was for the best. If they ever fell from grace—gave vent to their passionate natures—he'd be hard pressed to let her go.

"Tell me something, Nikolai."

Her voice was soft in the quiet room, and he turned his head a little, his lips just brushing her hair. "Yes, *drushenka*?" he asked.

"Do you regret . . . taking the step we did today?"

He was silent a moment. "No," he said at last. "As I told you before, an obligation exists, one my father is in no position to honor. And, even if he could do something, he couldn't afford to take the risk."

"Why not?"

Again Nikolai paused, as if weighing how much he ought to tell her. "He's not afraid for himself, but for Russia," he said. "Maybe you didn't know it, but he is one of the general secretary's strongest allies for *glasnost* and moderation. The balance of power is shakier than most outsiders realize. A blow to my father's credibility could send it toppling...along with all of our recent gains."

This time it was Katya's turn to look thoughtful. She hadn't imagined the look she'd seen on Dmitri Dvorov's face, then. *He doesn't want Nikolai to become emotionally involved with me, and I can't blame him,* she thought.

"So he knows what you're planning," she said at last. "I should have guessed."

Nikolai swallowed the last of his brandy, and she saw that he wanted her to know the truth. "Dmitri Alexeivich would never have allowed our marriage to take place if it didn't suit his purposes," he replied. "But you're not supposed to *know* he knows. I'm trusting you to keep that information to yourself."

Solemnly she gave her word. "But I still don't understand," she insisted. "If loyalty's so important to your father, doesn't he feel guilty, condoning my escape?"

Nikolai shrugged. "It isn't like that. Allegiance to one's country and the people one cares about conflict sometimes, but that isn't the case here. Letting you go won't harm the state."

"You don't think I'd be an asset to socialist progress?"

She posed the question with mock affront, and Nikolai smiled at her. "That's a different issue altogether, my dear Mrs. Dvorov," he said. "You want to return to your country, and I understand that completely. For myself, I could never leave Russia, wrongheaded as our ways sometimes appear."

Chapter 5

Outside, it started to snow in big, ragged flakes that feathered lightly against the windowpanes. The fire in the stove burned lower, and Katya burrowed even more deeply beneath the piled-up covers, allowing her head to rest on Nikolai's shoulder. Though his words had outlined all too succinctly the gulf that separated them, she felt comforted by his nearness. It wasn't long before she was fast asleep.

Easing her down against some pillows, Nikolai stoked the fire again and came back to lie beside her. She was curled up on her side like a child, trusting and oblivious. Rosy in the firelight with her sooty lashes resting against her cheek, she offered a temptation he couldn't resist. "Sleep well, my beautiful Amerikanskaya," he whispered, brushing her cheek with his lips. It was a long time before he too was lost in dreams.

* * *

Katya awoke to hot tea and spiced cardamom buns. As she sat up and took her steaming cup from Nikolai's fingers, she realized they'd slept on the floor all night. Yet oddly enough she felt more rested than she had since coming to Russia.

"Why didn't you wake me so we could go to bed?" she asked him and then blushed beet-red at the implication.

He couldn't help but enjoy her consternation. "You looked so comfortable I didn't want to disturb you," he said. "Hurry and eat your breakfast. I have a surprise for you."

The surprise turned out to be a borrowed troika. Three horses stamped and snorted in the new-fallen snow. "Oh, but it's like something out of a movie! Or a fairy tale!" Katya exclaimed, dancing joyously down the dacha's wooden steps to pat the nearest animal's neck. "Pinch me and say I'm not dreaming!"

Nikolai glowed fondly at her pleasure. "Perhaps it is a dream come true," he said. "Darling Katya, don't you think you'd be warmer if you fastened your coat?"

The endearment only increased the jubilation in her heart. Quickly she did as he suggested, putting on the fur hood he held out to her and tying it firmly beneath her chin. To her delight, the day was clear though cold, the sky over their heads an infinite expanse of blue. A pristine layer of new snow sparkled like sugar on the brooding firs and paved the winter-deep drifts with diamonds.

Taking Nikolai's hand with her mittened one, she let him help her into the sleigh. A moment later, he got in beside her, tucking the fur robes they'd used as bedding the night before around them. Then they were off, the bell-studded leather harness jingling merrily as Nikolai handled the reins with expert grace.

"But this is marvelous...marvelous!" Katya pronounced, her eyes glittering with excitement. "Like waking up and finding yourself in the Russia of *Dr. Zhivago.* I never imagined something like this!"

"I'm glad you like your surprise." Nikolai's cloud of breath mingled with hers in the frosty air.

For a mile or two, they kept to the snow-packed country road, meeting another troika and waving at its occupants. Several cars also passed them going the other way—black Volgas like Nikolai's and a Chaika limousine with gray curtains pulled shut inside its rear windows.

"Party bigwigs on their way back to Moscow," Nikolai explained. "A number of them have dachas in this district, but they don't like to flaunt it. I'm glad we don't have to go back to the city today."

As soon as he could, Nikolai cut over to the river, which was frozen solid beneath its blanket of snow. Ice fishermen, warming themselves with portable wood stoves, dotted its surface. The banks were an undulating drift of snow-laden, smoke-colored trees.

"It's so beautiful," Katya said, craning her neck in order to see everything. "The river makes a lovely thoroughfare through the woods."

Nikolai nodded. "I prefer it to the road...just as I prefer the knight and his capacity for deviousness to the more straightforward rook in a chess game. But as you'll see, the river doubles back on itself. It'll take us twice as long to reach our destination."

They had all day. Nikolai had chosen to take her to the Arkhangelskoye Estate, a green-roofed, yellow stucco mansion-turned-museum situated near the riverbank in a grove of trees. As a substitute for making love on one's honeymoon, it was as good as any, Katya supposed.

"The palace was designed by a French architect for Prince Yusupov, a wealthy czarist landowner of the late eighteenth and early nineteenth centuries," Nikolai said as he tied up the horses and helped her from the sleigh. "He was a politician and traveler…even governor of the Kremlin for a while. As you can see, he lived in lavish abundance. He also had an eye for beautiful women, or so the story goes."

Ascending the steps from ground level, they passed stately colonnades of pillars that surrounded the palace's front entrance. Inside was a dazzling artistic display. The mansion's many rooms and galleries contained fabulous porcelains, tapestries and sculptures as well as many exquisite paintings—some of them by the Flemish master Van Dyck.

According to Nikolai, Prince Yusupov had kept a menagerie of parrots and other exotic birds. Some of the large, ornate cages remained. Original glassware and china that had graced the prince's dinner table were also on exhibit.

After touring the house, they took a roundabout way back toward the river, deviating from the path now and then to inspect some of the outdoor sculpture and explore pavilions that lay half hidden among the trees. There were too many people about to engage in a snowball fight, though the urge to do so flitted through Katya's mind. She felt exhilarated walking in the sharp cold with Nikolai, her hand held tightly in his.

Wonderful as Arkhangelskoye is, the best part of our excursion so far has been the ride itself, Katya thought as Nikolai tucked the lap robes about them again and they were off on their return journey, the sleigh bells jingling and the troika's runners hissing over snow-covered ice.

Snuggling close to him under the heavy furs for warmth was almost too pleasurable to bear. Yet she felt anything but satisfied. She kept wanting more from him, more—to feel the prison of his strong arms around her, the sweet demand of his mouth as it plundered hers.

It seemed he was thinking similar thoughts. "Katya," he said, his voice barely audible over the scraping runners, jingling harness and frigid, heady rush of air.

"Yes, Nikky?" Expectantly she turned her face to his.

It was the first time she'd used the nickname that came so easily to others' lips, and a little flame of acknowledgement leapt in his eyes. "I shouldn't do this, but I'm going to anyway," he said in a smothered voice, covering her mouth with his in the way she wanted.

As uncontrollable as a forest fire, Nikolai's kiss touched off a conflagration throughout Katya's body. Though her cheeks were cold, hot blood thrummed in her veins, a life force suddenly gone mad in its need to mate with his.

No one but ice fishermen could see them and then only at a distance—two fur-swathed bodies, struggling to move closer in each other's embrace. Drawing the sleigh forward at a sprightly clip, Nikolai's borrowed horses didn't seem to mind his lack of attention to the reins.

Urged on by Katya's response, Nikolai parted her lips with his tongue. Heat suffused her, negating the bitter chill, as he slipped one hand inside her coat. Through the heavy cable knit of her sweater, he boldly explored her breasts, seeking and finding the hard outlines of her nipples. A gasp escaped her moments later when he moved his hand beneath the sweater to stroke her tautly aching peaks.

"I want them in my mouth, do you understand that, *drushenka*?" he muttered, his lips bruising hers with fierce, almost barbarous kisses. "To suck at them as an infant does . . . draw all the sweetness from your body."

His imagery seared her mind. The burning lava flow of desire it evoked took possession of her, its effulgence focusing between her legs.

"No, Nikolai . . . we can't! It's madness!"

Her body was screaming yes. Even as she denied him, Katya followed his lead, frantically fumbling with his buttons. Half mad with the currents of need that shuddered from the points of her breasts to her most feminine places, she wanted to feel him, touch him, taste him, merge with him unconditionally and completely in an untamed frenzy of delight.

With a little groan, he lifted her so that she was astride his lap. Her breasts crushed against his chest and her thighs gripping his, she could feel the tumescence beneath his trousers exactly where it excited her the most. Already she was slippery with wanting him.

We can't do this, she repeated to herself, unaware that she'd spoken the words aloud. Not here in the sleigh. Not ever. Yet she yearned with all the force of her being to merge her flesh with his.

Just then they hit a rough spot on the ice. Jolted, Nikolai felt about for the reins and pulled back on them, slowing the pace of the horses.

"You're right, Katya my darling," he acknowledged, leaning his forehead against hers. "As much as I might wish it, we can't make love."

Suddenly shivering with cold, she pressed closer against him. He held her protectively, ruefully. How can we sleep together in your bed in Moscow after this? she longed to ask. She blamed herself mightily for her feelings. Yet though it had brought her anguish, his was the touch she craved.

Gently Nikolai set her back in her seat. "It's my fault," he said, drawing her into the circle of his arm as if he couldn't bear for their contact to end. "I've wanted you since the first time we kissed outside your grandfather's apartment and I lost control of myself. You know I'm right, Katya. If we became lovers, we might not be able to let each other go."

Do we have to say goodbye? Katya thought. Can't there be some way around it? But no answer came winging to her on the rushing air.

The rest of their journey home was bittersweet, an exercise in futility and pent-up emotions. Though Nikolai's arm lay about her shoulder, she could almost feel him building a wall between them. The brilliant sunlight and jingling sleigh bells that had so entranced her now seemed cruelly to mock her mood.

When they reached the dacha, Katya thanked him and went inside. Nikolai didn't follow. He then returned the troika and horses to the affluent neighbor from whom he'd borrowed them and refused a ride home, preferring to trudge off his frustration in the snow.

From the frost-etched window of one of the glassed-in porches, Katya saw him stamp up the drive, then turn away toward one of the dacha's outbuildings. A few minutes later, the harsh ringing of an ax filled the air as he split an unnecessary cord of wood. Though she longed to go to him, she stifled the impulse. What are we going to do with ourselves in this solitude, she wondered? After what happened today, it will be so awkward for us to be together.

By the time Nikolai returned to the house, he emanated a quiet if hard-won control. Supper in the dacha's blue-and-yellow dining room was a modest affair of borscht, pickled herring and crusty bread they'd brought with them from Moscow. Conversation seemed stilted, and finally Nikolai put on the record player. A selection of themes from Tchaikovsky filled the room.

After dinner, Nikolai took a book from one of the shelves. Too distracted to read, Katya folded her hands in her lap and stared at the fire. Where will we sleep tonight, she asked herself. Together in Nikolai's room or alone in separate beds? Will state security people check the sheets for microscopic evidence that we slept together after we depart?

Finally the ormolu clock on the table beside Katya's chair struck ten. "It's been a long day," Nikolai noted, putting his book aside. "Perhaps we should turn in."

"All right." Katya gave him a hesitant look. "Do you think it would be better..."

"If we slept apart?"

She nodded, knowing that wasn't what either of them wanted but determined to take some of their shared responsibility on herself.

He regarded her silently for a moment. "Maybe I'm paranoid," he said. "But I really do feel we have to keep up appearances, even here. And anyway, the truth is, I want to hold you. I give you my solemn word: I won't repeat my behavior of this afternoon."

Filled suddenly with a tenderness that didn't negate the passion they'd shared but soared far beyond it, Katya laced her arms about his waist. "Maybe we can't be more than friends and co-conspirators, Nikolai Dmitrievich," she said. "But we can give each other comfort. I want to hold you, too."

For the remainder of their stay at the dacha, the affectionate compromise held. Once again, they had fun together, tramping the woods and building an American-style snow fort, picking out tunes on the guitar Yuri had left behind. Each night, they swapped childhood reminiscences by the fire.

Though desire was never very far from the surface, they kept it under rigorous control. A bit self-consciously, they shared the dacha's master bedroom. Strangely enough, once they were between the deep covers and luxurious feather mattresses of Yelena and Dmitri's four-poster bed, most of their awkwardness seemed to vanish. Warming each other's toes, they slept nestled in a cozy embrace.

Despite its undercurrent of frustration and regret, the contentment of those days followed them back to Moscow. It even accompanied them to the airport, where Katya went to see Nikolai off on his London journey.

On the day he left, it was spitting snow. As his KGB chauffeur watched, Katya put her arms around his neck and kissed him with enough actual fervor to convince even the most suspicious mind.

"I should go away more often," Nikolai whispered with a rueful smile. "Take care, my love. Don't do anything rash that would ruin your chances. I'll be home as soon as I can. And I'll call you. Just remember that our phone is tapped."

I'll remember, she thought—about that and a good many other things. Like the way you look when you wake up in the morning, with your hair all rumpled and your dark eyes sleepy on the pillow next to mine. The way you whistle when you shave and the firm, sure clasp of your hand. She found herself wishing they'd indulged their most primitive instincts while they still had the chance.

But he'd be back.

"You be careful, too, Nikky," she said, striving for a light touch. "Being married to a spy isn't exactly conducive to my peace of mind."

For a moment she thought he'd dispute her characterization of him, or demand to know why his safety mattered so much. Instead, he grinned, kissed the tip of her nose and let her go.

You might as well get the hang of saying goodbye to him, she thought as he joined several traveling companions on the runway. But she didn't leave even after he'd boarded. Instead, she remained on the tarmac as his plane took off, waiting until it had completely disappeared into low-hanging clouds.

For Katya, the following weeks were busy ones. Not only did she begin her night class at Moscow University, but the state in its beneficence found a job for her. The class, a study of Marxist-Leninist theory based on dialectical materialism, was boring in the extreme, its subject matter arcane and alien to her way of thinking. The job, as a translator for the Soviet news bureau *Tass*, turned out to be boring, too. Excited when she first learned of it, she quickly found herself in a back room, translating dry technical dispatches from English to Russian on the off-chance that they might contain something interesting. Still, it got her out of the apartment, and she found it a relief to be occupied again. So what if the manual typewriter that had been assigned to her was in dreadful repair? Her typing errors could be excused more readily that way.

Cautious at first, the other women in her translators' pool gradually accepted her. Several of them began stopping by her desk to gossip and ask her to eat lunch with them. Sometimes after work she lost to her grand-father at chess and cooked supper for him at his apartment.

Yet though her days were full, her nights were lonely. Often she simply came home alone, took a hot bath and ate some soup while she listened to classical music on the radio. Her overall sensation was one of being suspended, of waiting in a vacuum for Nikolai to return.

It's just that I'm anxious to go home to America, she rationalized as she reclined one evening in a tub billowing with some of the scented bubble bath Nikolai had mailed her from London. For her, the United States wasn't all race riots, drug raids and homelessness, the way it was portrayed on Soviet television. Instead, it was the freedom to come and go as one pleased, say what one thought and read newspapers that dared to tell the unvarnished truth about things. Most of all, it was her parents. Christmases that could be celebrated. The soil that had nourished her roots.

Nikolai wasn't part of that life. Yet somehow she found herself mentally pushing any chance to escape further and further into the future. She had to be practical, after all. It would be a year at least before they let her go with him to London.

Meanwhile, he'd be home in just two weeks!

She was humming a little tune and scrubbing her shoulders when a slight sound in the doorway to the cramped, old-fashioned bathroom caused her to glance in that direction. Her eyes widened to see him standing there, as if transported by a magician's spell. He was wearing his British-made topcoat, and his cheeks were ruddy with cold. He hadn't taken off his fur hat yet. Dark eyes gleaming, he gazed appreciatively at her bubble-bedecked nakedness.

"What...what are you *doing* here?" Katya exclaimed, her voice registering somewhere between a squeak and a croak. Suddenly realizing how she must look to him, she slid deeper into the suds.

Nikolai's mouth curved. "Enjoying the view. Since you ask, I do live here, you know."

"You might at least have let me know you were coming!"

"What? And spoil the surprise?"

Leaning casually against the door frame, he struck up a casual conversation about what she'd been doing in his absence. With a show of genuine interest, he inquired about her class and her new job. When finally those topics had been exhausted, he held forth at length on the pleasures of London during the winter season.

As he talked, Katya's bathwater cooled. Her protective layer of bubbles slowly deflated. A gentleman would step out of the room and give me a moment's privacy to get out of the tub, she thought. But though his manners customarily were flawless, Nikolai didn't seem to be aware of her plight. Instead, he regarded her with what might be repressed merriment and thinly disguised anticipation.

"Maybe I'd better dry off now," she prompted, afraid she'd catch cold if she waited any longer.

"Yes, of course," he agreed readily. "I'll get you a towel."

To Katya's consternation, she realized he had no intention of moving from the spot. Fine, she thought, her cheeks rosy with embarrassment as she got to her feet. Have an eyeful if you must. Because that's all you're going to get!

Lazily his gaze slid over the gleaming wet curves of her body. "Aphrodite rising from her scallop-shell to tempt mortal man," he murmured in tribute.

Instead of stepping toward the towel bar as she expected, he ducked behind the door frame. A moment later he was holding out a full-length sable coat.

"Oh, my God!" Katya blurted, forgetting herself. "It's gorgeous! Where did you get it?"

Nikolai gave her a slow smile, his eyes still grazing her wet, hardened nipples and curving hips as if they were trapped in a time warp. "I didn't steal it, if that's what you mean," he answered. "Actually, I ordered it for you before I went away... as a wedding present."

He continued to hold out the coat as if it were a thick terry bathrobe.

"Oh, but I'll get it wet...."

Abruptly remembering her nakedness, Katya snatched a towel from the rack herself and wrapped it around her, tucking one corner between her breasts. Seconds later she was thrusting her arms into the coat's silk-lined sleeves, hugging its luxurious softness and warmth about her body.

"It's absolutely beautiful!" she whispered. "May I really keep it? I've never owned anything as soft as this!"

Nikolai's smile broadened. "But of course you may, my darling," he said. "That was my intention."

The bathroom mirror was steamed, and eager to see how she looked, Katya started to waltz past him into the living room.

"I'm glad you like it," he added wryly, restraining her with a gentle hand. "But if you insist on going out there like that, I'd better tell Vanya to shut his eyes."

Who's Vanya? She gave him an uncomprehending look.

"Vanya Kutzov," he said in response to her unspoken question. "A colleague who works with me in London. I've invited him home to meet you...and share a meal."

He's serious, she thought. There's a strange man in the living room and I'm expected to feed him with nothing more than some soup and a little bread in the apartment.

"Oh, Nikolai..." she said. Despite their long conversation as she sat imprisoned in the tub, there was suddenly so much she wanted to tell him. Her thoughts seemed to stumble headlong into each other.

"Thank you for the beautiful coat," she settled breathlessly, "I'm so happy to have it. And to see you again. But since you've brought your friend, I have to get dressed and do some marketing...."

"Does that mean you wouldn't have bothered to get dressed if Vanya hadn't accepted my invitation?" he teased.

Her blush deepened again. "You know what I mean!"

They regarded each other fondly for a moment.

"First a welcome-home kiss and then the marketing," he insisted, taking her into his arms.

For a moment, the steamy bathroom, Katya's new coat and the presence of Vanya Kutzov in the next room dissolved as if they didn't exist. His mouth on hers after so many weeks of absence, Nikolai reclaimed lost territory, sending sharp stabs of desire to her very core. Boldly his tongue probed moist, secret places as if in a sweet preliminary to making love.

If his colleague weren't here, we'd go to bed together now, Katya thought as her tongue dueled eagerly with his. We wouldn't be able to stop ourselves. I'd let my towel drop and open myself to receive him. The image of

Nikolai entering her, thrusting deeply within to plant his seed, was almost more than she could take.

Knowing what dangerous ground they trod, he let her go. "Hurry up, then," he grinned, patting her on the derriere. "We're starving after our long flight. We'll drink vodka and tell jokes while you rustle a meal together."

Her mouth tingling with the delicious taste of him, Katya slipped hastily into the apartment's only bedroom while Nikolai poured a libation for his friend. A few minutes later, dressed in slacks, a sweater and her gorgeous coat, she was quickly introduced to Nikolai's admiring companion before dashing out the door.

Luckily their apartment was in a convenient section. Bypassing the state-run market with its interminable lines and rows of shelves that would be all but empty at that late hour, she headed for a *beriozka* shop, which was restricted to foreigners and high party officials.

With her identification papers as Mrs. Nikolai Dvorov and certificate rubles that had been earned abroad to spend, she was admitted. Nikolai's here, really here in Moscow, she exulted as she chose items not usually available to the average Soviet housewife, especially in winter. Quickly her string bag was filled with steak, lettuce, hot house tomatoes, pears out of season and a creamy round of brie cheese.

Nearby, a bakery was about to close, and she wedged inside just before they locked the door. Her guardian angel smiling on her, she managed to purchase the last *iablochnyi pirog*, or apple pie, of the day. You and your friend Vanya shall have a genuine American-style supper tonight, she promised Nikolai silently as she returned to the apartment and got busy in the kitchen.

The meal was a highly convivial affair. No small amount of vodka had been drunk in her absence and the cooking, particularly by their guest. Vanya positively radiated good will.

"Everything was delicious...superb!" he exclaimed when even the dessert had been reduced to crumbs. "You really know how to put a meal together on a moment's notice, my dear. And you've learned how to shop here...a far more impressive feat. I must say I envy Nikky his good fortune."

Their guest's expression made it clear he admired far more than Katya's housewifely skills. Nikolai took perverse pleasure in that, even though he'd denied himself the most profound joys their marriage could bring.

"It is rather remarkable, isn't it?" he said expansively, leaning back in his chair and eyeing Katya across the table. "You might say I'm a very lucky man."

After the dishes were cleared away and stacked in the sink to be washed later, Vanya set about entertaining them with a wealth of stories and jokes. Some of the jokes were at the expense of the Soviet system. After the frustration of learning to shop in Moscow's notoriously understocked stores, Katya particularly enjoyed an anecdote that poked fun at window displays touting unavailable merchandise. In the absence of salable items, she'd discovered, many emporia displayed one-of-a-kind treasures that couldn't be bought at any price.

"You've heard the one about the lapis lazuli figure of an ancient Chinese sage that decorated the window of one shop at GUM for years," Vanya said. "One day it turned up missing. People who were used to seeing it got upset. When they asked about it, the clerk said it had been sold. 'Who bought it?' a man dared to ask. 'The general secretary's wife,' the clerk admitted sheepishly. 'Well,' said the man with a shake of his head, 'we should be glad she doesn't go shopping among the art treasures at the Hermitage.' "

Though Katya laughed, she was careful not to reciprocate with a story of her own. Maybe this visit is a kind of test, she speculated. Vanya may be checking up to see if I'm serious about becoming a socialist—and truly in love with Nikolai. Or perhaps Nikolai himself has set up this meeting so his friend will carry back a favorable report.

Whatever the case, she wanted to make a good impression. She surprised her husband by slipping her arms around him and planting a kiss on his neck as she went to fetch another bottle of vodka from the cupboard.

Encouraged by their hospitality, Vanya continued his storytelling for several hours. Finally they hinted as graciously as possible that he should leave.

"Forgive me," he grinned, leering at them pleasantly as he put on his coat. "I forgot you're newlyweds who haven't seen each other for nearly two months."

Quiet with each other after his departure, Katya and Nikolai prepared for bed. He was already stretched out beneath the quilts when she returned from the bathroom smelling of cologne and toothpaste, her body barely grazing the folds of a voluminous flannel gown.

"If you're ready," she said, "I'll turn out the light."

Nikolai nodded his assent. Switching off the lamp, she got in beside him. The bed springs creaked as he turned toward her in the dark.

"You were a friendly little bear cub tonight," he observed, resting one hand on the curve of her hip where it turned inward toward her waist.

"I thought I should impress Vanya with our affectionate relationship," she replied.

A small silence hovered between them as they hesitated on the brink of something reckless. Katya could feel his warmth and allure attracting her like a magnet.

"Was that the only reason?" he asked softly, probing to the heart of the matter.

"No," she admitted after a slight pause. "You know it wasn't."

With that, Nikolai gave a little groan. Murmuring something perilously like "I want you," he enfolded her in his arms.

Chapter 6

Nikolai pressed Katya against the mattress, his kisses blunt and aching with need. The hard, sweet bulk of him and the rigid outline of his passion made her go weak with anticipation. "Yes, oh yes," she breathed, clasping him urgently against her body. "I want you too, so much that I've been dying of it." Just the thought of having him inside her, thrusting deeper and deeper until he'd gained complete access, touched off brushfires of longing in her blood only he could quell. She wanted him to possess her, fill her to overflowing, fuse their very souls together.

Wild to satisfy her dearest wish, Nikolai kissed her nose, her mouth, her eyelids. A moment later, he had unbuttoned the bodice of her gown to take one breast in his mouth. Sharp cries of pleasure escaped her as he cupped the rounded flesh to suck insistently at her erect nipple and lave its tight bud with his tongue. By some kind of instant transference, Katya could feel the dizzying, concupiscent sensation he was evoking directly between her legs. She felt as if she'd faint from the pleasure of it as he pulled and tugged at her other breast while pushing up the hem of her gown.

Nikolai was drowning in pleasure, too. Her thighs were slender and firm, the skin that covered them like satin. He could imagine them gripping him like a vise.

She hadn't worn panties to bed. Stroking upward to part the nest of honey-colored curls he'd glimpsed as she stood naked in the tub, he could feel her readiness. Damp and welcoming, it bade him enter. Not yet . . . not yet, he cautioned himself, his loins aching as he explored her velvet folds. First I'll set her off like a Roman candle. I want to feel the ecstasy of it rocketing through her body.

So skillful and inexorable at the nub of her femininity, Nikolai's touch banished all reason from Katya's mind. Arching away from the bed, she opened herself to him without reservation.

"Nikolai, please . . ." she begged, her fingers tangling in his thick, dark hair. "Not that way. I want us to be joined as a man and woman should."

She didn't realize she could have it all. Overcome by sudden speculation, he let her nipple slip partway from his mouth. "Katya, my darling," he asked in a raspy voice, slowing the rhythm of his caress. "Have you ever made love with anyone?"

Her answer was curiously American and as unstudied as a child's. "Not 'all the way,'" she confessed. "And I'm glad, Nikolai. I want you to be the first."

So he was right. She was a virgin: as innocent as spring lambs and new snow. Nikolai's hand stilled as a flood of guilt washed over him. Katya might be his wife under Soviet law, but that didn't excuse him. Theirs was a marriage of convenience. She was his charge, his moral responsibility. He had an obligation to honor Lev Petrovsky's trust.

I vowed to help her, not ravage her when she was at her most vulnerable, he thought. Whipping would be too good for me. I ought to be shot. Yet, try as he would, he couldn't stop wanting her.

"Darling, what's wrong?" Katya asked, immediately sensing his distress. "Please . . . say you want me. That you're not turned off by my inexperience."

The quaver of self-doubt he detected only deepened his sense of guilt. When he finally trusted himself to speak, Nikolai's voice was almost expressionless.

"We can't do this, you know," he whispered, reluctantly abandoning their intimate contact. "I'm supposed to be your protector, the man who delivers you back to your world unharmed. I can't violate your innocence this way."

"Not even if I want you to?" Anguish settled like a stone against the wellspring of her happiness.

In answer, he smoothed her gown back into place. "Don't think this is easy for me, Katya," he said. "I've never wanted a woman as much as I want you. But under the circumstances—"

"You'd rather I'd have slept with someone?"

The rejection and hurt in her question wounded him to the quick, and he steeled himself to accommodate it.

"No," he insisted, telling her the literal truth. "Even if I despise myself for it, I don't want that. It would have made things simpler, that's all. Allowed me to forget my responsibilities with fewer compunctions and take what you so generously give."

Tears were slipping unheeded down Katya's cheeks. He hadn't spoken of love, and she couldn't bring herself even to approach the word, though she was feeling something dangerously close to that all-consuming emotion as she fought to control her reaction.

"What are we going to do?" she asked.

"Hold each other." The answer came from somewhere deep inside himself. "I know it isn't enough, sweet girl. But it will have to do for us. In the context of a lifetime, we're fated to spend only a few short days together."

Finally it was spring. Living together in the small apartment, Katya and Nikolai had become the best of friends, though an undercurrent of frustrated desire was never far from the surface of their thoughts. Somehow, they had managed not to do anything they might regret.

They got a break from physical proximity when Nikolai was dispatched to London again, remaining for nearly a month. Now he was back, and their feelings had deepened. With jonquils pushing up in the parks and bushes everywhere leafing out in a delicate haze of green, their renewed tension was on the verge of spilling over. A dull ache of longing pervaded Katya's every breath.

Things were close to the breaking point one evening when Yelena called to invite them to Dmitri's birthday party. "We're having it at the dacha this year, thanks to the fine weather," her mother-in-law said. "If the day's sunny, we'll eat outdoors, under the trees. Plan on spending the night."

Like the New Year's gathering Katya had attended with Nikolai and her grandfather, the birthday party honoring her father-in-law was a delightfully spirited occasion. Temperatures had soared to an unseasonable high, causing the exuberant Dvorov men to roll up their shirtsleeves. Following Yelena's lead, Katya had worn a flower-sprigged, lightweight cotton dress.

She didn't own anything like that herself. Like her wedding gown, the dress belonged to Natasha, who was now pregnant and had outgrown last year's clothes.

"You next," her mother-in-law teased, causing a blush to rise in Katya's cheeks. "That is, if we can get Nikky to stay in Moscow long enough to do his part. I'll have to speak to him on your behalf!"

Katya knew her response was more from shame than embarrassment, and mixed in was an uncomfortable twinge of repressed desire. *So Dmitri hasn't told her about our arrangement,* she thought, avoiding Nikolai's gaze. *She thinks her son is happily married—sated and content with the woman of his choice. How small I feel, deceiving her this way.*

Despite the warmth in the air, the shade of the fir trees was cool. At Yelena's request, Nikolai and Aleksandra moved the family's crude wooden picnic table to a sunny spot. Joining the other women, Katya helped carry out the festive spread. Nikolai's oldest brother, Drosha, brought out a samovar and gathered up twigs for fuel.

Soon they were all gathered around the table, telling jokes and toasting Dmitri's health with tea and vodka as they attacked the caviar, skewered lamb and fresh spring vegetables from Soviet Georgia that Yelena had managed to obtain. The dessert was Dmitri's favorite—rich, buttery blackberry tart. Its purplish-red filling smeared his grandchildren's chins, causing their mothers to wipe indulgently at them with their handkerchiefs.

Katya's embarrassment over Yelena's remark had evaporated by the time Yuri picked up his guitar and began to play. But the mood of regret it had caused her to feel still lingered. Nikolai's so decent, so fierce in his emotions, she thought. He should have a real wife to nurture him, serve as the lightning rod of his passion and give him children. She couldn't bear to think of another woman having his babies, or lying drunk with pleasure in his arms.

In all their dealings, the word "love" had never passed his lips. She knew now that it probably wouldn't, though she wasn't sure whether he withheld it to protect her or simply didn't want to lie.

The fact is, I love him, she realized with a start as she watched him laughing and teasing with his family. Not just with some wildly romantic impulse, but deeply and totally, without reservation. Though I'm mad for his body, it's far more profound than that. What I feel is inextricably linked with friendship as well as passion. Its essence is the kind of commitment that brands the soul.

He wasn't hers to keep. But she didn't want to think about that. Instead, it shook her that her perception should have come at such a moment. Can he feel my shock, my complete absorption with what has happened, she wondered? Or is he impervious to them? In some obscure way, she expected him to guess the truth.

He chose that exact moment to catch her eye. "Come, Katya," he baited her affectionately. "You've eaten too much. Let's go for a walk in the woods."

Enduring a bit of good-natured raillery, they excused themselves from the table and disappeared together among the trees. His lips twitching with amusement at the suggestive comments that drifted after them, Nikolai took her hand and began to hum a little tune. As they walked, Katya's heart ached with the exquisite pain of her discovery. Just to touch him now was an agony of bliss.

The woods were lush with new growth, like something out of a fairy tale. Bluish in the afternoon haze, the firs provided the perfect backdrop for the delicate green foliage of the birches. Birds she couldn't identify flitted through the branches overhead, singing joyously as they mated and built their nests.

A tramp of several minutes brought them to a meadow that was shaggy with buttercups. The drone of bees gathering pollen assailed their ears.

"Would you like a bouquet?" Nikolai asked, slowing his steps. "Naturally these flowers belong to the state, but since I'm a Soviet citizen, I'm entitled to pick some for you."

What I'd really like is to lie down in the grass and make love to you here and now, she answered him silently. I'd beg you for the opportunity if I thought you'd relent.

"I'd love one," she replied.

Bending over, Nikolai gathered up a bunch of the sunny yellow flowers. "Here," he said, placing them in her hands with earth-stained fingers. "Don't let the Wild Women of the Woods see them. They're fond of human lovers and notoriously jealous of mortal maidens who cross their path. They might appear suddenly and tickle you to death."

Katya had heard the old Russian folk tale as a child. Casting down her eyes so he wouldn't guess how much she longed to have him tickle her that way, she buried her face in her nosegay of golden petals.

As he watched, something shifted in Nikolai's gaze. "Do you remember that waltz...the first one they played at our wedding reception?" he asked abruptly. "Wouldn't you like to dance to it again?"

"You mean...here?"

"Can you think of a better place? As for the music, I can carry a tune."

Bowing, he held out his arms. Her lips softly parted, Katya stepped into them. Holding her buttercups lightly against his shoulder, she followed his lead in the ankle-high grass. Untutored but resonant, his rich baritone provided all the accompaniment they needed. But it was their partnership, so heady and instinctive, that banished any remaining doubts. *I love him so much,* she thought. *More than life, more than anything! I wish I could preserve this moment in amber so it would never end.*

The dacha was quiet that night after everyone had gone to bed. Lying beside Nikolai in the dark, Katya stared fixedly at the ceiling. A rustling breeze stirred the lace curtains at the half-open window. *Why can't we have each other?* she asked herself miserably. *I'm his wife and he's my husband. All too soon we'll be forced apart.*

Like her, Nikolai was aching with need. Because of the clement weather, Katya had worn a flimsy cotton night-gown to bed. Her slender yet voluptuous figure had been all but exposed by its thin texture before she'd turned out the light. Watching her move about the room, he'd wanted to reach out and touch the dark shadows made by her nipples, push up her hem the better to caress her legs.

For what seemed an eternity he struggled with his thoughts. Then his emotions got the better of him. "Can you sleep?" he asked, his voice a low rumble beside her ear.

"No," she answered.

"Neither can I."

The admission hovered between them like a question, and Katya waited, her heart hammering against her ribs.

"It's insane," he whispered at last. "Wrong no matter how you look at it. But I want you, *drushenka*. I don't think I can go on this way."

Longing washed over her like a tidal wave. At the same time she felt light and powerful, able to have and be anything she wanted. "Oh, Nikolai..." she breathed, striving to keep her voice low, like his. "Don't you know how much I want you, too?"

Like a hand fitting into a glove, she came into his arms. What a boon it was finally to touch him as she wished! Half-intoxicated with the privilege, she smoothed the strong muscles of his back, letting them lead her down to his narrow waist and trim buttocks. Eagerly she inhaled the delicious man-scent of him, offered up her mouth.

But he didn't take her as she expected. Though one powerfully muscled thigh lay over hers so that she could feel his turgid readiness, he didn't part her lips with his tongue or attempt to remove her gown.

"We should wait until we're back in Moscow," he cautioned instead in a strangled voice.

"But why?" Distractedly she kissed the faint scratchiness of his jaw, buried her face against his neck. "Your family expects us to make love," she reasoned. "Even Dmitri. He must guess how difficult..."

"It isn't that."

"Then what? Tell me!"

"I wasn't planning this, Katya. I don't have protection."

It took her several seconds to register the full import of his words. If they made love that night, she might find herself carrying his child. A thrill of trepidation seized her, followed by acceptance as deep as the earth. *I don't want to play it safe*, she decided. *If we do, the moment will forever be lost.*

"We've waited for each other too long already," she told him. "I'm willing to take the risk."

Despite his rage to have her, Nikolai's scruples weren't that easily overcome. But she didn't frame her subsequent arguments in words. Instead, she began to touch him as instinct directed, feathering love bites and tantalizing little strokes of her fingertips over his skin.

Her delight and curiosity as she explored the shape of his generous male attributes wore down his resistance at last. With a smothered groan, he capitulated, crushing her to his body. "You," he gasped, his usually cultivated Russian speech almost guttural with desire. "Have you guessed, these many weeks, how much I've longed to ravage you? Rock you out of control until we both beg for mercy? I'm going to bury myself in you so deep...."

The bedsprings creaked as the rest of his impassioned promise was muffled against her mouth. But Katya was long past caring if anyone heard them. Yes! she thought, her tongue mating eagerly with his. That's the way I want you—moving inside me until we're part of each other.

Reaching under her gown, he met her moist readiness, the erect nub of her feminine response. With every atom of his being he ached to enter her without delay, bring her to a shuddering climax as he eased his own wild desperation. But it wouldn't happen that way if he didn't take his time with her. She'd never made love to anyone.

"Darling Katya," he murmured. "Let me look at you, sweetheart."

By now the moon had risen above the trees. Its silver hem splashed over the windowsill and across the bed, causing her skin to glow like alabaster. Clumsy in her haste, she pulled the thin nightgown over her head. His eyes glowed like live coals as he feasted them on her rounded breasts and dark, upturned nipples, her slender waist and womanly tangle of curls.

"You're so beautiful it hurts," he said, taking off his own things in what seemed to be slow motion. "Will you really let me make love to you?"

"Nikolai . . . please . . ."

Eagerly her eyes drank in his nakedness. He had seen her without clothes before, but she hadn't viewed him that way. He was magnificent—a beautifully made man with that broad-shouldered, narrow-waisted frame and the compact muscles that covered it. He was also the man she loved.

Wordlessly Katya held out her arms. He came into them without protest, his skin feverish with wanting her. Yet he refused to be hurried. When she strove to accelerate his response, he gently stayed her hand.

"Not so fast, little bear cub," he said, grazing kisses over her neck and shoulders before moving lower to claim her breasts. "There's an old Russian proverb: if you would sing a song properly, you mustn't neglect a single note. . . ."

That night, as he worshipped her with all the lust and tenderness at his command, Nikolai didn't omit the tiniest grace note, the most ephemeral crescendo of touch. Writhing at what he made her feel, Katya dissolved in a sea of reckless abandon. Her every thought transformed into the more basic language of feeling, she let waves of sensation break over her, lift her to new and dizzying heights.

She thought she'd go mad with pleasure when he began to stroke her between her legs. This time she didn't ask him to stop and enter her. The inexorable rhythm of his caress caught her by surprise, pushing her rapidly toward the breaking point. Spiraling upward with her thighs spread apart like wings, she broke free in a series of little shudders. A wave of gooseflesh spread over her skin the way a breeze casts its platinum sheen of ripples on a lake.

If she cried out, Nikolai didn't try to muffle the sound. His cheek resting against her stomach, he imagined what it would be like to experience those tremors deep inside her. No, he cautioned himself. Don't even think of taking her yet. First she must savor her appetizer completely. Only then can we satisfactorily devour the main course together.

The irresponsibility of making love to her without protection had just resurfaced in his thoughts when she stirred and took him in her hand. "Katya..." he reproved, even as his flesh sprang up, hard and throbbing with a will of its own.

"I won't let you stop us," she insisted, accurately guessing his intent.

With a half-articulate groan he gave in and let her wrap her legs about his waist. Pain flickered briefly as he entered her, ending her girlhood forever and making her his in the most intimate way possible. Moments later any discomfort was forgotten. As if he could tap the source of her being, Nikolai thrust deeply within, retreated and plunged once more into her body. Just the fullness of him was enough to set her off again. Though she'd returned to a state of reason just moments before, she felt renewed stirrings of desire.

This time, Katya's journey was an almost mystical thing. Unlike the sharp, localized pleasure his hand had evoked, her new burgeoning of delight promised to be deep and implosive. When it came, she guessed, the apex of their communion would rearrange her world.

As Nikolai rocked her, straining toward release, the bedsprings creaked in rhythmic protest. The rest of his family couldn't help but hear it. I don't care if they do, Katya thought. I want them to know what's happened. Joined like this, we're like primeval man and woman, the very essence of creation. There's nothing to be ashamed of in that.

With that thought, a second release caught her in its grip. Digging her nails into his shoulders, she let its fierce culmination take her, open her to him like a well as she drowned in paroxysms of delight.

Seconds later, Nikolai shook in his own rapture. His face a mask of ecstasy above hers in the moonlight, he pressed his thumbs against her sensitized peaks, causing little echoes of pleasure to ripple through her body.

Slowly they drifted down, the night air cooling the sweat that drenched them as they collapsed into each other's arms. I'm his, Katya thought, heat suffusing her cheeks. For now and always, though he doesn't know it yet. Somehow I have to make him see we must leave Russia together. I couldn't live without him, after this.

Whispering words of praise, Nikolai kissed her mouth, her eyelids, her breasts, before moving over to lie next to her and pull up the bedcovers. Contentedly she burrowed against him, enjoying their mutual nakedness. She could be pregnant, he thought, damning himself as he held her close. Yet even now I'm thinking how lovely it would be to wake up in the middle of the night and make love to her. I can't let this happen again.

In the morning, Nikolai was already dressed when she awoke. "I'm going downstairs to have breakfast with the family," he said. "Join us when you can."

What am I, if not family? Katya thought, stung by his matter-of-fact tone and polite, noncommittal smile. Still sans clothes beneath the bedcovers, she felt traces of the pleasant languor that had followed their lovemaking. Didn't it affect him too, she wondered? Or was he just feeling guilty? She didn't plan to let him get by with that.

After taking extra pains with her appearance, Katya went downstairs in a flowered blouse and her most formfitting pair of American jeans. She could feel Nikolai's brothers staring at her, the smoldering regard of her husband's dark eyes.

Damn it, she thought. I feel sexy. And I want him to be very much aware of that. "Good morning, everyone," she remarked casually in her most cultivated Russian as she took her place beside him at the table. "And you, Nikky...I hope you slept well?"

Speculation lifted Dmitri's shaggy eyebrows at her words. But he was too accomplished both as a chess player and a political strategist to give away his thoughts.

Meanwhile, Yelena's face was wreathed in smiles. "That's a good bed in Nikky's room," she said. "Very comfortable. Here, Katya...have some of these *pliushki* with cinnamon. Or a slice of this honey cake. You're a little too slender, my dear."

Nikolai's face had a closed look as they got into the car. "You didn't have to ask me how I slept," he complained as they pulled out of the drive. "Certainly not in front of everyone."

Katya shrugged. "Why not? I was worried about it. You acted as if you'd gotten up on the wrong side of the bed."

Apparently the colloquial expression didn't translate; he glanced at her with a question in his eyes.

"Feeling out of sorts," she supplied. "After last night..."

"After last night, I'm not very pleased with myself."

There was no time like the present to clear the air. "Why?" she demanded. "Because we made love? I thought you wanted that, too."

For several moments, Nikolai stared at the road ahead, unreachable behind his wall of silence. Then he gave her a sidelong look. "Not exactly," he said.

"For God's sake, what does that mean?"

Aching for the closeness they'd so recently shared, Katya felt her determination falter. He didn't want her any more. It was as painfully simple as that.

"It means that, when we get back to Moscow, I'm going to buy some little foil packets," he said.

Her eyes sparkled with renewed optimism. "In other words..."

"That's right. Birth control." Fiercely he pulled her into the circle of his embrace. "It was irresponsible for us to get involved, but since we have, it would be infinitely more foolish to make a baby. You didn't think, did you, I could keep from making love to you again?"

Back in their Moscow routine, Katya warned herself not to expect any declarations of love. Even if that was what he felt, she knew he'd never speak of it. He was much too honorable ever to set an emotional trap for her. Never mind what he personally might want. His every effort would be aimed at helping her escape.

Yet, despite the temporary nature of their relationship, she'd never been happier in her life. Now that she and Nikolai had crossed into forbidden territory, there was no turning back for them. Their days and nights dissolved in a frenzy of lovemaking. Mad for each other, they coupled on the floor, the sofa, in his old-fashioned bathtub—even over the sink one morning as they were getting ready for work. In between her job at *Tass* and her evening class at the university, she hurried home to him, shedding her clothes just inside the door of their apartment and teasing him to rapture before hastily assembling their evening meal.

I'm a wanton, she thought one evening as she stirred a pot of spicy Georgian *kharcho* wearing nothing but Nikolai's discarded and still unbuttoned shirt. So wild for his body I can't get enough of it. And he's the same way. Absolutely insatiable.

Yet she knew they shared far more than sexual obsession. During the months they'd been together, a much more profound union had supplanted their original marriage of convenience. Each night as she fell asleep, sated and dangerously content in his arms, she prayed that somehow the future would bring her everything she wanted.

In truth, she didn't let herself think very far ahead. Much as she loved her parents and wanted to return to them, she wasn't in any hurry to go home to America. In secret she practiced the arguments she'd use on Nikolai if and when a chance to leave Russia ever materialized.

Somehow you have to convince him to defect, she told herself repeatedly. Yet each time the subject was on the tip of her tongue she hesitated. Like a prophecy of failure, the words he'd spoken on their wedding night echoed and reechoed in her mind. I could never leave, wrongheaded as our ways sometimes appear, he'd said, and she knew he'd meant it. Despite the earthy yet spiritual relationship they shared now, she knew her chances of changing his mind were slim.

One day, without any warning, the ax fell. Katya came home from her office to find Nikolai on the phone. His dark brows were drawn together as if the conversation wasn't an altogether pleasant one.

"Yes...yes, I understand," he was saying. "Thank you, Comrade Gagarin. That's very good news."

He gave her an odd look as he put down the receiver. Suddenly apprehensive, Katya set her purse and string bag on the lace-topped dining room table.

"What's the good news that makes you frown that way?" she asked, fighting to ignore a sinking sensation in the pit of her stomach.

He didn't answer for a moment. Then, "That was my boss," he said finally, pouring out a shotglass-sized tumbler of vodka and downing it neat. "They're letting you accompany me to Helsinki and on to London in just two weeks."

Chapter 7

So soon? You can't be serious!"

Katya's heart leapt wildly as the first breath of freedom she'd drawn in months assailed her nostrils. The next moment she was plunged into despair. How can I give him up, she thought? How can I remain in Russia if there's a chance of escape?

"I don't get it," she protested, stalling for time as she let the unbearable choice she was facing sink freshly into her consciousness. "I didn't think you'd even asked Colonel Gagarin about taking me yet!"

Nikolai gave a fatalistic little shrug. He felt anything but resignation as he looked at her. How lovely she is with her cheeks all flushed and a thousand questions flashing in her eyes, he thought. And how necessary she's become—as difficult to get along without now as my right arm, the very air I breathe. After she's gone, my world will be like a tomb.

Almost as an afterthought, he switched on the radio and adjusted the dial to a thunderous symphony before he spoke. "I didn't really ask him," he said, belatedly answering her question. "The subject came up in passing yesterday, that's all."

His movements economical yet somehow blunted, like those of a sleepwalker, he poured out a second glass of vodka. "Here," he added, holding it out for her. "Drink this. It will calm your nerves."

Katya shook her head. "I don't need alcohol. I need to understand what's happening."

"So do I, my little bear cub. So do I."

The remark sent shivers of fear ricocheting along her spine. Downing the vodka he'd intended for her, Nikolai drew her to the overstuffed living-room couch that had been the scene of so much ecstasy in recent weeks. Some of its throw pillows were still disarranged from their romp the previous afternoon.

Katya felt anything but amorous now. There was a sick feeling in the pit of her stomach. Taking off her jacket and flinging it over a chair, she didn't sit on his lap or curl up beside him as she usually did. Instead, she camped on the floor with her feet tucked under her and her arms resting across his knees, the better to observe every flicker and nuance of his expression.

Something's wrong, something not limited to the pain of our personal dilemma, she thought, searching his face. From the way he looks, it must be something very serious.

"You're worried . . . aren't you, Nikolai?" she said.

He nodded as if relieved to unburden his thoughts. "I'm not comfortable with such a sudden change of heart. It's not like them to be so generous."

No, it isn't, Katya thought, recalling the impassive bureaucrats with whom she'd butted heads during her first weeks in the Soviet Union. *They're trying to trap us. Colonel Gagarin's unexpected cooperation is nothing more than a land mine tossed in our path as if it were a birthday gift. If Nikolai steps on it* . . .

"What do you think is going on?" she asked, suppressing the shudder of dismay she felt.

"I'm not sure. I can't quite remember how it came up, but I think the good colonel asked me how married life was treating me," he began. " 'Very well,' I told him. 'I can't imagine why I remained a bachelor so long.'

"He answered something to the effect that I seemed a very contented husband. 'You're even putting on a little weight around the middle,' he joked, patting his stomach. 'It must get lonely for the lovely Katarina, with nobody to cook for when you're away.'

"He isn't usually so friendly, and I suppose it threw me off balance. The words were out before I had a chance to stop them. 'One of these days, I hope to take her with me if it can be arranged,' I answered. He smiled at that . . . a very pleased smile, as I recall. 'Well,' he said. 'We'll have to see what we can do about that.' "

Soberly Katya considered his words. "It sounds like he set you up," she said. "But why? Just to catch me? Surely as your father's son . . ."

Nikolai shook his head. "It's precisely because I'm my father's son that I believe they're trying to trap me," he replied.

That night, the supper Katya had planned went begging as they talked for hours, examining each cleft and wrinkle of the precipice they were about to face. Nikolai concluded that the abrupt leniency toward Katya was part of a plot by his superior and others in the KGB to embarrass Dmitri for their own ends.

"They may actually be hoping you'll try to escape," he reasoned. "If you do, no doubt they'll attempt to lay it at his doorstep. He's too powerful for them to insist on his resignation over something like this, of course. But they might try to force him to abandon his support for *glasnost* and *perestroika* . . . to adopt a more conservative point of view."

Still Katya didn't fully understand. "But why would Colonel Gagarin want Dmitri to do such a thing?" she asked. "Is he an enemy of the 'new thinking,' then?"

"Not specifically, though he's a very conservative man. It's just that he wants to keep his job, get promoted once more before he retires. Don't forget . . . our chief of command at the KGB is engaged in a power struggle with the general secretary. This situation is made to order for him."

Comprehending at last, Katya didn't reply. Two of the things she'd most feared were inexorably coming to pass, and she couldn't think of a way to stop them. Nikolai and his father would find themselves in trouble for helping her. And she'd be forced to leave the man she loved.

"It doesn't have to be," she said finally, passing sentence on herself. "I don't have to go. Or if we decide that I should accompany you, so as not to arouse suspicion, I needn't defect."

"You may never have another chance."

Leave with me then, Katya told him silently. In the United States, we could be married for the rest of our lives. Raise a house full of children. Grow old together.

Instinctively she knew the time wasn't right for such a radical proposal. At the moment, Nikolai was much too worried even to consider it. His distracted air suggested he was thinking about his father and anyone else who might conceivably be affected by their plans—Lev, his colleagues in London, Katya herself if they bungled the attempt. In other words, he was concerned about everyone but himself.

"What are we going to do?" Katya asked.

With a sigh, Nikolai drew her into his arms. "I don't know," he admitted. "We'll try to get you out if possible when the time comes. But I can't promise anything. We'll have to play things by ear, I'm afraid."

Though the thought of home had an almost irresistible pull for her, Katya found a small measure of relief in his words. Yet as they lay in bed together that night, courting sleep, she couldn't relax. For once, they didn't make love. Instead, they simply held each other. For several moments Nikolai hugged her to him so fiercely she thought her bones would break.

"I don't want to leave you," she whispered, the words muffled against his shoulder.

"Do you think I wish it, sweet girl?"

It was his first admission in so many words that he might prefer she stay with him—even if he didn't think it was the right thing to do. Quickly he followed up his momentary lapse with a disclaimer, insisting she must return to her own country, no matter how great the cost.

"You don't want to live the rest of your life in Moscow, *drushenka*," he said. "You were meant to breathe the air of freedom, and I to serve Russia as my father's family has for many generations. Considering the barriers of geography and politics, we were lucky to meet at all. Incredibly lucky to share such joy, even for a little while."

He was right, of course. But Katya didn't feel like being grateful or reasonable. In a few short months, she had learned to love Nikolai with all her heart. To her, *that* was the most important thing.

I don't care what he says, she decided, listening to the creaks and groans of the old apartment building after he'd fallen asleep. I can't leave him. I can't use the Dvorovs this way, or tell my grandfather goodbye. Ruthlessly she pushed the mental image of her own concerned parents aside.

She realized Nikolai wouldn't let her make that kind of sacrifice without an argument. How I wish he'd say he loves me, she thought. That he wishes we could be married for a lifetime. Unless he does that, I don't have the right to insist we change our plans.

They broke the news to her grandfather the following afternoon. "I'm very happy for you, child," Lev said, putting his arms around her. "Every night when I go to sleep, I think of my Petra, so far away from me in a place called Wisconsin. I realize how much she must be missing her own daughter. She and your father will be very happy and relieved to see you again."

A blow-by-blow account of a sporting competition in Kiev was blasting from the radio. "I don't want to leave, Grandfather," she protested, following him into the kitchen as he heated water for tea. "If I go, I'll never see you again."

I'll never see Nikolai again, either, she silently added. She guessed her grandfather knew what she was thinking. His sharp glance at her and then at his favorite chess partner told them he wasn't oblivious to the change in their relationship.

"In these days of openness and *perestroika* you can't be sure of that," he soothed, his bright, bespectacled eyes resting on Nikolai's face.

"That's true," Nikolai agreed at once. "One never knows what the future might hold. It's better really . . . never to say goodbye."

As they drank their tea from mismatched tumblers, Nikolai brought Lev up to date on the political maneuvering between the KGB chief and the general secretary. He also mentioned his suspicions about Colonel Gagarin's change of heart.

Though the old man frowned, he nodded briskly in agreement. "In my opinion," he replied when Nikolai fell silent, "you're right to feel there's a great deal of risk involved in taking advantage of this opportunity. But like you, I believe the most serious mistake would be to wait. No one can say whether the limited freedoms we enjoy today will blossom and grow . . . or vanish tomorrow in a swamp of Stalinist-like repression. If you're right about their motives, it's doubtful they'll permit Katya to accompany you again."

Anything but comforted, she blinked back tears.

Katya was granted a leave of absence from her job with only a minimum of fuss. Her ease in obtaining the leave only fueled their speculations. During her final weeks in Moscow, she and Nikolai spent every free moment together. On several occasions she met him for lunch, flying into his arms outside St. Basil's or mauling him with fierce kisses when he picked her up in the Volga in front of *Tass* headquarters. Alone with him in their apartment, she wanted only to make love to him, somehow to forge a bond that would withstand their coming separation. He seemed to feel the same need, an answering desperation. Heightened by their imminent parting, those moments were the sweetest they'd ever known.

At the same time, she was almost sick with dread, losing her breakfast on several occasions. Aching at the thought of leaving him, she also mourned the pending severance of her warm relations with the Dvorov family. She'd grown particularly fond of Natasha and Yelena. The latter had become like a second mother to her.

Hour after hour she fretted over the price Nikolai and his father might have to pay for her foolishness. Endlessly she imagined what her life would be like without the man whose very existence filled her world. When the final moment comes, she thought, I'm not sure I'll be able to do it. I just might refuse to go.

Finally the day of their departure arrived. After she tucked one of their wedding photographs in her purse, Katya rode with Nikolai to Sheremetyevo Airport. From there, he told her, they'd fly by commercial jet to Leningrad, then board an overnight packet for their trip across the Gulf of Finland to Helsinki. He had business there, and they would spend a night in the Finnish capital before flying on to London the following afternoon. Grieving, Katya suspected he'd arranged the boat trip in place of a connecting flight to allow them a private farewell.

Lev came to the airport to see them off. The parting was fraught with tears. Though she'd never met her grandfather before coming to Russia, she'd developed a deep affection for him. As she clung to him, the old man's spectacles seemed to mist a little as well.

"Careful..." Nikolai interposed, restlessly eyeing the crowd. "You never can tell who might be watching. We mustn't make it seem as if your goodbye is intended to be a final one."

Somehow she managed to step back, though she clung briefly to her grandfather's hands. "Please ... take good care of yourself," she begged in a shaky voice. "I'll write...."

Lev drew himself up to his full height as if he were trying to look as robust as possible. "Better not, little one," he said. "After your 'treachery,' they'll never allow me to receive your letters. Or forward mine to you."

The true nature of their leave-taking thus succinctly stated, he ordered Katya to take Nikolai's arm. Blindly she did as she was told, as if she were an actress playing a part. Moments later, they were boarding the plane.

"Where is he? I can't see him," she cried softly, straining in an attempt to spot her grandfather's slight figure through their tiny double-glass window as the jet backed slowly away from the gate.

Gently but firmly Nikolai eased her back into her seat. "Lev has gone home, my darling," he whispered. "Like him, you must show courage. Instead of crying, try to behave as if you're excited and pleased. After all, you're going off on a second honeymoon with the man you love."

The flight to Leningrad took them about an hour. Katya caught only tantalizing glimpses of the handsome city Peter the Great had built at the mouth of the Neva River before they boarded their small packet at the waterfront. But she wasn't in the mood to appreciate the city's glories, anyway.

The early evening was sunny and surprisingly warm, though Leningrad was situated at nearly sixty degrees north in latitude.

"If it's all right with you, we'll eat with the other passengers and come back outside later to look at the view," Nikolai proposed. "Now that it's mid-May, we'll get a taste of the famous *bialy noch*, or white nights. At this time of year, the sun sets at about 8:30 p.m. and rises again at half past three in the morning. In between, there are several hours of full darkness. If we're lucky, we may see the northern lights."

Katya wasn't hungry. Perhaps the natural motion of the boat on the Gulf's relatively calm waters had taken away her appetite. In any event, she felt a return of the nausea she'd experienced during the past several weeks.

Many of the other passengers grouped around the dining salon's rough tables were tourists, some of them from the United States. Mindful of listening ears and feeling light-years removed from them, she didn't attempt to strike up a conversation. Instead, she confined herself to the use of Russian and said very little throughout the meal.

Afterward, wrapped in her sable coat against a chill breeze that was whipping up off the water, she let Nikolai lead her out to the rail. Churned up by their progress, waves splashed and boiled against the hull. As he put his arm around her, the sun was sinking slowly in the west. Like some departing deity, it trailed a deep crimson and purple pall over the Gulf's dark surface. *I'll never see the Soviet Union again,* Katya thought, *even if I live to be very old.*

"'Pushed off from one shore and not yet landed on another,' aren't you?" Nikolai whispered in her ear, quoting an old Russian saying. "I can imagine how all this must seem."

"Can you really?" She turned to face him, her amber eyes glittering with sudden intensity in the gathering dusk. "If that's true, how can you let me go?"

An expression of pain crossed his face and was quickly hidden. "How can I do otherwise?" he said, as usual answering her with a question. "When I made love to you that first time at my parents' dacha, I never intended you should be shackled to my fate. It's unfortunate we must play by the rules, sweetheart, but we can't change them . . . just bend them a little for your sake. When the time comes, you must go and I must stay. We belong to separate worlds.''

Not answering, she buried her face against his shoulder.

At that latitude and in that season, the night stole softly into being, seeming to rise up from the water until it cloaked heaven and earth. One by one, the stars came out. As Nikolai and Katya watched, the first flickerings of the aurora borealis washed the sky with light.

It wasn't what she expected. Wide bands of light luminesced and faded, reappearing in glowing striae and splotches of color. Dancing and shimmering, they waned and then waxed again. Iridescent with ghostly brilliance, the firmament announced the illusion of sunrise after sunrise and praised by imitation the pyrotechnics and slow dissolution of a thousand sunsets.

Despite their seeming magic, Katya knew the northern lights were a natural phenomenon, caused by ionospheric disturbance and solar flares. Yet their majestic effulgence tore at her heart. It's as if our life together is going by on some gigantic stage even as we watch, she thought. Each minute brings our separation that much closer. All this beauty, all the love I feel as I stand here sharing it with Nikolai, only make the pain of leaving him that much harder to bear.

''Watching this display makes me think of the fire bird legend,'' Nikolai said. ''According to the old Russian storytellers, there once was a young girl named Marushka who could embroider more beautifully than anyone in the world. The sashes and shirts she adorned with her work were priceless, yet she demanded only what those who wished to buy them could afford.

"Gradually Marushka's fame grew. From the four corners of the earth, rich merchants came, begging her to go away with them and work under their patronage. But she always refused. 'I shall never leave the village where I was born,' she said. 'There are no fields and woods as sweet as those in the land of one's birth.'

"At last a wicked sorcerer learned of her reputation and became covetous. He wanted the beauty Marushka created all for himself. But when, like the merchants, he tried to persuade her to leave with him, he received the same answer. Realizing he planned to trick her, she changed into a fire bird. But his evil magic was too strong. Becoming a great black falcon, he lifted her up in his talons...."

"And so," Katya whispered, "the sorcerer won."

Nikolai shook his head. "The maiden outwitted him, though it cost her life. Bit by bit, she shed her brilliant plumage. Her fiery feathers lit up the sky, gradually drifting back in a shower of beauty to the land she loved."

A small silence rested between them.

"So it's Marushka, reaffirming her loyalty to the fields and woods of her birth, whom we've been watching tonight," Katya said. "No wonder I feel so sad."

"Ah, *drushenka*. I didn't mean..." His arms tightened around her.

Yes, you did, she thought, holding him close. At some subliminal level, you chose that fairy tale to emphasize allegiance to one's native land, not just as a metaphor for the spectacle overhead. You want me to realize that you can't come with me, no matter how much you might wish it. But I won't accept that kind of an end for us. If I did, any hope I have for happiness would be lost.

It was as if Nikolai could read her thoughts. "I don't want to spoil our last days together," he said. "But there's something I must say to you. As soon as you're free, you must divorce me, my darling. Your whole life in the West will be waiting for you."

Crushed at his mention of divorce and exhausted from both the heavy dose of fresh air and her own conflicting emotions, Katya slept briefly aboard the packet with her head on Nikolai's shoulder. It was already light when they docked in Helsinki shortly after 3:00 a.m. To her surprise, the harbor was teeming with activity at that hour. Close beside the docks, in the Kauppatori, or market square, numerous trucks and carts were unloading produce, fresh fish and flowers. Vendors were haggling with suppliers beneath yellow canvas awnings. Ducks and geese were setting up a racket in their crates at the poultry-sellers' stalls. Watching over it all like a benign patron saint was Havis Amanda, the city's famed bronze water-sprite.

A car from the Russian embassy slid noiselessly to the curb, and a chauffeur got out to pile their bags into the trunk. "Good morning, comrades," he said humorlessly as they climbed into the back seat. "If you ask me, it's too early for man or beast."

Snuggling down beneath the covers in their bed at the embassy, Katya slept like the dead. It was as if she hoped to negate reality by sinking into a deep, deep well. She wanted to hide from the pain of what was about to happen in a subterranean cavern of her own making.

At last she felt someone jarring her lightly by the shoulder. She sensed immediately that Nikolai was gone from her side.

"Mrs. Dvorov," a feminine voice called gently. "It's almost noon. Your husband asks that you meet him in Kaivopuisto Park at one. Would you like some coffee or hot chocolate while I draw your bath?"

The speaker was Russian, a smiling young woman about her own age. Katya remembered the park she mentioned vaguely from their drive to the embassy the night before.

"This is the first time I've traveled abroad with Nikolai," she said, rubbing the sleep from her eyes. "Is it permitted that I go to the park alone?"

"Yes, of course." Setting a silver tray with coffee and hot chocolate service on the bed, the maid disappeared into the bathroom to turn on the water taps.

So, thought Katya, trained to suspicion. They're acting as if they trust me now. I wonder what this is all about.

Seated on a bench overlooking Kaivopuisto Park's spreading lawns by a few minutes to one, Katya pretended to read from one of Lenin's works. Although her gaze blurred as she stared at the Soviet founder's dry and convoluted prose, she hoped to convince any onlookers that she was a serious student of communist doctrine, keeping abreast of her university class during a foreign holiday.

Quickly she was approached by a man she was certain was KGB. They're giving me enough rope to hang myself, she thought, masking the chill she felt. How convenient it would be for them to catch me out in Finland where the government must stay on amicable terms with the Russian Bear. They'd prefer not to wait until we've reached the United Kingdom—America's closest European ally.

She wasn't surprised when, after glancing at her book and asking her the time, the man struck up a casual conversation. Abruptly he asked if she was American.

"Say, aren't you the woman who was detained in Russia last fall against her will?" he asked in his blameless Midwestern accent. "It was in all the papers. If you need any help..."

Katya gave him her most forbidding look. "I don't know who you are or what you're talking about," she answered coldly. "I'm a Soviet citizen, and I'm waiting for my husband. If you don't leave me alone, I'll call the police."

London was a tonic to her nerves despite her sense of time running through an hourglass. As they drove from the airport to the Soviet embassy, she was heartened by the city's sights and sounds, its melee of colors. Most striking to her eye was the blithe, jaunty air of the pedestrians. And the signs! They advertised everything from new cars to toothpaste. Despite the 'new thinking,' Russian billboards and neon lettering were still apt to tout Party slogans.

Upon their arrival, Nina Mikoyan, the wife of the embassy's chargé d'affaires, Andrei Mikoyan, took her in hand. She's probably been assigned to keep an eye on me, Katya thought, doing her best to smile. She'll pretend to let me slip away while summoning a couple of embassy thugs. Wave goodbye as I'm hustled back to the Soviet Union in disgrace. Her husband will get a promotion in exchange for her handiwork.

"Of course, you'll want to go shopping," handsome, dark-haired Nina laughed as she poured tea for them in an embassy drawing room. "That's all we do here, it seems . . . satisfy our greed for nice things and fill orders for family and friends."

Politely Katya refused an offer of buttered scones. "I'm sure I'd enjoy the chance to make a few purchases," she responded without enthusiasm. "But it isn't a high priority. Nikky's very good about picking up anything we need."

The following day, Nikolai and Katya went walking in Kensington Gardens amid throngs of nannies with prams, exuberant plantings of spring flowers and children sailing their toy boats.

"Here, by the fountain," he motioned, leading her to a bench and sitting close beside her.

With a start Katya realized that, even in the out of doors, he was afraid they'd be overheard. The rushing water of the fountain would make that impossible. Her heart caught in her throat as she registered the glittering intensity of his gaze.

"What is it?" she asked, her lips barely forming the words.

"Good news or bad . . . depending on how you look at it." Something hardened in his face as if he were willing himself to keep a tight rein on his emotions. "Your escape has been arranged. Tomorrow evening, there'll be a reception at the Dutch embassy, where I have a good friend on staff. The Dutch ambassador's daughter has just gotten married, and she'll be moving back to The Hague. My friend will smuggle you out with Margit Beenhaaker's furniture."

Gasping, Katya felt as if she'd been hit by a truck. For a moment, she thought the pavement would rise up to meet her.

"Darling, please...you must get hold of yourself," he insisted, steadying her with his hands on her shoulders. "We won't have much time away from the embassy together, so I want to make sure you understand. From the movers' truck, you'll be transferred to a U.S. Air Force van. If all goes well, they'll fly you out of the country from a military airstrip."

Still stunned, Katya tried desperately to make sense of what he was saying as he described what would happen at the party and outlined the part she would play.

"Don't go shopping with Nina this afternoon," he said. "Plead an upset stomach. Maybe that will throw them off the scent."

"How can you hope to pull this off, when you know they're expecting it?" she exclaimed. "That it's what they want? Even if I manage to get away, they'll ruin Dmitri. Your career will be over...."

"I can't discuss those ramifications with you," he answered. "I can only say that we're setting it up to look like CIA."

Who is we? she thought. But she knew he wouldn't tell her—probably for her own protection. Her sudden outburst was frantic. "No...I can't do it. I can't leave you!"

Nikolai pulled her close. "You must," he said. "You don't want to grow old without seeing your country again."

For several seconds, the only sounds that met their ears were the splashing fountain and the playful cries of children. The city traffic was a distant roar.

"Then come with me," Katya begged, the words she'd longed so desperately to speak spilling over. "Start a new life with me in America. They could take us both."

Slowly Nikolai shook his head. His eyes were sadder than she'd ever seen them. "No," he said. "It's not that easy, my love. Even if I wanted to leave, my family, particularly my father, would suffer for it. I couldn't do that to them.''

His reasoning left her without hope. *If only he'd tell me he loves me,* she thought. *That he wants our marriage to last. I'd plead with him to find a way—one that wouldn't put his family in jeopardy. Surely some solution can be found so that it needn't end like this!*

Lacking any such assurance, she pressed her lips together. *Tomorrow night, I'll have to turn my back and walk away from him,* she thought. *Leave the person I love best in all the world without a backward glance.* The nausea that had been churning in her stomach since breakfast only intensified.

As the contingent from the Soviet embassy prepared for the Dutch ambassador's party the following evening, Nikolai and Katya made anguished, fevered love. Their need for each other exploded like wildfire, flaring with the spectacular brilliance of a thunderstorm as it rips through a darkened sky.

Coming upstairs from some meeting or other, Nikolai heard the shower running. He stepped into the bath's tiny cubicle. Through the steamy glass of the tub enclosure, he could see Katya standing beneath a torrent of water. Though her eyes were shut as she faced directly into the stinging spray, tears were streaming down her cheeks. In seconds he had stripped off his clothes and tossed them aside. His beautiful eyes blazing with passion and torment, he got into the tub beside her and imprisoned her in his arms.

"Oh, Nikolai," she pleaded. "Say you won't let—"

He laid one finger against his lips. The next moment his mouth was crushing hers. Wet and soap-slicked, she clung to him, meshing her fingers in his drowned tangle of hair and pressing her erect nipples against the hard wall of his chest.

Sliding down her back, his hands gripped the gleaming muscles of her buttocks and hauled her even more intimately against him. She moaned at his readiness and shifted a little to accommodate it.

This time would be their last. Invading her mouth, his tongue was greedy, insistent. Not stopping to taste, he devoured her sweetness as if he'd been dying of hunger and thirst. Though he'd spoken of divorce, it was a merging of their separate selves he seemed to want, a passionate blending of identities that would make her forever his.

Loving him from the depths of her soul, Katya tried to push the chalice of their parting from her lips. Irrevocable, it hovered there, a bitter draught that in a few short hours she must quaff to the dregs. There's no time now to sing every note of the song, a poignant memory whispered. You have only a half hour at best. Frantic with need, she wrapped her legs around him.

As if in slow motion, Nikolai turned her beneath the shower's flood. Like dancers moving as one or a latter-day version of mythology's two-backed beast, they clung together beneath the rushing water as they sought the only antidote that would ease their pain.

With a groan he scooped her up and carried her dripping to the bed. They weren't able to draw out the preliminaries for long. Like an avalanche he entered her, filling her so completely that circles of rapture spread from the point of union to encompass her being.

Nikolai! she wanted to shout as he began to move, building their crescendo with deep, ever more rapid thru   so that it rapidly approached the breaking point.

The only truth I know is you. You're my man, my love, my anchor in the universe! But the room was bugged, and she had to stifle even the wordless cries and whimpers that rose to her lips.

When it came, their release was almost simultaneous, a shuddering cataclysm of ecstasy that pulled her taut as a bowstring and threatened to sunder her from consciousness. Shivers of gooseflesh spread over her skin as they gasped together, both shaken to their depths by the force of what they'd experienced.

"Katya," Nikolai whispered when it was possible once more to speak.

"Yes, my love?"

"Just Katya. Not another thing in all the world." Like a mighty stag falling to the hunter, he collapsed in her arms.

Nina Mikoyan chose that precise moment to knock on their door. "Almost ready?" she called a fraction too brightly, as if she knew very well what she had almost interrupted. "We have to leave in less than twenty minutes, you know."

"Yes, all right." Nikolai's voice was gruff but rigorously polite. Rolling off the bed, he got to his feet.

"Stay," Katya protested, clutching at his hands.

"We'll be late, my darling." He reminded her in pantomime that others were probably listening to their conversation. "Please, get dressed."

She didn't move. Picking up a towel, he dried his hair and blotted the sweat from his body. "Please, Katya," he repeated.

He's really going to go through with this, she thought, all the warmth and languor draining from her body.

Nothing I can do or say will stop him. It's too late to tell him how much I love him. Because of the listening devices, we can't even talk about what lies ahead.

Chapter 8

Though her deepest convictions argued otherwise, Katya forced herself to get up, put on some makeup and towel-dry her hair. All the warmth and healing magic of their fierce coupling had evaporated, leaving her sick at heart. As she stood before the bedroom mirror in her lacy undergarments, she felt like a condemned woman, putting on a mask of bravado as she prepared to meet a firing squad.

After donning his snowy evening shirt, beautifully tailored dinner jacket and trousers, Nikolai arranged his tie with steady hands, then stepped back to watch as she put on the sapphire-blue silk gown and matching pumps she'd borrowed from Nina Mikoyan. How lovely she is, this wife of mine, he thought. A long-stemmed American beauty with a complex Russian soul. When we make love, her thighs grip me like the gates of Paradise. Yet how rebellious she could be too.

Somehow, though it ran counter to every mute cry of brain, blood and marrow, he had to make her go. It would be madness for her to stay, and he knew it. He didn't want her to endure the deprivations of a Marxist society for his sake.

With the lures of her former life in the West beckoning, he believed, she'd learn to regret it if she stayed. Ultimately that regret would extend to him.

"We have to go, Katya my darling," he said, burying his feelings as deeply as he could. "Nina will be impatient with us."

Anguished, she shook her head.

Sweetheart, we *must*. The words formed by his lips were soundless. As if in apology, he held out his arms.

Katya went into them and rested her head against his chest. Storing up memories, she listened to the strong, steady rhythm of his heartbeat. He was alive with passion and energy, this man she loved so much. And soon he'd be lost to her. She'd never make love to him again.

With a little moan, she lifted her head. Lightly but desperately she kissed him on the mouth, felt the light brush of his tongue against her lips. It was a goodbye kiss. Yet, imminent though she knew it to be, their parting still didn't seem real to her. Moments later they were walking out of the room they had shared and descending the curved staircase of the embassy's living quarters.

"Don't you look lovely, my dear." Nina greeted her, smoothing her own rose-colored *peau de soie* skirt as if she regretted not wearing the blue herself. "But you're a little pale. Aren't you feeling well?"

Katya met Nikolai's gaze. Quickly he answered for her. "Her stomach's still a bit upset," he supplied.

Nina shrugged on her gray chinchilla wrap, claiming his polite assistance as her due. "Perhaps she ought to stay home in bed," she remarked.

"I suggested it," he answered promptly. "But you know how a bride can be. She wants to prove a credit to her husband."

Nina wasn't inclined to let Katya so readily off the hook. "Sore throat, too?" she demanded. "You haven't spoken a word since coming downstairs."

I'd *prefer* to stay here in bed, Katya thought. More than you can possibly guess. I don't want any part of what this evening has in store. But she didn't dare contradict Nikolai or throw a monkey wrench into their plans.

"I'll be all right," she lied in a small voice. "I'd only feel worse if I stayed behind."

Just then Andrei Mikoyan stepped out of the embassy library where he'd been conferring with several representatives of a British trade association. Like Nikolai, he was dressed in evening clothes. "Ready?" he asked, absently stroking his thin, wiry mustache.

Everyone nodded. As they got into the limousine, Katya realized afresh that she and Nikolai would have only an hour or so more together. Her knuckles showing white, she held his hand tightly.

The Dutch embassy ballroom was ablaze with light. Like a wave, the heightened, liquor-induced chatter of London's sophisticated diplomatic set assailed their ears. At one end of the room, a three-piece combo was playing. Katya noted several elegantly clad couples swaying in desultory fashion to an American dance tune. Threading their way through the crowd, waiters bustled about with brimming cocktails balanced lightly on their silver trays.

"Would you like a vodka?" Nikolai asked after checking their coats. "Or perhaps something Western, like a martini? Naturally the Dutch stock an excellent gin."

How can you be so nonchalant, so detached? she reproached him with her eyes. Can't you see that my heart is breaking? "Maybe I'd better not," she replied, her voice shaking a little. "Do you think they'd have mineral water instead?"

Briefly he spoke to a waiter. When he turned back to her, his beautiful eyes were momentarily naked of safeguards as she could glimpse the torment in his soul. All the anguish he felt, all his concern for her safety shone forth like a beacon. Though he deliberately shuttered them from view a split second later, she felt oddly comforted.

"Let's dance," he said, his voice brusque with repressed emotion.

Without being told, she knew he wanted to hold her. And with all her heart she wanted that, too.

Nina intervened. "Come now," the older woman smiled, the benevolence she was attempting to convey not touching her eyes. "There's nothing to be afraid of, Katya my dear. You must learn to mingle at these events if you want to be an asset to your husband."

Determinedly Katya shook her head. Refusing to make the rounds with Nina might incite suspicion, but they'd just have to deal with that. With only minutes remaining to them, she didn't plan to leave Nikolai's side.

"Sorry, but I'm still a bit queasy," she insisted. "Let me get my bearings first."

Shrugging, the Soviet chargé d'affaires' wife drifted off in the direction her husband had taken a few moments before. But she didn't go far. As she chatted with a succession of acquaintances, Nina appeared to be keeping an eye on them.

Keenly aware that they were about to be separated, Nikolai watched Katya's face as she sipped at her Perrier and lime. Quite consciously he was trying to memorize every feature, every flicker of expression. In a short time—less than an hour by his reckoning—they'd be parted as effectively as if one of them had died. I can't imagine what my life will be like without her now, he thought. Empty, I suppose. Like a desert. Yet I have to let her go.

They were speaking to one of Nikolai's London contacts when a young blond woman approached. "Katya, I'd like you to meet Johanna Schuyvelt, from the Dutch embassy staff," Nikolai said. "Johanna, this is Katya. Of course, you and Ian already know each other."

Like a blow to her solar plexus, the reality of what they were doing hit home. Shaking hands with Nikolai's lithe, fresh-faced friend, Katya felt herself go clammy and cold all over. In the park, Nikolai had described Johanna in detail and made Katya repeat her name several times. The smiling young woman would be her passport to freedom.

"Half an hour after the two of you are introduced," Nikolai had said, "Johanna will approach us for the second time. She'll mention that she's going upstairs to the powder room because all the downstairs lavatories are in use. Your part is simple. You have only to mention that you're not feeling well and offer to accompany her. Johanna will take it from there."

It had boggled her mind that Nikolai expected her to leave him with the most casual of au revoirs. I don't know if I have the strength, Katya thought now. Maybe I'll just refuse to go.

When Johanna drifted away from them, Katya invited Nikolai to dance. "I want to hold you, my love," she whispered. "Feel you next to me one last time."

Mercifully no one overheard. Coming into each other's arms, they meshed like matching pieces of a jigsaw puzzle, separate spheres blending to form a universe. A veritable panther of a man in his superbly tailored evening clothes, Nikolai drew her close. As they moved together through a set of romantic dance numbers, she inhaled deeply his scent, let the warmth that radiated from him seep into her every pore. God, but I love this man, she thought. Maybe there'll be a hitch in our plans.

When the combo took a break, they found themselves standing next to the Mikoyans. A torrent of icy water dashed Katya's fevered hopes when she spotted Johanna, advancing for the second time in their direction. No, she thought. I'm not ready for this. But then she'd never be. A lifetime with Nikolai wouldn't be enough.

"Would you believe it?" Johanna complained to all and sundry when she reached their little group. "All the downstairs lavatories are full. And the office area is locked, of course. Looks like I'll have to go upstairs to the ambassador's quarters if I want to powder my nose."

Katya didn't speak, and unobtrusively Nikolai caught her fingers in an iron grip. Say it, my love, he willed. Quickly, before you arouse suspicion. This may be our only chance.

Like a puppet who merely serves to convey the thoughts of others, Katya obeyed his silent plea. "I believe I'll go with you if Nikolai doesn't mind," she answered. "I'm still not feeling up to par."

Relinquishing his hold in what she would later think of as infinitely slow motion, Nikolai murmured his approval. Katya didn't dare look at him or even glance at

Nina Mikoyan. An automaton with feet of lead, she turned and accompanied Johanna up the stairs, half expecting the chargé d'affaires' wife to follow them.

A contingency plan had been worked out to cover that possibility, of course—one that would allow her to escape within a whisker's breath rather than a comfortable safety margin. But though Katya could feel both Mikoyans' gaze like a hot poker between her shoulder blades, Nina didn't move.

I can't do it! I can't! she raged as each step took her further from Nikolai. If I go now, I'll never see him again! In her mind a tape was running: the conversation Nikolai would be having with Nina. *Anything wrong?* Nina would ask, her sharp eyes probing his for the slightest hint of treachery. *First trimester of pregnancy,* Nikolai would explain, his voice filled with unmistakable pride. *She gets queasy at the oddest moments.*

Still skeptical, Nina would start after them, pretending to offer womanly support. Lightly Nikolai would detain her. *"It's a secret yet,"* he'd confide with every apparent expectation of being understood. *"She doesn't want anyone to know."*

What will happen to him when they find out the truth? Katya asked herself as she followed Johanna into a luxurious bath that connected two family bedrooms. Will they question him for hours? Try to beat the truth out of him? Will he be sent home in disgrace?

Hurriedly Johanna locked the hall door and another that had briefly offered a glimpse of heavy masculine furnishings.

"We haven't a moment to spare," she urged in her Netherlands accent. "Quickly, through there into Margit Beenhaaker's room. They're moving her things down the back stairway, and they have their instructions. Good luck!''

I can't! Katya said to herself again. But she knew any protest at that point would be futile. In the scheme of things, Nikolai was already lost to her. It had been their bargain, after all. And maybe it was what he wanted.

With a wan ''thank you'' to Nikolai's friend, she stepped into the dismantled bedchamber. Most of the furniture was already gone. Two workmen in blue uniforms were getting ready to roll up a large Oriental carpet.

''Miss Dane?'' one of them inquired, startling her. His tone was kind but urgent. ''Lie down, please,'' he directed. ''We'll roll the carpet around you.''

Cleopatra was smuggled in to see Julius Caesar like this, Katya thought wildly as the men tumbled her over and over inside the musty-smelling carpet. And there was a pianist who defected from Czechoslovakia this way. But all her real thoughts were for Nikolai. What will happen to him when they discover I'm missing? she thought again. I can't bear it if he has to suffer for my sake.

Fear for her own safety was nonexistent as the men lifted her and started down the service stairs with their burden. Please...don't let them punish him, she thought as she smelled the sharp night air, felt herself being stowed in some kind of a truck. The floor beneath her was cold as a tomb, and something hard, like a chest of drawers, rested firmly against her backbone.

Somebody shut the truck's rear doors with a clang of metal, and she heard a bolt slide home. Moments later, the engine caught and she was speeding through the dark streets of London, away from the man she loved.

To her amazement, nobody followed them. The transfer Nikolai had told her about would take place in a suburban parking lot. They lurched to a stop and almost immediately the truck's rear doors were flung open. The roll of carpet in which she lay hidden was lifted. She swung wildly as several men carried her to another vehicle.

"Hold tight, Miss Dane," an American voice reassured as she was lifted inside. "You're with the United States Air Force now. We'll have you out of that rug in a jiffy, just as soon as you board the plane."

At the Dutch embassy, Nikolai had begun to fidget. He hoped it wasn't too noticeable. As a precaution, he had extricated himself from the Mikoyans' company and engaged an East German official he didn't really like that much in conversation. As the man droned on, his heart was aching. But he nodded encouragingly at every pause. He wanted to give Katya as much lead time as he could.

Not to be shaken off so easily, Nina joined them a few minutes later. Pointedly she looked at her watch. "I wonder if Katya's all right," she said. "She's been gone almost half an hour. I'm going upstairs."

This time, Nikolai didn't attempt to stop her. If everything had gone as planned, his bright, pretty wife was no longer in the embassy building—or in London proper, for that matter. With luck, she might already be in the hands of the American military.

Seated on the edge of the tub in the family bathroom where she'd taken Katya and repairing a damaged nail as she waited, Johanna Schuyvelt jumped as Nina's knuckles rapped sharply on the door.

"All right, all right," she called. "I'm about finished." Squaring her shoulders, she put away her nail file and unfastened the lock.

Peremptorily pushing her way inside, Nina glanced into the tub enclosure and into Margit Beenhaaker's empty room. She buttonholed Johanna as the latter was about to go back downstairs.

"Where is Mrs. Dvorov?" she demanded accusingly, her breath an almost tangible thing in the younger woman's face. "She came upstairs with you. Tell me where she's gone!"

In response, Johanna merely shrugged. "I haven't the faintest idea," she answered, stepping back as if she found Nina's proximity unpleasant. "She said she was feeling much better. I presume she rejoined her husband ages ago."

Katya could hear the low roar of engines, smell the pungent aroma of jet exhaust as she was loaded aboard the plane. A hue and cry will be raised by now, she thought. The Mikoyans will have everyone searching the embassy for me. Moments later she was unrolled from the carpet by two fresh-faced young airmen in flight suits. One of them extended a hand to her, and she got stiffly to her feet.

"You'll want to clean up, ma'am," he advised politely. "The lavatory's this way. Please try to hurry, though. We'll be taking off in just a few moments."

Alone in the plane's tiny washroom, Katya washed her hands and combed her hair. All the color seemed to have drained from her face, but she didn't bother to reapply her makeup. Tears welled up as she stared at Nikolai's garnet and her plain gold wedding band.

Already worried she wouldn't be able to remember his face, she took their wedding photograph out of her purse. Looking at it didn't seem to help. The picture snapped by Vasily at the Palace of Weddings had recorded the events of another time and place. It didn't seem to have any relevance to their current situation. During her hasty exit from the embassy and jolting ride inside a roll of carpet, she realized she'd crossed into another life dimension—one in which Nikolai had ceased to exist. They hadn't even had a chance to say goodbye.

By then, the crowd at the Dutch embassy was buzzing over Katya's disappearance. Though the building had been thoroughly searched with its ambassador's co-operation, no trace of her had been found. Even her magnificent sable coat was missing from the cloakroom.

Enraged, Andrei Mikoyan had placed a call to Scotland Yard. He was closeted now with Nikolai, Nina and several high Dutch officials in the Dutch ambassador's study. Angrily Nikolai was placing the blame for his wife's disappearance on U.S. agents. He was demanding an immediate investigation.

"I spotted several thugs known to work for American intelligence near the embassy tonight," he said, his expression a study in mixed fury and regret. "I should have known they'd try to pull something. Her disappearance is all my fault."

"The Schuyvelt woman says Katarina Dvorov walked out of the bathroom in the family living quarters under her own free will," Nina insisted, giving him a cold, disbelieving look. "It doesn't sound to *me* as if she'd been snatched by the CIA."

At that very moment, the air force jet carrying Katya was lifting off British soil. Strapped into a roomy seat with a pillow behind her head and a blanket over her knees, she watched the shapes of buildings and trees contract to scale-model dimensions, the lights below them shrink into a patchwork of luminescence. Overhead, an ink-dark sky was pierced by the pinpricks of stars.

There could be no going back now. In a few minutes, they'd be traversing the Atlantic Ocean, leaving London behind, along with any part she might have in the drama that was unfolding there. Numb with grief and worry, she covered her face with her hands.

"Welcome home to America, Miss Dane."

Glancing up, Katya focused on a tall, redheaded man in civilian clothes who was holding out a cup of coffee. Despite her heartbreak, it smelled delicious and she accepted it with trembling fingers.

"I know you've been through a lot," he soothed, taking a seat beside her. "And we'll want to hear about that as soon as you've recovered a bit. Meantime, I'd like to introduce myself. Will Chalmers, U.S. State Department. I flew in yesterday when we got word this was going down."

"How do you do?"

The polite rejoinder came automatically to her lips. She realized suddenly that, despite his selfless efforts to get her out, Will Chalmers and his colleagues would deeply distrust Nikolai and everything he stood for. They'd ply her with questions, hoping to glean some tidbits of information to use against him. Patriotic American though she was, she didn't want that. The very last thing she wanted was to betray the man she loved.

Covertly the redheaded State Department official studied the play of emotions on her face. "By the way," he said gently, "Dvorov managed to liberate something besides yourself."

Katya's heart did a crazy little leap. "Who... what is it?" she asked.

Will Chalmers grinned, for the moment keeping any questions he might have about her relationship with Nikolai to himself. "A sable coat," he said. "It appears to be very valuable. You'll have to check it through customs when we reach the States."

In London, the inquisition over Katya's disappearance had shifted to the Soviet embassy. Scotland Yard had proved very little help, and the mood was an angry one. Everyone—including two men Katya definitely would have classified as thugs—was crowded into the ambassador's ornate, old-fashioned office. The ambassador himself, who had attended a gala performance at Albert Hall that evening instead of accompanying them to the Dutch reception, glared at the assembled company from beneath bushy brows.

By now, Andrei and Nina Mikoyan were looking sick. Clearly they'd been charged with keeping Katya in their sight and forestalling any attempted defection on her part. No one gave the slightest hint they'd been ordered to give her enough rope to hang herself, but Nikolai knew his suspicions were just. Andrei, who played nervously with his mustache, was sweating. Nina continued to take refuge behind a show of righteous anger. But her complexion was the color of dirty snow.

They would get theirs later, Nikolai knew. At the moment, the ambassador's pointed questions focused on him. "It's as I told you, Comrade Rochenko," he avowed, sticking to his story and keeping any fears for his physical safety to himself. "My wife would never have left me of her own free will. We were very happy. She's going to have my baby."

Would the latter assertion were true, he thought. Katya's departure caused a profound ache in the vicinity

of his heart. A child would have forged a permanent link
between us. But, except for that first time at my parents'
dacha, we were very careful. Any irresponsible wishes I
might have along those lines must remain frustrated.

Anatoly Rochenko's brows drew together in an even
more ominous frown. "And the CIA men you supposedly saw . . . you say they were driving a moving van?"

Nikolai nodded, keenly aware of his superior's mis-
trust. That much of the truth, at least, he could offer
them. The two U.S. intelligence officers who had bribed
the real movers to take their places couldn't be traced
back to Johanna Schuyvelt or the colleague who'd assisted her. His friends would be safe from reprisals.

"As we later learned," he said, "the Dutch ambassador's daughter is in the process of moving back to The
Hague. It's my belief they muscled in on the real movers
and grabbed Katya as she left the powder room."

The ambassador's skepticism was an almost tangible
thing. "And the names of these two men?" he demanded for perhaps the dozenth time.

Nikolai shook his head. "As I told you before, sir, I
don't know them. But I could identify them from a
photograph."

Anatoly Rochenko's fist came down on the desktop
with an unexpected crash, causing everyone in the room
to jump. "Fool!" he shouted. "Why didn't you report
the sighting at once?"

They had him there, and Nikolai knew it. As a highly
trained KGB officer, he was obliged to pass along such
information immediately. Not daring to ask, he wondered if they'd contacted his father yet.

"It didn't occur to me," he responded as convincingly
as he could. "My wife was feeling ill, and I was con-

cerned about her welfare. I accuse myself of careless-ness.''

The slight nod Nikolai had been expecting made Anatoly Rochenko's double chin quiver slightly. Seconds later, rough hands seized Nikolai by the shoulders, half hoisting him out of his chair.

"Now," said the ambassador, a glint of cruelty surfacing in his steely gaze. "Let's have no more lies. This time, I want the truth."

As the plane chased the night across the Atlantic, Katya slept fitfully. Each time she woke, huddled beneath her regulation air force blanket, she experienced her separation from Nikolai as a fresh wound. By the time they were making their final approach to Washington, D.C., her eyes were red-rimmed and swollen, her pillow rumpled and stained with tears.

Alex and Petra Dane were waving from the tarmac as her plane touched down. My parents! she thought, stumbling toward the exit with her beautiful coat flung casually over one arm. I never expected to see them again. Her father met her midway down the portable metal steps, to crush her in a fierce bear hug. "My little Katushka!" he cried, his voice breaking beneath its heavy load of emotion. "I can't believe it's really you!"

Sobbing, Petra Dane inserted herself into their embrace the moment they reached the ground. I'm back home in the United States, Katya thought wonderingly, returning her mother's kisses. This is American soil beneath my feet. She was only peripherally aware of news photographers' cameras and a horde of print and electronic media representatives with notepads and microphones pressed in their direction.

"No interviews," Will Chalmers said firmly, ushering them to a State Department car. "Miss Dane is exhausted from her ordeal. We should have some kind of statement for you by tomorrow afternoon."

As they got into the gleaming black Lincoln, Petra kept touching her daughter as if she were a vision—one that might vanish the moment she turned her head. She bristled visibly when Will murmured something about a debriefing session.

"I can understand that a number of questions must be asked," Alex said. "However, I think I speak for both my wife and me when I say that anything resembling an interrogation at this point would be grossly premature. Our daughter is in desperate need of a few days' rest."

As the State Department car containing Katya, her parents and Will Chalmers headed into the Virginia countryside, Nikolai was being helped aboard a plane. His destination was Moscow, and his collarbone was broken. Close observation would reveal several bruises on his head. The worst of them were hidden by his clothing.

Yet he'd won insofar as that was possible, given the situation. They hadn't been able to thrash a confession out of him. And his father had intervened before Anatoly Rochenko's goons could do any permanent damage. Though he was going home in disgrace for not preventing Katya's disappearance, he wouldn't be blamed for engineering the whole affair. There wouldn't be any prison time or a stint in Siberia to look forward to. So far, Dmitri was unaffected by what had happened. And nobody would dare fire Nikolai from the KGB as long as his father continued to wield power in Party circles.

As his punishment, he'd be given a boring desk job, together with an opportunity to redeem himself. And he could handle that, perhaps even find a way to turn it to his advantage. It was life without Katya he didn't think he could take.

The State Department safe house where Will Chalmers had taken Katya and her parents was much too quiet for her taste. A white-pillared, red-brick mansion of Georgian design, it was set back behind high walls and a fortified gatehouse in a venerable stand of oaks. The hum of honeybees that filled the air reminded her of the meadow where she and Nikolai had danced near the Dvorovs' country house. A profusion of dogwood and forsythia were in bloom.

The quiet gave her too much time to think about what she had lost. To make matters worse, even after a full day's rest, she felt tired and ill. When Will Chambers suggested sending an Army physician from Walter Reed Hospital to examine her, she agreed at once.

At her request, she saw the military doctor alone. Their session together was brief but thorough. "Well?" she asked when he'd finished poking and prodding. "Will I live?"

The uniformed doctor, who was about Nikolai's age, put away his stethoscope and smiled. "There's nothing wrong with you that rest, relaxation and a proper diet won't cure," he remarked. "You do realize that you're pregnant?"

Katya's mouth flew open. To her amazement, the nausea she'd experienced during the past few weeks hadn't stemmed exclusively from nervousness. Nor was it simply a convenient distraction to fool the Mikoyans. She really *was* going to have Nikolai's baby!

"I see you didn't know," the medical officer observed dryly, patting her on the shoulder. "Well, you seem healthy enough, Miss Dane. I wouldn't worry too much. Naturally you should consult a qualified obstetrician at your earliest opportunity."

Katya was in a daze as she bid him goodbye. It must have happened that night at the dacha, she thought, when Nikolai took me so passionately and sweetly between the featherbed and comforters! Afterward we were always so vigilant. When we talked in the park of giving the Mikoyans that excuse, we never guessed....

Far from feeling trapped, she was ecstatic at the news. Though Nikolai was lost to her, she'd always have a part of him. Already she loved their unborn child with all her heart.

It made her sad to realize Nikolai would never hold their baby. I hope we have a little boy with dark hair like his, she yearned, hugging herself in the bedroom window seat. His father's generous and loving spirit. Those melting, beautiful eyes.

Breaking the news to her parents wasn't an easy task. Both Danes greeted the revelation with a mixture of sorrow and outrage.

"How dare Dvorov use you that way?" her father spluttered, pacing furiously back and forth across the room. "What kind of hero does he think he is, impregnating a twenty-three-year-old girl who's been entrusted to his care?"

"I'm not a girl anymore, Papa," Katya replied, trying not to lose her temper. "I'm a woman now. Nikolai's wife."

"You said yours was a marriage of convenience!"

"It started out that way. And then we fell in love. Nikolai isn't to blame for what happened. *I* am. I begged him to make love to me against his better judgment. We did it only once without protection.''

And how many times otherwise? Though Alex Dane didn't pose the question aloud, Katya could read it on his face. Imagining how her parents must feel, she tried to be gentle with them. But when Alex mentioned the possibility of getting an abortion, her resistance solidified into a wall of stone.

"That's Nikolai's and my baby you're talking about!'' she retorted, more adamant than she'd ever been about anything in her life. "*Your* grandchild, Dad. Lev's issue to the third generation. I'd never consider getting rid of it ... not for a single moment!''

But though she flatly refused to discuss the subject again, Katya decided to take her parents' advice where her plans for a career were concerned. Instead of attempting to look for a job in Washington when her debriefing was finished, she agreed to return with them to the family farm. There, she could walk in the apple orchard and dream of Nikolai, awaiting their baby's birth.

PART TWO

Chapter 9

Kissing, kissing, *kissing*. They were kissing each other in the falling snow. Twisting in the big bed, Katya felt Nikolai's mouth importuning hers, demanding the very essence of her soul. His skin smelled clean and warm and sexy, the way she remembered. She wanted to crawl inside his coat.

Please, she begged the powers greater than herself. Don't let him stop. I can't bear it if this has to end.

As they pressed against each other, the sound of a siren frayed at her consciousness. With each moment it seemed to come closer. The police are on their way, she thought.

"Aren't you *ever* going to wake up?" a child's voice asked.

Groggily she blinked the sleep from her eyes. The siren, or rather her alarm clock, had been shut off by a small but expert hand.

"Is Aunt Midge going to take me to nursery school? Or are you?" three-year-old Davey demanded. There was a touch of exasperation in his voice.

"I've already fed him breakfast," smiled Katya's housemate, Midge Carruthers, from the open doorway. "A poached egg and a blueberry muffin. He wanted Sugar Toasties. I can drop him if you like."

Katya had dreamed about Nikolai again. Though it had been more than four years since that chill October evening when he'd first kissed her outside her grandfather's Moscow apartment building, it seemed like only yesterday. She felt the familiar ache she always suffered when that memory surfaced.

"Thanks, that would be great," she said. Swinging her legs over the edge of the bed, she hunted for her slippers.

"It's no bother." Midge, a forty-five-year-old widow who worked at the Library of Congress, ruffled Davey's hair. "I made you an egg, too," she added. "I don't have to leave yet. While you eat it, I can lay out the cards."

So she guesses about the dream, Katya thought. Or at least that Nikolai's on my mind. For all the plodding detail of her job, Midge Carruthers was amazingly psychic. She offered to tell Katya's fortune whenever she felt something extraordinary was in the air.

Vrooming as he went, Davey raced his latest toy car around the kitchen floor while Katya and Midge settled in the breakfast nook with its blue-and-white upholstered window seat. Outside, in their tiny garden, the trees were as bare as sticks in the dead of winter. Inside, a pot of narcissus bloomed, and the aroma of fresh-brewed coffee filled the air. The room was typical of a Georgetown row house—simple, elegant and narrow with a very high ceiling.

As Midge poured them each a cup of Colombian special roast, Katya gave her housemate's familiar pack of Tarot cards an obligatory shuffle. She didn't expect the cards to turn up anything particularly astonishing about the future. Her dream and every waking thought that morning were firmly rooted in the past.

"Don't forget to cut the cards," Midge reminded.

With a desultory gesture, Katya complied. She knew it was useless to resist her friend's enthusiasm. Quickly Midge slapped the oversized cards with their other-worldly medieval designs into place.

"Aha!" Midge exclaimed, surveying the way they had fallen. "I knew it! The Knight of Pentacles is in your immediate future. I thought that was Nikolai Dvorov's card."

"Who's Nikolai Dee-voroff?" Davey asked.

Staring at the card in question, which had turned up facing the card that represented her, Katya didn't answer him. She couldn't deny it affected her to hear Nikolai's name on their son's lips.

"A good friend of your mother's...one she hasn't seen for a long, long time," Midge supplied. "Want another muffin, sweetheart?"

Bored with grown-up conversation and not the sort of child to stuff himself, Davey shook his head.

"I don't see how he could be in my future," Katya said, keeping her tone matter-of-fact so as not to re-awaken Davey's curiosity. "According to our best information, Nikolai's been stuck in Moscow ever since I escaped. I don't have a prayer of seeing him again."

Midge shrugged as if she didn't subscribe to that kind of absolute. "The cards say what they say," she advised. "Let's start from the beginning and see what's going on."

Her chin propped on one hand, Katya tried not to display her skepticism too much. She had almost convinced herself she didn't believe in fortune-telling. But her friend had been right on more than one occasion. What could it hurt?

"In this case, the Fool represents you, the questioner," Midge began. "It's a good card...signifying a choice or decision to be made. The Fool stands at absolute zero on the numerical scale, indicating that the questioner can go one way or the other. You're crossed by the Lovers..."

"Nikolai and I," Katya whispered.

"Yes, that feels right. Here, in your immediate past, is the Six of Cups. A child playing in a garden. Davey perhaps...the fruit of your relationship. And Nikolai is here, in your future, as we have said."

Her face solemn, Katya continued to gaze at the Knight of Pentacles. A dark-haired man, strong and handsome, he rode his horse with an air of confidence. Would that the cards didn't lie, she thought.

"The Tower is below me," she said.

"Yes," Midge acknowledged. "It's reversed and stands for destruction. That's the worst possible outcome. Above you is the Ace of Cups, the very best you can achieve. It's a healing card. Notice that the cup is overflowing. And the dove symbolizes love."

Not answering, Katya looked at the knight again. If Nikolai really did turn up in her life again, she'd be the happiest woman on earth. But she didn't believe it was possible. It didn't make her feel any better to note that the Death card had appeared in Midge's layout.

"The Eight of Swords in seventh position," Midge continued, "indicates how you'll be tempted to handle the situation. It's reversed. Like the woman it portrays...bound, blindfolded and surrounded by swords stuck in the mud, you may believe you lack options. If so, you'll be mistaken. Here in your home and hearth, we find the Chariot. It indicates travel, a trip you hadn't planned.

"In ninth position—your hopes and fears—we find the Three of Swords. A heart is pierced by swords, indicating an almost unbearable sadness. You fear the desolation you might suffer if you found Nikolai, only to lose him again."

"What about the Death card?" Katya asked, staring at the image of a skeleton in armor seated on a black horse. "Certainly *it* can bode no good."

Midge shook her head. "Not necessarily. Turning up in tenth position, the ultimate outcome, the Death card *can* mean the demise of the questioner or someone close to that person. But it can also indicate the end of something, with a corresponding fresh start. Maybe it stands for a new life—one you and Nikolai can share."

Don't I wish, Katya thought. But she remained silent.

"Don't forget that my interpretations are individual ones," Midge added. "Someone else might read the cards differently."

More than anything, Katya wanted to set store by her friend's predictions. But for her and Nikolai, she feared, "hello" would prove even more impossible than "goodbye."

"Yikes," she exclaimed suddenly, glancing at her watch. "It's nearly eight o'clock. You really will have to take Davey now. If I don't make a run for it, I'll be late for work!"

Katya's job as an assistant to an assistant in the Soviet affairs division of the U.S. State Department had been hard won. Though she'd used her acquaintance with Will Chalmers, the new division boss, to land it, she'd first had to undergo an interrogation that made the debriefing after her escape from Russia seem like an embassy tea party.

There had been veiled suggestions that she was a "mole," programmed to infiltrate and undermine American operations. Several interviewers had suggested—not too subtly—that her loyalties lay with the man she'd married in the Soviet Union, not the United States.

Gritting her teeth, she'd endured one lie detector test after another and remained unwavering in her desire to work for the U.S. government while cultivating a thick skin toward its petty bureaucrats and their unreasonable distrust.

Ultimately Will's bosses had believed her and allowed her to go to work for him. But she'd paid a price for her Soviet connections. With a master's degree in international relations emphasizing Soviet affairs, she'd been forced to start as a lowly clerk. Her current status was the result of several promotions. Because of her sojourn in Russia and intimate relationship with a KGB officer, she still felt the need to prove herself.

All the way in to work, as she bucked rush-hour traffic and peered into the rearview mirror to put on her makeup, Katya couldn't get Nikolai out of her mind. Though she'd begun to date other men casually during the past year, she was still madly in love with him. She had remained physically and emotionally loyal, though she didn't expect to see him again.

As she pulled into her parking space in the huge State Department lot, she couldn't help but wonder what Midge's reading portended—if indeed there was any validity to that sort of thing. Did the Death card apply to Lev? Since her escape from Russia, none of the Danes had heard from him. Not for the first time she worried about her grandfather's welfare. She hoped he hadn't suffered for her foolishness.

She couldn't bear it if any harm came to Nikolai. Please, don't let it be him, she thought. I couldn't bear a world without my darling in it, even if we can't be together.

The Chariot, with its sly prediction of unexpected travel, offered another puzzle to taunt her brain. She wasn't planning any trips, certainly not one to the Soviet Union. And Nikolai hadn't been out of that country since he'd fallen from grace.

All right then, she asked herself, threading her way through the crowded parking lot. What about the Fool? He's supposed to imply decision-making. That didn't seem to fit, either. Though their office *was* dealing with a political hot potato at the moment, she wasn't directly involved. So why did she have the funny feeling it was all connected somehow?

The situation was this: a Russian couple living in Chicago had become disenchanted with America and decided to return to the Soviet Union. Their eleven-year-old son had refused to accompany them. His request for asylum was being backed by former neighbors and several relatives who were committed to staying in the U.S. Originally a coup for the Soviets, the Vronskys' change of heart had deteriorated into a propaganda nightmare. They were demanding the boy's immediate release and, thanks to public opinion, State Department officials were hedging. If negotiations between the two sides broke down, the federal courts would have to decide.

Naturally the press was having a field day. The story positively dripped with human interest. Anyone who was a parent would have to sympathize with the Vronskys despite his or her politics, Katya thought. The boy's a minor. He belongs with them. Yet, with his love for hot dogs and the Chicago Cubs baseball team, freckle-faced Mischa had tugged effortlessly at American heartstrings.

Will Chalmers and his assistant, Katya's immediate superior, Joe Bruscelli, were handling the case. They'd be flying to Chicago in the morning with a Soviet delegation in hopes of working out a compromise.

Though she would remain on the sidelines, the dilemma spoke to Katya on a deeply emotional level. She'd discussed it with Will over the dinner table several nights before. Lanky, red-haired and somewhat on the diffident side, Will was no match for Nikolai. Still, hungry for friendship if not romance, she'd said yes when he'd asked her out several months before. He was a nice guy, and the fact that she was seeing him kept well-meaning acquaintances from telling her it was time she got on with her life. Unlike a computer technician she'd dated only once, Will was very understanding. He didn't pressure her to make their relationship something more than platonic, even though she guessed he'd like to—very much.

To Will, the best possible outcome in the Vronsky case would be for Mischa Vronsky to return voluntarily to the Soviet Union. "If we can get him to change his mind, there won't be any recriminations," he'd told Katya over coffee and dessert. "But we aren't going to look much better than the Soviets if we turn a kicking, screaming child over to them."

Katya didn't think Mischa should be bullied into going home against his will. Expediency was one thing and human decency quite another. Mischa felt American, just as she did. In her opinion, sending him back to Russia despite his objections would be nothing short of criminal.

When she entered the office, she was surprised to find Joe Bruscelli sitting at her desk. He was smoking a nasty-looking cigar, and his feet were propped up beside his coffee cup. The first draft of a report she'd been writing was scattered over her desktop.

Groaning inwardly at the thought of putting it to rights, Katya wrinkled her nose with distaste. "Joe," she began, "if you don't mind."

"Yeah, yeah, I know. You hate these smelly things. But if you're going to Chicago and I gotta finish your damn report—"

A frisson of apprehension feathered over Katya's skin. She froze in the act of putting down her briefcase. "*I'm* going?" she asked. "But I thought..."

Joe gave her a level look. "Will wants to see you in his office," he said speculatively. "I understand the Russkies have asked for you by name."

Katya couldn't help shivering again. Oh, no, she thought. Do they want to discredit me? She could feel the old chasm of distrust yawning at her feet.

Or could it be...?

Hope and fear held firmly in abeyance, she knocked at the door to Will's private office and went inside. As usual, he was on the phone. Speaking in a series of "uh-huh's" and "mmmn's" that revealed very little, he waved her to a chair. A trip, Katya thought, her mind racing. And a tricky decision. All of it associated with...

Abruptly Will put down the receiver. "Kat," he said. "I don't know quite how to break this to you. I may as well give it to you straight. Apparently Nikolai Dvorov has been rehabilitated. He's been appointed leader of the delegation that's arriving from Moscow this afternoon. He specifically asked that you be on our team.''

Katya felt the color drain from her face. There was a ringing sensation in her ears, and her heart was hammering wildly against her ribs. She was actually going to see him! The sweet unbelievability of it nearly took her breath away.

''Do you want some water?'' An expression of deep concern furrowed Will's forehead. ''Or maybe a breath of fresh air? The stuff they circulate in this building could asphyxiate you if you dragged it too deeply into your lungs.''

With difficulty she focused on what Will was saying. He knew most of the story about her and Nikolai—more than she'd told anyone but Midge and her parents.

''I'll be fine in a minute,'' she said.

The Soviets—Nikolai!—would be arriving that afternoon. Katya racked her brain trying to recall the schedule. Dulles Airport at four, she was fairly certain, followed by a brief meeting at the Swiss embassy. An early flight in the morning to the Midwest.

''I'm sorry about this, Kat,'' Will said.

Are you still in love with him? his eyes had asked as he broke the news. She wasn't sure what answer he'd read there. Lord knew she'd tried to hide what she felt.

Now he was being thoroughly professional, her boss again. ''I know this rakes up old memories for you,'' he said. ''And that meeting Dvorov again may be difficult. But we have to do whatever we can to straighten out this mess. I hope you understand.''

Katya nodded. She was still pale, though her color was gradually returning. Her eyes glittered with an amber light.

Will regarded her without speaking for a moment. "The fact that he asked for you might raise some sticky questions. Is there . . . anything you need to tell me about that? Anything I should know in case the subject comes up?"

Katya wasn't sure how to answer him. She knew Will was being extremely fair, even if he couldn't keep a certain wariness out of his voice. He didn't want trouble from higher-ups or a scandal on his hands, and she could scarcely blame him. Under the circumstances, he was displaying a great deal of confidence in her.

"If you're asking whether there's any collusion between Nikolai and me, the answer is no," she said. "I haven't seen him or heard from him since I returned to the United States. I don't agree with his politics, and my loyalty is to this country, one hundred percent. But I won't pretend I'm not grateful to Nikolai, or that we didn't have an intimate relationship. You've met Davey, so that should come as no surprise."

Will nodded as if satisfied. "Okay," he said. "I believe you. Just keep me informed if anything develops. In the meantime, why don't you take the morning off? Walk around a little. Go home and pack your bags. You might even throw in some ski things. The weekend's coming up, and if we can settle this . . ."

Right now, a cozy tête-a-tête with Will was the last thing she wanted. And he probably knew it. Murmuring something she hoped was tactfully appropriate, she started out the door.

"Oh, and Kat . . ."

"Yes?" she answered.

"Be back here by one o'clock. The undersecretary's coming down to talk strategy before we leave for the airport."

Katya's hand shook slightly as she dialed Midge's number. "Margaret Carruthers, Early American collection," her housemate answered in a cool, businesslike tone.

Midge was gasping a moment later as Katya related the news. "Here?" she exclaimed. "Nikolai's coming here, to Washington?" There was a brief pause. "I'll pick up Davey, of course. And look after him while you're away. Nikolai won't be coming to the house, will he? He doesn't know?"

She was referring to Davey's existence, of course. And his parentage. "No, I don't think so," Katya replied.

Desperate to get away, to think, she quickly ended the call and almost ran out of the building. She had four hours to put her emotions in some kind of order before their meeting with the undersecretary. She had seven hours until Nikolai's plane touched down. It was precious-little time to bridge the gap of geography and years that had separated her from the man she loved. She found herself hanging back, savoring her unexpected boon and letting the reality of it settle. Every minute would be an eternity until she could see his face.

As she started the engine of her Volvo station wagon, Katya's mind was brimming with possibilities. Her heart leapt to think that Nikolai had asked for her. Hold on, she thought, attempting to play the cautious diplomat. His request doesn't translate to a pledge of undying love. When you were together, he never declared himself. Maybe this request was politically motivated.

Her inner self promptly rejected the notion. Nikolai would never use her that way; she would stake her life on it. But even if he cared for her, she realized suddenly, there could be complications.

By now, he could be married to someone else. Katya grimaced with the blinding pain that idea caused. He's a virile, sensuous man, and you can't expect him to live like a monk just because you've chosen that path, she told herself. He might simply be checking up on you as a favor to your grandfather.

Unable to keep herself calm and afraid that, in her state of mind, she might get into an accident, Katya parked in a lot by the Lincoln Memorial. She got out to walk beside the famous reflecting pool. In the distance, the Washington Monument soared against a cloudy sky.

Freedom's still at the crux of things, she acknowledged, sitting down on one of the benches. It's something Davey and I can't live without. But she wasn't sure she could live without Nikolai, either, now that she was about to see him again.

The meeting with the undersecretary dragged on for nearly two hours. Trying to pay attention and to field the pointed questions that were aimed at her, Katya kept seeing Nikolai's face in her mind's eye. She kept remembering the way he moved. The shape of his hands. The taste of his mouth on hers. The fierce, sweet splendor of his lovemaking.

She longed feverishly to touch him again, drink in the scent that was uniquely his, feel his heart beating next to hers. At the same time she realized there might be no opportunity for that. Neither side was likely to encourage intimacy between them.

Katya was outwardly composed as she stood beside Will at Dulles Airport later that afternoon, watching Nikolai's plane land. It was gray and rainy, the absence of light prophesying an early dusk.

I wonder if he's very different, she thought. He's thirty-eight now. Have the years of disfavor taken their toll?

Equally open to question was the way she'd look to him. Would he still see her as the impulsive girl who'd snuggled with him during a sleigh ride on the Moskva River? Or would she seem unapproachable—an unfamiliar Washington career woman in her expensive business suit? When she'd run home to pack her bags she'd impulsively snatched up her sable coat. Perhaps he'd guess that whenever she wore it she thought of him.

As the plane's jets reversed, slowing its forward motion as it swept down the runway, Katya was gripped by sudden dread. What if she did something foolish, like flinging herself madly into his arms?

After taxiing slowly back toward the VIP terminal, the huge jet came to a halt. Its massive engines shut down with a sigh. At a signal from the pilot, several workmen rolled a set of portable metal steps to the forward exit.

The first passenger to emerge was a stout woman with grim, set features. She was wearing a suit and coat that could have passed as Red Army issue. Nikolai's unofficial watchdog, Katya surmised. She wasn't terribly taken aback when the woman's eyes fastened on her with an accusing look.

Next in line was Vanya Kutzov, the man who'd dined with them one memorable night in their Moscow apartment. Katya recognized him with a start. All the soaring happiness of that occasion, the flood of desire Nikolai's early return from London evoked, came back to her in a little rush.

Vanya seemed to remember her, too. But her eyes lingered only a second or two on his face. All her real attention was for the third passenger to disembark—

Nikolai himself, a bit thinner than she remembered, in his dark suit and overcoat. He looked tired, his eyes faintly shadowed from jet lag or lack of sleep. With a pang she noted a few strands of silver had woven themselves through his thick, dark hair.

Yet he was the same handsome, alluring man she so vividly remembered. Beloved, she thought, restraining herself with difficulty. You're here in America! Just this morning, I thought we'd never see each other again!

As if drawn by a magnet, his gaze sought hers and held it. A powerful current of electricity seemed to pass between them, painful yet healing in its intensity. Touched by time and separated by continents, they were in essence unchanged—a man and a woman who reached instinctively for each other. How she loved him still!

Nikolai wondered if she could guess how he felt. During so many long winter nights, he had dreamed of her. With something close to despair he'd tossed in his bed, remembering her fragrant hair, the warm, silken curves of her body as she'd fitted it passionately to his. Each successive spring, with its echoes of spiritual communion and fevered lovemaking, had broken his heart.

She's so beautiful, he said to himself, with the same honeyed hair and tawny eyes. Not a girl any longer but a woman—with a woman's poise, maturity and grace. She hasn't run forward impetuously, the way she once might have done. Yet it was no secret to him that she was affected by their meeting. He could sense the tumult of emotions as if they were his own.

Katya had a moment's respite as Nikolai, shaking hands with the undersecretary and Will, introduced his colleagues to them. Then he was holding out his hand to her.

"Hello, Katya," he said in his deep, heavily accented voice, not bothering to hide the fact of their past relationship from anyone. "You're looking extraordinarily well."

Though both their hands were gloved, she could feel the old magic like a physical bond between them. Though his handclasp didn't waver, she could feel hers tremble. Tears glittered against her lashes.

God but he's wonderful, she thought. Those eyes and the laugh lines that furrow his cheeks. And his mouth! I'd give anything to kiss it. Oh, I do love him so!

"Hello, Nikolai," she answered quietly, allowing her hand to remain in his. The gesture would probably look bad—both to her State Department bosses and the other Soviets—but the last thing she cared about at that moment was maintaining a prim facade.

A pair of limousines was waiting to transport their party. Somehow, as if to satisfy the predictions of the tarot, Katya and Nikolai ended up together in one of them. The undersecretary would ride with them, she learned, while Will accompanied Vanya and the unpleasant-looking Soviet woman in the other.

Her knee grazed Nikolai's as they took their seats. "Your grandfather sends his love," he whispered, taking advantage of a brief hiatus before the undersecretary joined them.

Katya's heart turned over at the words. Already tremulous at his nearness, she couldn't keep her lower lip from quivering. "Then he's well?" she hazarded urgently under her breath.

Nikolai nodded. "Retired now. Politics and a heart condition. But surprisingly active nonetheless. There's a letter..." Unobtrusively he slipped a much-folded missive into her hand.

Diplomatic immunity had made its transfer possible. Not glancing at it, Katya stuffed the letter into the silk-lined pocket of her sable coat. For a moment she could imagine herself in the drab Moscow apartment where Lev had brought them together. Those moments were precious, she thought. We'll never see their like again.

"What of your parents?" she asked, instinctively lapsing into Russian with him. "Did Dmitri...suffer as a result of my escape? How is Natasha? And Yuri? All the rest?"

"Later," Nikolai cautioned.

Getting into the limousine with them, the undersecretary nodded to the driver. Seconds later they were on their way to the Swiss embassy, encountering the first signs of rush hour traffic.

"Well, Colonel Dvorov," the undersecretary said, giving Katya her first hint of Nikolai's promotion, "it's a pleasure to meet you at last. Your father and I were at Geneva together last year, as you may remember. Ironic, isn't it, that the opportunity should arise from such a ticklish situation...."

His tone relaxed and affable, Nikolai murmured something noncommittal in reply. His nearness was driving Katya to the point of desperation. With the accumulated longing of nearly four years, she ached to touch him, caress him, hold him. But she didn't dare make a move in that direction—not unless she wanted to be banished from her job and lose any chance she had of seeing him again.

To her astonishment, Nikolai was ready to circumvent the rules. Keeping his gaze politely trained on the undersecretary's face, he reached for Katya's hand under cover of his briefcase. Little currents of desire swept through her as he stroked her palm with his thumb. She almost moaned with relief when he stopped, only to lace their fingers sensuously together.

Chapter 10

The conference room at the Swiss embassy was discreetly elegant. It was paneled in mellow, dark wood and warmed by several bouquets of fresh flowers and a collection of old silver. A uniformed butler took their coats.

With an air of wary nonchalance, the participants settled around a gleaming oval table. In addition to carafes of ice water, a waiter offered coffee, tea and various alcoholic beverages. There was a rustle of notes as the representatives of each side prepared to state their positions and demand concessions.

A small but rotund man with twinkling blue eyes, the Swiss ambassador himself was present to help smooth over any tensions that might erupt. Perhaps realizing her inexperience in such situations, he gave Katya a wink of encouragement.

By contrast, the Soviet woman, who had been introduced to Katya as Dr. Irina Maximova, continued to regard her with a hostile air. *She's obviously dying to know* if we still care about each other, Katya thought. No doubt she's aware that Nikolai asked for me. I pray he won't get into trouble for that.

She couldn't keep her eyes off him long enough to be discreet. How wonderful it is, she thought, just to re-acquaint myself with the planes and angles of his face, those broad, sweet shoulders. His luminous gaze met hers over the briefcases and water glasses, and she wondered for a delirious moment if he planned to defect. Reason argued otherwise. He hadn't said or done anything to support such a radical conjecture. As far as she knew, all the old barriers to his ever leaving Russia were still firmly in place.

Nobody can fault me for feeling the way I do, Katya thought. I won't get my hopes up. The truth is, I'm abjectly grateful just to see him again.

She wondered if they'd have any time alone together. "Later," he'd said, as if he planned to arrange a private meeting. If anyone could bring it off, she knew Nikolai could. For the first time since they'd parted in London, she felt protected and cherished, free to place every detail of her existence into his capable hands.

With both sides observing the usual niceties, the meeting began. Even the most casual observer couldn't fail to note the obdurate position that underlay Nikolai's opening remarks on behalf of the Soviets. Nothing would satisfy them but young Mischa Vronsky's immediate return to his parents. Will and the undersecretary were much less definitive, more conciliatory in their approach. But in reality they didn't give an inch, either, Katya realized.

Thanks to their briefing earlier that afternoon, she knew no fall-back position had been arrived at on the American side. But we have a distinct advantage in this, she thought. Possession is nine-tenths of the law. And we have the Vronsky child. When I was trapped in Moscow, the Soviets certainly viewed things that way. Hanging on to Nikolai's every word, every gesture, she tried with only partial success to focus on the business at hand.

For forty-five minutes or so, discussion ranged back and forth, its outcome nebulous and its harsher elements suitably sugar-coated. At Katya expected, Nikolai and his colleagues pointed to international law and the traditional right of parents to govern their children. In answer, the Americans spoke feelingly of human rights.

"We agree that you should see the boy," the undersecretary told Nikolai at last. "Let him explain in his own words how he feels. If you still want him to return to the Soviet Union—and you can persuade him to do that without exerting undue pressure—we'll have no quarrel with that. If you can't, then the matter may have to be settled by our federal courts."

Until that moment, Irina Maximova had kept a relatively low profile. Suddenly that changed. "What right has an American judge to decide such things?" she asked, fixing Katya with a malevolent stare. "Since his parents have returned to Moscow, Mikhail Vronsky is once more a Soviet citizen. Your courts have no jurisdiction over him. Perhaps we should kidnap the boy...as the illustrious Kathryn Dane was herself supposedly snatched by the CIA."

Irina's outburst had been in Russian. Quickly Katya translated for Will and the undersecretary, her cheeks flushing scarlet in the process. Will gave her a sympathetic look.

Barking a curt order, Nikolai effectively put Irina in her place. She didn't look as if she planned to stay there permanently, however.

"I apologize for my colleague, Miss Dane," he said. "She's a recognized legal specialist in the international rights of children and personally very concerned about this issue. I hope she hasn't given offense."

"None was taken," Katya whispered. She felt hot and cold all over. As if they'd never been apart, Nikolai's dark eyes had briefly yielded up his innermost secrets. For the first time, she realized how much he wanted to make love to her—right there on the conference table if that was their only option.

The meeting ended on a tentative note. The Soviets would spend the night at their own embassy as planned. Despite an invitation from the undersecretary, Nikolai informed everyone that they would dine there as well.

Disappointment settled over Katya like a pall. We won't see each other until tomorrow, she accused him silently. How could you waste even a second of your visit this way? Still, she acknowledged, it might be better for them to take things slow. If at first Nikolai appeared to toe the line, perhaps they could more readily escape detection later to share a few stolen hours.

They were drifting toward the door, well within earshot of each other, when the undersecretary placed a fatherly hand on Katya's shoulder.

"I neglected to thank you before, Miss Dane, for participating in what must be a difficult assignment for you," he said. "You handled the situation with Dr. Maximova like a true professional. And your Russian skills are most impressive. With a child of your own, I'm sure you'll bring much needed insight to a very complex and delicate situation."

Katya wanted to sink through the floor. "Thank you, sir," she responded in a small voice. "I appreciate your confidence. I promise to do my best."

Without glancing in his direction, she knew Nikolai had paused to listen to the undersecretary's comments. His shoulder brushed hers as they started down the embassy's front steps.

"You have a child?" he asked intently, the words close beside her ear. The underlying premise of his question wasn't difficult to guess.

She wasn't prepared for it. "Yes, a son," she admitted, frantically trying to decide what to do. If Nikolai guessed Davey was his, would their son find himself torn between two countries the way Mischa had? She didn't want that, no matter how much she loved his father.

"He just turned two last month," she added, making up her mind to lie.

"I see."

Expecting him to quiz her further, Katya was surprised when he apparently decided to take her at her word. The pain and acceptance she saw in his eyes wounded her to the quick. Thanks to her dissembling, he believed she'd been able to forget him in another man's arms when for nearly four years she'd dreamed of nothing and nobody but him.

In the morning, they'd fly to Chicago together. Somehow during the brief time they'd have together, Katya vowed, she'd set things right. She had to make him see nothing mattered but their feelings for each other.

"Good night," he said softly, turning away toward the big black automobile that was waiting for him. "Sleep well."

"Good night, Nikolai," she responded. In her own opinion, she didn't deserve to sleep a wink.

After dropping off the undersecretary at his Georgetown address, Will took her home in the other limousine. "I'll have someone pick you up at 7 a.m.," he said. "Be ready. And Kat . . ."

"Yes?" she asked.

"I hope this situation isn't too painful for you."

Really, she thought. Does a bed of nails hurt? Or a dagger through the heart? Thanks to her conversation with Nikolai on the embassy steps, he had no earthly idea how much she loved him. At that very moment, he was probably downing his first vodka of the evening and tormenting himself about her supposed affair.

It was cold comfort to realize he'd probably had several liaisons of his own since they'd been together. Deliberately she let the thought twist like a knife in her imagination.

"I can't pretend this afternoon hasn't reawakened some difficult memories for me," she replied at last. "But I think I can handle them."

His face filled with concern and another emotion she didn't want to recognize, Will accompanied her to the door. "You know I care about you, Kat," he said awkwardly. "As your boss and, well, as a friend. Please let me know if there's anything I can do to help."

Katya's initial conversation with Midge was brief. Returning Davey's hug with several fierce kisses, she sent her son back to play with his toy cars.

"Yes, he's as gorgeous, wonderful and amazing as I remembered," she admitted, half lost in a dreamworld of her own. "By sheer coincidence he found out I have a child, and I told him Davey was two his last birthday. He thinks I had an affair with someone else just a few months after we were separated."

"Oh, Kat . . ." Midge's brown eyes filled with sympathy.

"I wanted to protect Davey," she explained, wondering if she'd made a terrible mistake. "We'll talk more about this later. Nikolai brought me a letter from my grandfather. I have to read it and call my folks."

The letter, in Lev's shaky script, was difficult to decipher at first. With some effort, she managed to piece together its meaning.

My dearest Petra, Katya and Alex,
I thank God for this opportunity to write you. I hope my letter finds each of you well.

What can I say in this space so generously allotted to me? How can I convey the overwhelming love and good wishes I feel?

Petra, my angel . . . please know that many times during each day that passes I think of you. Often I remember you as a small girl, helping your mother light the Hanukkah candles. Your eyes were bright as stars. Sometimes I think of your marriage to Alex and the day you went away on the concert trip with him, never to return. He's a good man, and I'm glad that you have each other. It's a great comfort to me to think of you in this place called Wisconsin, free and secure and loved.

Katya, always remember that you were the unexpected joy of my last years. Though our time together was too brief, I'm thankful we could share it. No man could ask for a granddaughter more loving or dutiful than yourself. I beg you, precious girl, believe I am well. It goes without saying that the advancing years take their toll.

No harm came to me because of your escape. As Nikolai will tell you, I was forced to retire from the university. But I had planned to do so anyway. My

pension was not affected. I am content in having
known your love.

I realize you cared very deeply for Nikolai, my
dear. Knowing him as I do, I'm certain he won't read
this letter before placing it in your hands. Thus I feel
safe in saying that, though you will never forget him,
you must love again. Carry our family's heritage
forward into the next generation. It's what I, Nikolai and your parents would want. My deepest bless-
ings on you, child.

Her grandfather's signature was scribbled in a down-
ward scrawl at the bottom of the page. Sitting in the
window seat of her Georgetown kitchen, Katya burst into
tears.

Her phone call to her parents caused more tears to
flow. Petra cried, too, muffling her sobs against Alex's
shoulder. Katya could picture them comforting each
other, deeply secure and caring after so many years. It
was the way she longed to picture herself and Nikolai.
Oh, Grandfather, she thought. If only you knew the
truth! Nikolai and I *have* carried your seed into the next
generation. But they won't allow us to live together in
peace.

That night, as she tucked Davey into bed, Katya
grieved to think Nikolai would never know their son.
He's a beautiful child, my love, she thought, kissing the
boy's smooth forehead. Davey looks a lot like you. He
has the same dark eyes and hair, and your warm smile,
just the way I hoped he would. He's impetuous sometimes. And demanding, as I can be. But he has your daring, your bright intelligence. In a better world than this,
the two of you could be together.

Her sorrow extended to Davey, too. All his life, he'll lack a father, she thought, when in reality he has the very best. If only they could meet, get to know each other. Were it not for ideology and the arbitrary lines drawn on maps by politicians, Davey could be part of the Dvorov clan. How his aunts and uncles and cousins would dote on him! And how he'd thrive in their exuberant company!

"What's wrong, Mom?" Davey asked with a frown. His eyes were heavy with sleep. "You look like you're about to cry."

"I'm fine." Leaning over, Katya gave her son an extra hug. She had tried to be everything to him, but what he needed was Nikolai. "Guess I'm being sentimental, baby," she said. "I love you so much."

She was wiping away tears a few minutes later as she packed her bags.

"C'mon in the parlor," Midge said, watching her from the doorway. "I've fixed us some hot chocolate. Whenever you're feeling down, chocolate is good for the soul."

Curled up on a chintz-covered Georgian sofa with a cup of Midge's excellent chocolate in her hand, Katya shared the day's events and her feelings with her friend.

"What do you want Nikolai to do? Leave his job, his family and his country to come live with you in America?" Midge asked when she'd finished.

Katya hesitated. It sounded so selfish, stated that way. But her friend had accurately described the deepest desire of her heart. "Yes, that's what I *do* want," she admitted.

Midge was silent, and the complaisant ticking of a grandfather clock filled the room. "Loyalty to one's country is very important," she said at last. "But I think people are the most valuable thing. Parents, friends, the teachers who open the world to us. Most of all our mates, who become like one flesh with us. And our children, of course.''

''In my opinion, we have too much to learn to be limited to a single lifetime. If we must return over and over again, why not do it in conjunction with those we love?''

''That makes sense to me,'' Katya replied.

''At least it's one way of looking at things. The point is, we could find ourselves living anywhere the next time around...a Russian in South America, for example. Or a North American in the Ukraine. Who's to say *people* aren't our real connections in the universe?''

As Katya had expected, she slept poorly that night. On one hand, she was much too excited about Nikolai's presence in Washington even to think of shutting her eyes. In the morning, she would see him! At the same time, she was besieged by guilt. But though she hated herself for deceiving him, she still concluded it had been her only choice.

By the time her alarm clock went off at a quarter to six, her eyes were tired and red. Will looked at her with concern as she got into the car.

''Sure you're okay?'' he asked.

Though she nodded, she didn't speak.

''I wish you wouldn't wear that damn coat,'' he fussed. ''It makes you look like a celebrity or something.''

''Come on, Will. It's cold in Chicago. I don't want to freeze.''

''So wear a parka. The Russkies might resent...''

Katya gave him a swift, disparaging look. ''Because my coat was 'kidnapped by the CIA' at the same time I was? Maybe because you don't like the fact it was a present from Nikolai?''

He could hardly admit to jealousy. "If you mean, 'do I trust you despite your past relationship with Colonel Dvorov,' the answer is yes," he replied, sidestepping any concessions. "But it's anybody's guess how the other side feels. I'm sure I needn't tell you to be circumspect."

Nikolai seemed thoughtful and a little remote when they met at the airport. He didn't speak to Katya except to wish her a quiet "Good morning" as they boarded the chartered jet. All the intensity she'd felt, reaching out to her from the moment they'd laid eyes on each other, now seemed damned up behind an emotional barricade.

It's my stupid so-called "affair" that has ruined everything, she thought. Nikolai pictures me in bed with my phantom lover, and the thought of it is too much for him to bear. He won't be angry or even blame me—that's not his style. But he won't hold hands with me in secret or arrange an opportunity for us to be together, either. If he treats me with polite reserve, it will break my heart.

Will offered her a window seat next to him, and she buckled herself into it without comment. They took off a few minutes later, rising above a low ceiling of ragged, dirty-looking clouds. Always restless, he wandered off to the lavatory just as coffee was being served. At first Katya didn't glance up when she felt someone slide into his place, thinking he had returned. Continuing to cradle her coffee cup in both hands, she stared out the window.

"Katya," Nikolai's voice said.

She jumped. The coffee sloshed a little, and she steadied it, keenly aware of the erratic beating of her heart. "Oh, Nikky..." she whispered.

"I've only got a minute," he said. "Your Mr. Chalmers will be back soon. I need to ask you something."

Tense with anticipation, she waited.

"Your son's father," he continued. "Did you marry him?"

At first she thought the question was a riddle designed to expose her falsehood. Looking into his beautiful eyes, she saw that wasn't the case. As always, he was being open and honest with her.

"No," she lied, wanting to weep on his shoulder.

A small silence rested between them, filled with unspoken thoughts. The clean scent of his after-shave tantalized her nostrils. His hand lay achingly close to hers, on the armrest between the seats.

"When did you divorce me?" he asked.

Katya gave him a startled look. "I didn't," she blurted. "I thought..."

"That I'd take care of it?"

Mutely she nodded, her mind reeling at the sudden possibilities. As if they'd never been parted, their gaze merged and held, deep brown eyes invading honeyed topaz.

"Ah, but I didn't," Nikolai revealed, his expression softening. "Darling Katya, it seems we're still man and wife."

A second later, he was returning to his seat, brushing past Will as they met in the aisle. "What did Colonel Dvorov want?" the latter asked, returning to Katya's side.

"Nothing." Adrift in a private maelstrom of emotion, she could barely answer him. "A word of greeting, that's all," she prevaricated. "From Lev Petrovsky, my grandfather."

This time, lying didn't bother her a bit. Will had no right to cross-examine her about her personal life. And her relationship with Nikolai was as personal as things could get.

Her answer had the desired effect. Will relaxed visibly, making her want to scream at him for being so transparent. "Well," he said, "that sounds harmless enough. I hope the old gentleman's all right."

Though Nikolai was seated just behind her and across the aisle, Katya couldn't see him without turning her head. Unwilling to endure another lecture from Will, she refrained from doing so, though the urge was all but impossible to resist. Responding to her boss's question in as few words as possible, she went back to looking out the window.

We're still married! He's still my husband! she thought, the words a litany of astonishment in her head. He even called me his darling! She wanted to shout her exultation from the rooftops until she remembered she was on a plane. Okay, she thought, a smile playing about her lips. I'll broadcast it over the PA system. Suddenly, irrationally, she was filled with hope.

In Chicago, the temperature was twenty-eight degrees. Heavy snow conditions prevailed. Their plane skidded slightly as it touched down on the runway. The huge, gaunt terminal was hidden by a blur of white.

Just like Moscow, Katya thought. The night we first kissed...

"The weather reports aren't good," Will informed Nikolai as they disembarked. "I'd suggest stopping here for a bite of lunch to let the snowplows catch up, but things are only expected to get worse. According to the latest reports, the expressways have slowed to a crawl."

Nikolai gave him a condescending look. "In Russia, we're used to such weather," he said. "I assure you, it won't bother us. Why don't we press on with the task at hand? Perhaps by this evening we'll have something to celebrate."

Fate, in the form of one of the Vronskys' former neighbors, had decreed otherwise. They had just emerged in the gate area when a tall black man in a crisply tailored dark suit identified himself to Will. Katya stood beside Nikolai, making small talk with him and his colleagues while the two men conferred.

Will rejoined them a moment later, looking embarrassed. "Ladies and gentlemen," he said, "this is Herbert McWilliams, assistant chief of the Federal Bureau of Investigation's Chicago office. Mr. McWilliams informs me the Vronsky child has been spirited away from his aunt's home on the city's North Side. The FBI and police in five states are investigating. We should have something soon."

Quickly Nikolai conferred with his associates. "What do you propose we do in the meantime?" he asked.

Will cleared his throat, apparently somewhat at a loss. "Perhaps we could speak with the aunt," he suggested finally. "We might learn something."

An assistant U.S. attorney assigned to the case joined their party as they left for Mrs. Svetlana Vronsky's residence. This time, Katya and Nikolai rode in separate cars. Yet, though the smallest separation seemed onerous now, most of her despair had lifted. They were still married, and she was secure in the knowledge that they'd have to talk. Somehow, without betraying the truth about Davey, she had to let him know how she felt about him. They'd be lovers again, if she had her way—husband and wife, in the truest sense of the word. And the ache in her heart would subside.

Mischa Vronsky's aunt was small, wiry and extremely closemouthed. To Katya, it was obvious she approved of the conspiracy to hide her nephew from his Soviet visitors, whether or not she'd actually taken part in it.

But she wasn't a citizen yet, and she hadn't been gone from the Soviet Union long enough to lose her respect for authority. Under questioning by the federal prosecutor, she admitted that the neighbor last seen with Mischa had friends in Wisconsin. The friends were farmers, she believed. Their place was situated somewhere north of Chippewa Falls, between Spooner and Rice Lake.

"No," she answered when the attorney questioned her further. "I can't remember their names."

Requesting permission to use her phone, Will called the Wisconsin State Police, who promised to check out the lead. Turning away from them, Svetlana Vronsky switched on her TV set. A weather bulletin was being telecast.

"A severe snowstorm has the city in its grip," the bespectacled announcer reported. "O'Hare International Airport shut down just moments ago, and ground transportation is becoming increasingly difficult. Many schools have closed early. Persons with no urgent need to travel are advised to remain at home."

"We may as well stay in Chicago tonight," Will said as they returned to their limousines. "In the morning, perhaps we'll have something to go on. Meanwhile, everyone will be the guest of the U.S. State Department for dinner and a hotel."

With a show of reluctance Katya suspected was for Dr. Maximova's benefit, Nikolai agreed. Vanya shrugged philosophically, but the good doctor herself continued to glare.

Will's choice turned out to be the Richmont, an exclusive smaller hotel situated close by at the corner of Ontario and St. Clair. It had excellent food, he assured them. They wouldn't be forced to brave the inclement weather in search of something to eat.

As she dressed for dinner that night, Katya hesitated over her choice of clothing. She had brought two suitable dresses—one of them a sensible gray wool, the other a slightly low-cut silk with little cap sleeves in a rich sapphire. Though it wasn't the gown she'd borrowed from Nina Mikoyan on that fateful evening four years ago, the similarity between the two dresses was striking.

She didn't want Nikolai to get the wrong impression. If he thought that in choosing the blue gown she was trying to play havoc with his emotions, it would do more harm than good. But if he guessed that what she wanted was a return to intimacy...

Meeting her own eyes in the mirror, she decided to take the risk. A few minutes later she was wearing the blue dress and demure pearl earrings when she met Will in the hall outside their adjoining rooms.

"You look ravishing," he said, surveying her lightly from head to foot. "Almost good enough to eat. Wish I could convince myself such a splendid gown came out of mothballs for my benefit."

That's right, she remembered. He saw me in Nina's dress, too. Thanking him for the compliment, she refrained from pointing out his error.

Though Nikolai's praise was silent, she hugged it to her heart. They'd agreed to meet in the hotel bar, and now, as she and Will walked in, he paused in the act of raising a glass of vodka to his lips. Abruptly he set it back on the counter.

He didn't make Will's mistake. The dress she was wearing was more revealing and far more sensuous than Nina's had been, though it preserved a ladylike air. His eyes acknowledged that. She felt his gaze brush her swell of bosom, dip to caress the hollow between her breasts. Because of the closeness they'd once shared, Katya could almost guess what he was thinking. He'd like to push down my bodice, she thought, and play my nipples against his tongue.

The stab of desire her thoughts evoked only intensified when they were seated across from each other in the hotel's dimly lit French bistro with its pristine white napery and vase of fresh flowers on every table. Though they said very little to each other during the excellent meal, his smoldering looks left Katya in a fever of arousal. Oh, for half an hour in bed with you, she thought! Or even in the maid's closet on our floor if you can't come to my room.

She was crushed when he excused himself and his colleagues early, pleading travel fatigue. Helpless in the face of protocol, she lingered over coffee with Will, doing her best to make polite conversation. Perhaps because of the "off limits" signals she unconsciously gave out, Will didn't broach any awkward topics. Finally they went upstairs, bidding each other a somewhat formal good night.

Nikolai's just three doors down, and I can't go to him, Katya thought, tormenting herself as she fitted her key into the lock. Yet soon he'll be gone again, back to a country I don't dare visit and a life I can't share. There isn't any justice in this world.

Moments later she was stifling a gasp. To her astonishment Nikolai was waiting for her. "Vanya agreed to cover for me," he said, inviting her with his eyes.

Chapter 11

The way a storm surge hurls itself against the shore, Katya flung herself into Nikolai's arms. Hungrily he enfolded her. She knew it would mean the end of both their careers if they were discovered. But though she feared for his safety, she didn't care what happened to her. She was ready to suffer any reproach, pay any price barring harm to Davey, just to be with him again.

"If you knew how I've longed for this..." he groaned, kissing her eyelids, her nose, her mouth.

"*You* have! Oh, Nikolai..."

"It's been hell." His arms tightened around her until she thought her bones must break. "Without you, Moscow might as well have been Siberia. The nights..."

If he thought she'd consoled herself too easily in his absence, Nikolai didn't tell her so. She didn't have the slightest doubt he still wanted her. Though he'd been back in her life little more than a day, already her anguish and loneliness were receding like the half-forgotten wisps of a bad dream. She was wide-awake now—free to accept the marvelous boon fate had granted them.

"I know, my darling," she whispered, her gratitude encompassing the earth. "It was awful for me too, not knowing what had happened to you."

This time, she vowed, we won't let each other go so easily. We'll find some way to make a life together.

Parting her lips, Nikolai's tongue claimed moist depths that had always belonged to him. If only she dared tell him that! To confess no one but him had ever touched her. Admit it was his baby she'd carried for nine months beneath her heart.

Aching with love and arousal, she molded herself to his body. Desire rose up in a flood as he gripped her buttocks, gathering her to firsthand knowledge of how much he wanted her. The pressure of his readiness against her abdomen was as intimate as a kiss.

"Can you stay?" she asked breathlessly.

"Long enough to make love to you." He reinserted his tongue into her mouth.

He's my life, my love—together with our son, everything that matters to me, she thought, going weak at the pleasure of it when he took off her gown and carried her to the bed. I want to slake his thirst, be manna for his hunger. Heal the pain of our separation and never be parted from him again.

Katya hadn't been wearing a bra, and Nikolai unconsciously wet his lips as he gazed at her rose-tipped loveliness. How beautiful she is, he exclaimed to himself. My stunning Aphrodite of the bath has become even more a woman. Cupping her in his hands, he laved first one pink bud and then the other lovingly with his tongue.

She felt as if she would die from wanting him. "Nikolai . . ." she moaned, her fingers tangling in his thick, dark hair. "Take off your things, I beg you. I want to touch and taste you too."

He was sucking at her now, tugging with insistent demand at one erect nipple, and he released it with a smacking sound.

"Whatever you say, my little bear cub," he agreed. "You know I want to please you."

But instead of unbuttoning his shirt, he slid his hands down her body, to unfasten her stockings and garter belt. Feathering over her heated skin, his kisses left a trail of delicious shivers in their wake as he removed her bikini pants. Desire translated to white-hot need when he inserted one knowing finger into the tender folds beneath her tuft of light-brown curls.

"Nikolai, please!" she cried, unable to quell her sudden, sweet delirium. "I want *you* there... filling me... rocking me..."

But plead though she might, he refused to stop caressing her until she'd burst the bounds of sanity in little shudders of delight. "Ah, *drushenka*," he murmured, resting his cheek against her stomach. "How I've missed making you do that."

Even as he spoke she could feel his longing, unabated. "Take off your clothes," she repeated as a fresh tongue of desire curled to life inside her. "Let me give you everything."

This time, he did as she asked. She cried out with pleasure at his nakedness—feasting her eyes on the way his taut, smooth muscles rippled in the lamplight. Lightly she ran her fingertips over the dark chest hair that narrowed to an uneven line when it reached his hard, flat stomach. It was his turn to exclaim, though he tried to muffle it, when she took his generous male attributes in her hands.

"At night I would dream of doing this," she said. "Lie in my bed and imagine myself guiding you into me. Touching you to my heart's content."

He hadn't come to her unprepared. As he assumed protection, the thought that he'd planned everything over the rainbow trout and crème brulée acted as an aphrodisiac. Katya went hot and cold with anticipation.

Then he was inside her, claiming her with a single thrust and holding them briefly motionless, as if the very act of possession had nearly pushed him over the edge. We're like one person again, Katya exulted, cradling him lovingly with her arms and thighs. She felt as if a missing but essential part of her had been fitted back into place.

With a sigh, he began to move—slowly at first and then in a mounting rhythm that rapidly carried her out of herself. Fused to him, she felt the force of their implosion build in ever-widening circles. They were one with creation, joined in the cosmic shout that had created the universe.

Aching for release, she gave way suddenly, burned to an ingot of rapture in the crucible of his embrace. Following her by seconds, Nikolai was lost in his own culmination. Yet their union held, deepened, as if they could share the same skin. We're primeval man and woman, she thought as the heavy languor took her. Soul mates for as long as life will last.

But even the multiple lifetimes Midge sometimes talked about wouldn't be enough.

"Ah, love…" His body gleaming beneath a light sheen of perspiration, Nikolai pressed her to the mattress. "It was good, wasn't it?"

"So good." Deeply she drank in his scent, wanting to make the moment last forever. "Please, darling...stay with me."

"Only until you fall asleep."

Tears stung her eyelids, and she blinked them back unshed. Nothing's changed, she thought. He still can't leave his father for fear of reprisals. But what about me? And Davey? Aren't we his family, too?

"What will happen to you if they find out where you've been?" she asked. "Dr. Maximova doesn't like you. I think she'd ruin you if she could."

Rolling off her, he cuddled her tenderly against his shoulder. "Irina's a fool," he said, his voice soft and deep beside her ear. "She'd never understand what it's like for two people in love. She's also Nina Mikoyan's cousin, which explains her hostility. Don't worry, I can handle her."

As she sifted through his reply, one phrase stood out above the rest. "Do you mean," she whispered, "that you..."

Nikolai caught her meaning instantly, though he seemed incredulous at the question.

"You're asking if I love you, *drushenka*?" he said.

Feeling a fool herself, she nodded.

He shook his head. "What did you think, sweetheart? That I'd give up any thought of other women, put my head back in the noose of danger the minute you were within reach if I wasn't crazy in love with you?"

"Oh, Nikolai!" She was suffused with more joy and hope than she'd thought possible. "I love you, too."

They'd have only a few short hours at best until he had to return to his room. But perhaps tomorrow... Stubbornly willing a future for them, Katya drew him fully into her arms.

* * *

Kissing her lightly so she wouldn't wake, Nikolai got out of bed and dressed hurriedly in the dark. They'd made love three times, and he hungered for more. But a glance at the luminous dial of his watch told him it was nearly 3 a.m. Whether he wanted to or not, it was time for him to go. At least by now Irina's watchful eyes would be shut in sleep.

To his consternation, the woman's door opened as he passed. "Please come in, Comrade Colonel," she said, giving him a look of grim satisfaction. "I want to talk to you."

Like her cousin Nina's, Irina Maximova's tone could sting like dry ice against the skin. Shrugging, Nikolai stepped past her into the luxurious capitalist hotel room. It was the mirror image of the one where he had just spent several delirious hours loving Katya and satisfying his most primitive urges. The beds were back to back, separated by a wall.

I wonder if she heard anything, he thought, noting that her sheets were only slightly rumpled. Perhaps she'd lain rigidly awake, straining to catch the slightest sound. But aside from a condemnation of Irina's mental powers, he hadn't said anything that could incriminate him. His only sin had been to make love repeatedly to an enemy of the state.

Selecting one of the room's two easy chairs so that his face would remain in shadow, he sat down, careful not to indicate the slightest defensiveness. "What's on your mind?" he asked with the Western-acquired casualness he knew infuriated her.

Irina's face assumed an even more forbidding expression. Probably she found the idea of him and Katya in bed together distasteful, too.

"The question is, comrade, what's on yours?" she asked, confirming his speculation. "Sexual games? Or your assignment? Our superiors in Moscow will be very interested to learn how you've spent the past several hours... and in whose company."

"I can't think why."

He could feel her rage grow in proportion to his nonchalance. "Surely you jest," she said. "The woman betrayed you. And our glorious country..."

"That's where you're wrong."

In contrast to his colleague's ire, Nikolai seemed relaxed, totally at his ease. But then Mikhail Gagarin had once called him a master of artifice. "The CIA snatched her, as I maintained from the beginning," he went on. "Once she was back in the U.S., her family pressured her to stay. General Taratchikov and the others know what I'm doing. If my plan is successful, she *and* the Vronsky child will return with us."

Stirring, Katya reached for the man she loved. But the place beside her was empty. A moment later the phone on her bedside table trilled—her 6:30 a.m. wake-up call from the hotel desk.

The sense of loss she felt was overwhelming. What will happen today, she thought? Will they find Mischa Vronsky and have their talk with him? If so, Nikolai will soon be on his way back to the Soviet Union. After what they'd shared the night before, she couldn't bear to be separated from him again.

Maybe if she made a clean breast of the truth about Davey, he'd defect—stay in America with them. But she didn't dare take the risk. I don't want our son to be a pawn like Mischa Vronsky, she thought as she dressed to go downstairs. In addition, there was the small matter of her pride. Much as she loved Nikolai, she didn't want him to remain in the U.S. primarily for Davey's sake.

Outside, the snow had stopped. More was on the way, Will informed them. According to forecasters, he said, they could be in for the snowstorm of the century.

Nikolai listened politely, not offering any comment. Last night was paradise, he thought, though loyal communists don't believe in such things.

Katya knew Nikolai well. She could sense his profound contentment. It permeated her being, too, like a deep inner glow. Yet, despite the memory of what they'd shared, just to see him was to want him again. If he's the man I remember, she promised herself, he has similar yearnings. And he'll find some way to satisfy them.

They decided they would drive to Wisconsin and check in with Wisconsin state troopers in their District Seven headquarters in Spooner. Police were scouring the area. They were bound to locate the farm in question soon.

"We'd better get going while we can," Will advised. "I've rented two cars, for comfort's sake. I'll take one. If Major Kutzov could drive the other..."

"I'd be happy to oblige." Nikolai shot Katya a look and said, "Perhaps Miss Dane could accompany me. Since she grew up in Wisconsin, she can provide directions. As I'm sure everyone realizes, we have a lot of catching up to do."

It was too late, Katya knew, for Will to bug the car. About to object, he glanced at Dr. Maximova. Though her mouth was set in a stern line of disapproval, she didn't say a word. He didn't get any help from Vanya, either.

"How do you feel about that, Kat?" Will asked at last. A reminder of her promise to report anything interesting was written all over his face.

With sudden clarity she realized he'd hired two cars as a way of separating her from Nikolai. The last thing he'd wanted was for them to be together. Stunned by Nikolai's bold ploy and aware that a satisfactory outcome to whatever he was planning hung in the balance, she kept her voice casual, almost expressionless.

"I don't mind."

Will gave in gracefully, as she'd hoped he would. Of course, he'd expect them to keep visual contact.

"That's settled then," he said with a shrug. "We'll take Interstate 90—the Kennedy Expressway—to Eau Claire, then Route 53 north to Rice Lake. I've arranged motel rooms for us there."

The drive promised to be a lengthy one, given the weather. Under normal conditions, Katya knew, it took more than an hour just to reach Beloit from downtown Chicago. Eau Claire was another four and a half hours to the northwest, through rolling farm country. Rice Lake was at least an hour's drive beyond that. If the roads had been cleared following yesterday's storm and if they outran the new front, it would take them at least seven hours to reach their destination—longer if it started to snow.

She wanted to make every second last.

"How did you manage this?" Katya demanded as they drove up the expressway ramp between mounds of freshly plowed snow. "I didn't dream for one minute that Dr. Maximova would let you get by with it."

She was wearing her sable coat, and he rested one hand on her knee, stroking the fur, despite the unfamiliar route and heavy traffic.

"We had a talk last night," he said.

Her eyes widened. "After you left my room?"

"She was waiting up for me." His mouth curved a little, causing his laugh lines to deepen. "No, *drushenka*, she wasn't jealous. Quite the contrary. She plans to report me to our superiors for fraternizing with the other side."

"And?"

"I told her I needed some time alone with you, so I could convince you to return with me to the Soviet Union."

Wondering if he was serious, Katya didn't quite know how to answer him. Perhaps I'd take him up on that, she thought, if it weren't for Davey. Things are changing in Russia now, becoming more open, more democratic. Yet she knew that country would never be home to her, despite her love for Nikolai and her fondness for the Dvorov clan. She was unalterably American, despite her heritage.

"I couldn't do that," she said slowly. "My son..."

Thoughts of Davey hovered between them, and she could sense the questions Nikolai was too much of a gentleman to ask.

"Well, then," he remarked, dismissing them, "perhaps you could come to work for us."

Katya turned to him in surprise and outrage. "If you think for one minute," she said heatedly, "that just because I love you I'd betray..."

He laughed outright, and she realized with a start that he'd been teasing her. "Come, my little bear cub," he said. "It's me, Nikolai, remember? Why don't you snuggle up to me? We're going to have a very long ride."

Sheltered by his affection and her beautiful coat, Katya did as he asked. He was so solid, so real, and he was there with her—not just a memory or a figment of her imagination. I want to make love to him over and over again, she thought. Feel him moving inside me the way he did last night. I'm wild just thinking about the way our bodies fit together.

Unfortunately Will, Dr. Maximova and Vanya were in the car ahead of them. They couldn't very well pull off the road and check in at some motel.

Gradually they left the city and its far-flung suburbs behind. The rolling hills, farmhouses and silos that were the icons of Katya's childhood surrounded them. The sky was a leaden gray color, heavy with the promise of snow.

As they drove, they talked—striving to fill in the gaps created by almost four years of separation. Katya held tightly to his arm when he spoke of the rugged questioning he'd undergone in London after her escape. But though she insisted, he wouldn't give her more than the sketchiest details.

"You didn't tell me there was a chance you might be hurt as a result of what we did," she reproached him.

"If I had, would you have agreed to go?"

The answer was obvious, and reluctantly she withdrew her protest.

"I was lucky to escape with a broken collarbone and some bumps and bruises," he said. "Rochenko, Mikoyan and company might have done a lot worse if someone hadn't alerted my father. Thanks to his intervention, I was allowed to return home instead of being shipped off to Siberia. The desk job they gave me was boring, but I didn't mind that so much. Unfortunately it gave me a lot of time to think . . . mostly about you. . . ."

Glancing at Katya's face, Nikolai saw she was fighting back tears.

"Don't cry," he said. "Things are looking up. When our chief of the KGB lost his power struggle with the general secretary last year, my situation changed radically for the better. With the general secretary now our President, my father was finally able to pull some strings, and I was rehabilitated. I even got a much-delayed promotion. There's no telling what rank I might attain if I 'bring home the bacon' this trip."

When it came to the issue of Mischa Vronsky, she and Nikolai were on opposite sides. But she didn't want to go into that. There was something endearing about his use of Western slang, and she had the uncomfortable feeling Nikolai knew it. She guessed he was employing it to distract her from thinking too much about what had happened to him or what the future might hold as a result of his recent conduct.

"Haven't you put yourself in jeopardy by requesting my presence and then maneuvering to spend time alone with me?" she pointed out. "Irina won't keep her mouth shut when you return to Moscow. You'll have to answer a low of awkward questions."

"I'm not worried about that."

Though she raised her eyebrows, Katya didn't speak.

Like her, he was silent a moment, staring at the car ahead of them. "What I told you a little while ago was true," he said at last. "Before I left, I asked permission to contact you. I told my superior, General Taratchikov, that I hoped to convince you to return . . . to live with me in Russia as my wife."

Their eyes met briefly, and for Katya, at least, the pain of their situation returned full-blown. "Is that what you really want me to do?" she asked.

For one heartrending second she thought his answer would be *yes*. Then he appeared to clamp down on his emotions.

"Of course I wish that," he conceded lightly, turning on the radio for a weather report. "But you know it's impossible, my love."

They stopped for lunch at a diner in Tomah, ordering coffee, hamburgers and french fries. Nikolai and Vanya each had a slice of cherry pie. But Katya was too excited and tense to eat very much. She made a point of avoiding Will's troubled gaze.

When they hit the road again, she and Nikolai were in the lead. Perhaps to forestall any further discussion of risk-taking on his part, he asked her to tell him about her return to the United States. As she described her departure from the Dutch embassy in Margit Beenhaaker's Oriental rug, the clandestine transfer to the air force van and her flight to America, he nodded several times with approval.

"I'm glad everything went well," he responded with obvious satisfaction.

He didn't seem too surprised when she described the heavy debriefing she'd undergone.

"What did you expect?" he asked. "A beautiful young woman of Russian descent is detained in the Soviet Union, supposedly against her will. Her grandfather—elderly, Jewish and therefore vulnerable—is still living there. Suddenly she manages to get out, with the help of a KGB agent whose father just happens to be a confidant of the general secretary.

"To make matters worse, the young lady in question has married her Russian spy. She's been living with him in his Moscow apartment. If you represented the American government, wouldn't you be a little suspicious of her story?"

"Maybe so," she acknowledged. "But I had to go through it all over again when I applied for work at the

State Department. Somebody suggested I could be a mole. Even Will..."

Nikolai sighed at her mention of the redhaired division chief. "Will Chalmers appears to be a good man and an able diplomat," he said. "I suppose it's no secret that he's in love with you."

Twenty minutes north of Tomah it started to snow. Nikolai was telling her the latest news about his family when the first flakes appeared, rushing like tiny white kamikaze pilots toward their rental car's windshield.

Quickly the wind-whipped flurries turned into a full-scale blizzard, fulfilling weather forecasters' worst predictions. By the time they left the interstate and headed north on Route 53, driving had become extremely hazardous. The road ahead of them was shrouded in a blur of white.

At the wheel of the second rental car, Will slowed to a crawl. He was obviously unfamiliar with winter driving conditions in the upper Midwest. By contrast, Nikolai was an old hand at snow and ice. Switching on the headlights, he kept up a respectable pace. Gradually the distance between the two cars lengthened until the one containing Will and the rest of their party had fallen some distance behind.

Out of nowhere, a railroad crossing appeared. They had just driven across it when a freight train approached. Behind them, the train's whistle split the air as the automatic crossing gate lowered. Katya and Nikolai looked at each other, suddenly aware that their traveling companions were trapped on the other side.

Glancing in the rearview mirror, Nikolai hesitated, then pressed down on the accelerator. "Is there another way to Rice Lake?" he demanded urgently. "One that would let us get lost for a while?"

His unspoken question hovered between them: where can we go to be alone?

Hurriedly Katya got out the map Will had given them. Nikolai will have hell to pay if he runs off with me the way we're contemplating, she thought, scanning the maze of crisscrossing routes—even if his mission to bring Mischa Vronsky back to Russia is a success. But she was unable to refuse him, even for his own sake.

They could always say they'd gotten lost in the snow.

"We're almost to Route 64," she said. "When we get there, turn east, then north on Route 40. It'll take us most of the way to my parents' place. According to Mom's last letter, she and Dad will be in Minneapolis for the next few days. We should have it all to ourselves."

The drive to the Dane farm near Round Lake was the most arduous Katya could remember. But she didn't have any fear with Nikolai at the wheel. Nestled against his shoulder, she watched the snow come down in a lacy curtain that was barely disturbed by the steady slap of their windshield wipers.

In a day or two, she thought, we'll have to face the music for what we've done. But right now, the only thing that matters is that we're together. I want us to shut out the rest of the world for as long as fate allows.

It was still snowing when they reached the gate, turning in by the mailbox her father had decorated with a miniature onion dome. To Katya's relief, the private lane that led to the black-shuttered, white wooden farmhouse was innocent of vehicle tracks. Not even the volunteers who assisted the Danes in their battle against Soviet censorship had stopped by to work for several days.

Her excitement grew as they secured the rental car inside her parents' garage. Kissing her once, twice and then a third time for good measure, Nikolai removed their luggage from the trunk. "So, my love," he said. "If luck is with us, I'll spend a few days in your world."

Snow stuck to Katya's hair and lashes as she ran ahead of him to retrieve the spare key from the bird feeder and open the door. He caught up with her at the threshold.

"What does this remind you of?" he asked, setting down their bags in the stone-paved entryway and taking her in his arms.

Half a globe apart and quite different in aspect, her parents' home and the Dvorovs' country place exuded the same atmosphere of security and warmth. Each of them is everything we could want in a lovers' hideaway, Katya thought.

"You don't mean the dacha?" she teased, slipping her arms around his neck. "And our wedding night?"

Briefly Nikolai crushed her to him, as if his hunger was so fierce he must take her on the spot, without the sweet preliminaries they both loved so much. Then, "I'll go after some firewood," he offered, glancing at the field-stone hearth that dominated her parents' large, comfortable living room. "Why don't you see about getting us something to drink?"

It was anybody's guess how much time they had. Flinging her coat onto an overstuffed chair upholstered in soft, flowered chintz, she set out small balloon-shaped glasses of brandy. A moment later, he returned, stamping the snow off his shoes as he carried in an armful of logs. The cheerful blaze he kindled imparted a ruddy glow to the walls of books and the satiny wood of her father's grand piano. Beyond the room's French doors, snow was falling in a tranquil clearing bordered by birches, cedars and oaks.

"It's perfect, isn't it?" Nikolai asked, tossing his coat down beside hers and accepting the glass she gave him.

"I want to make love to you here in the firelight, *drushenka*. Taste you, savor you, the way a connoisseur savors his brandy. In the course of a lifetime, it seems, we're fated to spend too many hours apart."

Chapter 12

Flickering over Katya's bare skin, the firelight kissed her rosy nipples and pointed out the golden highlights in her light-brown curls. How beautiful she is, how responsive, Nikolai thought. Little cries escaped her as she writhed with pleasure in his arms.

Wanting to please her, to make her wild with wanting him, he ran his hands lightly over her body. Though he knew she found it almost too delicious to bear, he excited her sensitive peaks even further. Bold and loving, his tongue made swift forays into her most private places the way a hummingbird tastes a flower.

Finally, after so much longing and a few stolen hours in a hotel bed, they could sing every exquisite note of their song of love. Sensuously, without the slightest hurry, he would take her. In the same spirit of abandon, she would give to him. Their union would be complete.

Ultimately, of course, they couldn't make it last. Nikolai's thrusts would quicken, his demand become excruciating, imperative. Katya would press down with the small of her back, lifting her hips and gathering purchase. The shudders that shook them would rock their very souls.

Katya was thinking similar thoughts. We'll have each other again and again, she reveled, opening herself and guiding him into her. Only the physical limitations of our endurance can inhibit desire.

As they loved and slept, whispered words of praise and loved again, the heaviest blizzard of the century continued unabated. Isolated on its country road, her parents' farm provided the perfect haven. Only a raccoon, its fur hoary with snowflakes, pressed a curious bandit's mask to a window.

Dusk had long since fallen when Katya wandered into her mother's cozy but spacious kitchen to fix them something to eat. Though it was cold outside, the house was comfortably warm, even toasty. Her feet thrust into a pair of woolly slippers, she raided the refrigerator wearing nothing but Nikolai's unbuttoned shirt.

A little too tall for Alex Dane's blue robe, he leaned in the doorway watching her. "My sweet, domestic wife," he murmured, wishing they owned the rambling farmhouse and could live there together for a lifetime. "I must admit I've missed your cooking, darling. But it's your bedroom skills I love the most."

Affectionately she inserted one hand into the robe to caress his crisp chest hair. "Glutton," she accused. "Don't you ever get enough?"

"Not where you're concerned." Gently he pinched her buttocks, enjoying her smoothly rounded flesh.

You're my best friend, she answered him silently. And my beloved husband. Oh, I do love you so much!

Taking down a neatly wrapped packet from the freezer, she waved it under his nose. "Meat *piroshki* Petra Dane-style," she informed him. "Now you'll find out what the best Russian cooking is like . . . right here in the United States!"

They slept in the canopied four-poster bed Katya had occupied as a child. Though the wind whistled around the farmhouse eaves, she was safe and warm with Nikolai. I'd like to make another baby with him, she thought dreamily as they lay in each others' arms. We could live forever in a place like this. Raise kids and dairy cattle, keep out of politics. Put all our energy into making a home together.

More snow fell through the night, obliterating their tire tracks and piling up against the stoop. When they awoke it was still drifting earthward, muting everything it touched. By tacit agreement, they didn't turn on the television or the radio. Instead, they made love again, devouring several plates of scrambled eggs and bacon afterward, and set out for a walk in the woods.

Wearing her oldest jeans and her mother's shapeless down jacket, Katya led Nikolai to the beaver pond where she'd played as a child. Next stop was a woodlot clearing where deer sometimes grazed. A silent but bright-eyed sparrow hopped from one heavily laden branch to another, shaking little clumps of snow into their eyes.

Lying down in a pristine drift, Katya spread her arms to make a snow angel impression for the man she loved. As he watched, a flame of desire leapt into Nikolai's eyes. Moments later he was covering her with his body.

Instantly she thought of the time the militiaman had accosted them as they'd stuffed each others' coats with snow. I can't be part of that world anymore, she thought. But Nikolai has a choice.

"Stay with me. Stay!" she burst out, surprising herself as much as him. "If you asked for asylum, the United States would have to grant it. Will would know what to do...."

The minute the words were out, she wanted to bite her tongue. She hadn't meant to bludgeon him with the idea like that. At first, Nikolai didn't answer as he continued to hold her. When he finally spoke, she could hear the sadness in his voice.

"Even if I wanted to leave my country, I couldn't," he said. "My family would suffer. Please, darling...let's not talk about it. We don't want to ruin what little time we have left."

The sun came out around noon—weakly at first through a break in the clouds and then with a burst of radiance that spangled the new-fallen snow. Desperately trying to hide the misery she felt, Katya bustled about with forced cheerfulness, straightening the house in case her parents decided to come home early. It was as if she'd had a premonition. Nikolai had just drawn her down on the couch to insist she forget him when their car pulled into the lane.

"Ivor? Betty? Is that you?" her mother's voice called, naming two of the volunteer translators who had keys to the house.

"No, Mom...it's me." Shaky from butting heads with Nikolai on such a painful subject, Katya stood up and advanced slowly in her mother's direction.

"Sweetheart, I thought ..." Petra hesitated, catching sight of Nikolai, who had risen to greet her as well. "We saw your smoke coming from the chimney," she said. "But we never dreamed ..."

Coming up behind her, Alex Dane stepped into the living room. He looked distinguished yet somehow arty in his sherpa-lined jacket with suede patches on the elbows. As Katya expected, his somewhat stern, still handsome face wore a question.

"Mom, Dad, I want you to meet Nikolai," she said softly, praying they'd understand. "He's here in the U.S. because of the Vronsky situation. We were on our way to Rice Lake so he and his colleagues could talk with the boy when we got lost in the snowstorm. We ended up here."

Katya looks like her father, but she has her mother's eyes, Nikolai thought. Both of them are very refined, intelligent people—the sort my parents would enjoy knowing as friends. "I'm very pleased to make your acquaintance at last, Dr. and Mrs. Dane," he said in a quiet voice.

Swiftly the Danes exchanged a look. Katya's "lost in the snow" story was patently false, and they quickly rejected it. She watched as, with the wordless communication of the long-married, they asked each other what was expected of them.

Immediately after her escape from the Soviet Union, Alex had wanted to tan Nikolai's hide. Throughout the long months of his daughter's pregnancy he'd inveighed repeatedly against the sort of man who'd abuse Lev's trust and take an inexperienced young woman like Katya to bed. None of her protestations that she'd talked Nikolai into making love to her had changed his mind one bit.

Now she wondered if he could let bygones be bygones, allow his gratitude to come to the fore. It was thanks to Nikolai that I returned at all, Dad, she reminded him silently. You don't know what he went through on my behalf.

But Alex Dane had left Russia for a reason. And perhaps he could guess. Slowly he held out his hand. "At last we have the opportunity to thank you for helping our beloved daughter regain her freedom, Major Dvorov," he said, taking Nikolai's hand in a firm grip.

"It's 'Colonel' now," Katya corrected, beaming at him with relief and pride.

Embracing their unexpected guest, Petra telegraphed a message to her daughter. What about Davey? she demanded. Does Nikolai know?

Aching with guilt that she must keep their son's parentage a secret from Nikolai, Katya shook her head. But she still had what she considered good reasons for not confessing the truth. Our private time together is at an end, she thought as her parents engaged him in conversation. But I'll be able to see him, even touch him, for a little while yet.

She, Nikolai and her parents were talking by the fire when Will and a state trooper arrived. Keenly attuned to his surroundings, Nikolai was the first to hear them approach. "I think your friend has found us," he said, giving Katya a look.

Will was furious, as she'd expected, though he hid it well. A career diplomat, he was too professional to castigate Katya in front of Nikolai and her parents. Yet he couldn't keep a trace of bitterness from his voice.

"What happened?" he demanded once the social niceties had been observed. "We've been cooling our heels in a Rice Lake motel while the highway patrol searched for you and Mischa Vronsky."

Knowing he wasn't likely to believe her, Katya repeated the story she'd told her folks. "We must have taken a wrong turn," she theorized. "We were almost here before I realized our mistake. The weather was so awful it seemed prudent to stay."

Will's expression didn't change. "Why didn't you call, then?" he said reasonably. "You knew our destination."

Katya swallowed. There goes my job, she thought. But considering the way I feel about Nikolai, the trade-off was worth it. "The phones were down," she said, hating herself for the lie.

There was an instrument on the table beside her father's chair, and Will lifted the receiver. "It's working now," he shrugged.

The young policeman who'd accompanied him glanced from her to Nikolai and back again. He didn't say a word.

The Danes had known their daughter's boss since her dramatic return to the United States. In addition, they'd met him several times in Washington since she'd gone to work for him. Both considered him likely husband material, Katya knew. Sensing things were amiss and no doubt guessing the reason, Petra offered a fresh pot of coffee and slices of her famous walnut sponge cake.

"I'm sorry, Mrs. Dane, but we'll have to pass." Though his tone expressed polite regret, Will was clearly adamant. "The roads have been plowed, and they've located the Vronsky child," he added. "I'd appreciate it, Colonel Dvorov, if you and Kat could get your things together."

Holding hands but saying very little, Katya and Nikolai followed Will and the state trooper to the latter's headquarters in Spooner. Another day or two and he'll be gone, she thought. I may never see him again. Why can't people who love each other come and go freely in this world?

There was a tense moment with Irina Maximova when they arrived. But though the woman glared at them with actual hatred in her eyes, she didn't say anything. Vanya greeted them with a tolerant look.

Fortunately everyone agreed on one thing: they should visit Mischa Vronsky as soon as possible. Arranging it so Katya traveled with Vanya and Dr. Maximova in one car while he, Nikolai and the state trooper led the way in another, Will escorted them to the Vladimir Povich farm.

The sun was a flat, red disk sinking slowly toward the horizon when they arrived. Unlike the Dane acreage, the Povich place wasn't prosperous. A gaunt house and sagging barn were surrounded with tumbledown outbuildings and a few half-dead trees.

From Vanya, Katya learned that the neighbor who'd been hiding Mischa had taken refuge there with her married sister. Both women were hostile and fiercely protective of the boy when they opened the door.

The brother-in-law, a burly, plain-spoken man, also seemed ready to do battle for him. "I'm not sure we should talk to you. We plan to hire a lawyer to handle Mischa's case," he announced, as if even the intent might offer them some protection.

Katya doubted any of them had the money for a retainer, let alone a protracted legal battle if the U.S. government sided with the Soviets. Mischa himself—the charming, freckle-faced boy whose likeness she'd seen on numerous telecasts before getting personally involved with his case—merely stared at them without a word.

These people wouldn't even let us in the door if it weren't for our friend the state trooper here, she guessed. And I don't blame them. We don't have a court order.

But she knew a kidnapping charge had been mentioned, and the Poviches would be aware of that. Eyeing them warily, Vladimir Povich invited them into his shabby, old-fashioned living room.

What a far cry this is from Geneva and the blue-ribbon disarmament talks that are carried out in that illustrious city, Katya thought, noting the neatly mended slipcovers and faded pictures on the walls. The fate of the world doesn't hang in the balance here, just one boy's destiny. But he has a right to live as he chooses. The thought that she and Nikolai would be denied that right brought tears to her eyes.

Fortunately nobody was paying much attention to her. His voice gentle, Nikolai had begun to question the boy. As if he were a passerby with no stake in the situation's outcome, he asked Mischa what he liked best about America and the Soviet Union respectively.

"You say Russia's not so bad, but the U.S. is better...am I correct?" he asked without a hint of disapproval. "And that's why you want to stay?"

Mischa nodded sullenly.

"Well, let me tell you something, son. In this life, you get only one set of parents. That's all. Right now, yours are inconsolable. Your mother cries all the time. And your father can't sleep...."

"I can't help that. I told them they shouldn't go back!" For all his bravado, a flicker of concern crossed Mischa's face.

Nikolai gave a fatalistic shrug. "Maybe you were right and they were wrong," he said. "Who knows? The fact is, they did go back. Your parents love you, and the Soviet Union is still your country. You belong there, with them."

"No! America is my country!"

Though Nikolai had spoken in Russian with Katya translating for Will, Mischa answered him defiantly in English. He was obviously close to tears.

"You're too young to decide such matters," Nikolai asserted. "Don't you love your parents? Don't you want to see them again?"

The boy's tears spilled over at that, and he brushed them aside with clumsy fingers. Katya wanted to shake Nikolai and take Mischa into her arms. He was only eleven, after all. Just a baby. Though they looked nothing alike, he reminded her of her son.

But Mischa didn't give in. He faced Nikolai as if they were two adults, squaring off against each other. "Of course I do!" he cried, unconsciously falling back on the use of his native Russian in his distress. "Don't you know anything? Here in this country, I'm an orphan. But if I go back with you now, I'll never have another chance to live as I wish."

"He's right, Nikolai," Katya put in, violating the dictates of protocol. "You know the boy is right."

For a moment their eyes met, and she saw that, in some respects at least, Nikolai felt as she did. Not answering her, he proposed that he and his fellow Soviets step outside for a moment. She watched through the window as the three of them stood deep in conversation beside the Poviches' front stoop, their profiles harshly outlined by a bare bulb that hung overhead. By now the sun had set and the temperature was dropping. Their breath smoked and plumed on the air.

While the Soviets conferred, the Poviches and Mischa withdrew to the dining room to wait. Katya noted a lingering aroma of cabbage and some kind of meat. To her chagrin, she was left alone with Will in the living room.

"We have to talk, Kat," he said.

"I suppose you're right," she answered. "No doubt you'd like my resignation. But it'll have to wait."

A moment later, Nikolai and his colleagues filed back into the room. "I have an idea that may solve our problem," he announced, not glancing in Katya's direction. "Tell me something, Mischa... would you agree to return to the Soviet Union if I could get an ironclad guarantee that when you're eighteen you'll be allowed to live where you choose?"

For a moment, nobody said a word. Clearly the boy was stunned by the idea. "How can you do that?" he asked at last.

"I'm not sure I can," Nikolai admitted. "But I'm willing to give it a try."

Again dead silence filled the room. "Maybe...I don't know," Mischa answered in a shaken voice.

As wise as Will in the ways of diplomacy, Nikolai didn't press his luck. Instead, he turned to Vladimir, who obviously hadn't quite assimilated what was happening.

"I can't arrange things tonight," he confided, as if the two of them had sworn to cooperate. "It's 3:00 a.m. in Moscow, and top party officials don't like being rousted out of their beds. But in a few hours, it will be possible to call them. I'll be back sometime tomorrow with an answer, if you permit."

Reluctantly, after conferring with the two women and the boy, Vladimir gave his consent.

They spent the night at the Rice Lake motel. Will had dinner sent in, and Katya ate alone in her room. She was asleep when Nikolai placed the initial call to his father at midnight from Will Chalmers' phone.

The call took nearly an hour to go through. As they waited, Nikolai and Will watched a late-night movie on television. Its subject was the French revolution, and they traded a few barbs about the meaning of freedom and democracy. Will had provided the liquor, and he sipped morosely at a Scotch while Nikolai had a few vodkas.

"Look, Chalmers," Nikolai said finally, stretching out on the bed. "We need to set something straight. In no way did Katya Dane betray you or her country. The storm...our need to be together..." He shrugged. "What happened, did. We're still man and wife; neither of us ever divorced the other. Tomorrow I'm going to tell her she must go ahead with that. Hopefully she'll be ready to love again someday."

As he watched his American counterpart through narrowed eyes, Nikolai gave no hint of what he felt. By contrast, Will's face was a battleground of conflicting emotions. The phone rang, and with an expression of relief, Will picked it up. "Your party in Moscow is on the line," he said, passing Nikolai the receiver.

The conversation with Dmitri was brief. Quickly understanding what was needed, Nikolai's father agreed to see what he could do. They would have to wait until he could arrange a meeting with the Soviet President.

"If possible, I'll call you back by 10:00 a.m. Wisconsin time," he said, taking down the number of the highway patrol office in Spooner where they would be at that hour. He advised Nikolai to get some sleep.

Their group ate an early breakfast at a small cafe— ham, toast, coffee and orange juice, eggs over easy. Nobody said very much. Katya had dark circles under her eyes.

They arrived at District Seven headquarters around nine, parking outside the low stone building. The day was clear, windy and cold. Atop twin poles, the Stars and Stripes and the Wisconsin state flag snapped briskly in the breeze.

The dispatcher informed them that nobody had called yet. Nikolai glanced at Will.

"Come, Katya," he said, guessing Will wouldn't object. "Let's stretch our legs while we wait. Somebody can hail us if my father calls."

With Dmitri expected to phone at any moment, they couldn't go far. Huddled in her sable coat, Katya strolled at his side, not really seeing the state highway maintenance equipment yard, nearby motels and scattering of mobile homes that lined the road.

"I know what you're going to say," she told him, taking the initiative away from him. "You're going to insist that I divorce you. Well, you can save your breath. I won't."

Pain flickered in his eyes. "Be sensible, *drushenka*," he said. "You know I love you more than life itself. But our situation is an impossible one. This may be the last time we'll ever see each other. You owe it to yourself— and your son—to find some happiness."

Davey's my best argument, she thought. But I don't dare use it. Besides, I want Nikolai to stay for my sake.

"Let me tell you about my housemate," she said, trying a different tack. "Midge is psychic, and she has some far-out ideas. But some of them make sense to me. She has a theory that we live many lifetimes, because we have so much to learn.

"Midge thinks that . . . if we must return to this earth over and over, we should be able to do so with those we love. But in subsequent lifetimes, she points out, we could find ourselves living anywhere. She believes that people, not countries, are our connections in the universe."

For the first time, Nikolai appeared to hesitate. "Don't you think I want to be with you?" he asked. "Never mind countries...during the past few days, I've reassessed their importance in the scheme of things. But my family, Katya...how can I betray them? My father's career would be destroyed if I did what you're suggesting!''

I'll be destroyed if you don't, Katya thought as they turned and headed back toward police headquarters. I don't think I can take thirty or forty years alone.

Just then, they saw Will waving to them from the parking lot. "Colonel Dvorov!" he shouted. "Your father's on the phone!"

Dmitri had good news. When Mischa reached eighteen, he would be allowed a choice of citizenship. The Soviet President had given his word. It's settled then, Katya thought, feeling something close to despair. If Mischa decides he can believe what Nikolai tells him, the two of them will be leaving...perhaps today.

They returned to the Povich farm at noon. Several reporters had gotten wind of Mischa's hiding place, and they shoved microphones and cameras at Will and Nikolai as their party pulled into the drive. Only the presence of several more state troopers on the property kept them from barging into the house.

Tensely Mischa and his protectors waited for them behind tightly drawn curtains. As Nikolai relayed his father's message, the boy's eagerness to see his parents became painfully obvious. Yet he didn't comment immediately. Instead, he spoke in a low voice to Vladimir Povich and the two women for several moments.

"How do I know I can trust you?" he asked Nikolai at last.

Katya could see the man she loved had already decided how to handle that question. "We'll hold a press conference in Washington before departing for the Soviet

Union," he promised without hesitation. "The world will witness our contract."

Ultimately Mischa agreed to go along with the plan. Katya could see it was a relief for him not to defy his parents any longer. With a quick call from Will to the undersecretary and another to the airport in Hayward to charter a light plane for the trip back to Chicago, they were on their way.

"No comment," Will shouted at the reporters, shielding Mischa as they emerged from the house. "The Poviches have asked not to be disturbed. We'll have a statement for you this evening in Washington."

A stout, unyielding presence, Irina sat beside Nikolai on the plane. Will had arranged that Katya accompany Mischa, perhaps hoping a woman's presence would have a calming effect. Trying to set the boy at his ease, she encouraged him to talk about his aunts, uncles and cousins in Russia.

My child has relatives there, too, she longed to shout. But he won't ever see them. Or his father. Nikolai *can't* go away like this, with so much unsaid between us! But she still wasn't ready to use the one argument that might change his mind.

In Chicago, they were obliged to dodge the press again as they gathered Mischa's possessions and waited while he said goodbye to relatives and friends. Somebody brought him a Chicago Cubs' sweatshirt. As a farewell gesture, they had hot dogs for lunch.

The flight to Washington landed at dusk. This time, an even larger contingent of reporters was waiting for them. They got off the plane to face floodlights and a battery of microphones.

"Good work!" the undersecretary greeted Will, including Katya in his praise. "The secretary is pleased."

TV cameras were grinding away as he announced to the waiting crowd that an agreement had been reached. Jovially he elaborated on its nature, stepping back so Nikolai could confirm the details. At reporters' urging, they allowed Mischa to say a few words.

Once that was done, the undersecretary offered to answer questions. Indicating he didn't have anything further to say, Nikolai moved to stand by Katya's side. "I love you," he whispered, surreptitiously catching hold of her hand. "Never forget that, my darling. But you must divorce me. Make a life for yourself."

She was about to refuse again when a small boy darted between the military police who were keeping back the media and a group of protesters within bounds. To Katya's astonishment, it was Davey—a miniature Nikolai with his mop of dark hair and melting brown eyes.

"Mommy, Mommy!" he cried.

A second later, Katya's son was tugging at her skirt. Though her heart turned over, she tried to smother her dismay. "It's all right . . . he's mine," she told a frowning security guard.

"Sorry," Midge apologized in a whisper, once the guard had let her pass. "He wanted to come to the airport to meet you. I never dreamed he'd pull something like this."

Pausing briefly at the flurry of activity, the undersecretary proceeded with the comment he was making. In the meantime, Nikolai was staring at Davey.

"Your son is older than you said," he observed, a look of recognition dawning on his face. "Why don't you introduce us?"

"Davey, this is Nikolai Dvorov," she said, wishing she could sink through the pavement.

Solemnly Davey held out his hand. "Hi. I'm David Nicholas Dane," he told his father.

There wasn't time for them to do anything more than smile at each other. All too quickly, the Soviets' plane was ready to take off for London, where they would spend the night at their embassy before flying on to Moscow.

"Nikolai..." Katya began, words suddenly inadequate to the situation.

"He's my son, isn't he?" he asked.

"Yes," she admitted. In that moment, pride ceased to mean anything. "Please...stay with us," she begged.

Irina and Vanya were motioning him to get aboard the plane.

"I have to go," he said, looking at Davey again and then at her. "But I'll try...if there's a way, I promise I'll try, my darling. I love you so much."

She couldn't even kiss him goodbye. A few minutes later his Aeroflot jet was lifting off the runway. Tears ran down her cheeks as it gained altitude, shrinking to a tiny cluster of lights against a lowering sky.

"Take your son and go home," Will murmured sympathetically at her elbow. "I was way off base, getting upset with you the way I did. Everything turned out all right, and the job is still yours if you want it. I don't expect to see you in the office for at least a week."

At the Georgetown house she shared with Midge, Katya took a sleeping pill. Drained, weary and incredibly lonely for Nikolai already, she sunk into a state that was more coma than dream. Yet the recent scenario involving them, Mischa, Will and the others repeated endlessly, like a film loop in her head. Each time it became more distorted. In the end, Nikolai disappeared.

The following day was Saturday, and Midge kept Davey busy so she could sleep. Though Katya woke off and on throughout the day, each time she found oblivion preferable to reality. Nikolai had said he would try, and hope shot through her whenever she thought of that. But the odds were against them, and she knew it. He wouldn't expose his father to ruin. Barring some miracle, they'd have to live apart.

It was nearly six-thirty when Midge finally persuaded her to get up and have some coffee. Davey was eating a plate of spaghetti when she wandered into the breakfast room. Her housemate had just turned on the evening news.

Both she and Midge tensed when a segment came on about Mischa's arrival in the Soviet Union. The boy's reunion with his parents was an emotional, touching one. But to their surprise, Nikolai didn't get off the plane.

"In an odd twist to this already unusual story," the CBS anchorman said, "Nikolai Dvorov, the delegate who arranged the deal that led to Mischa Vronsky's reunion with his parents, didn't return with his Soviet colleagues to Moscow. Remaining behind in London, he was killed by an IRA bomb blast this afternoon. Investigators from Scotland Yard speculate that the blast was a mistake. Apparently it had been aimed at an unidentified British cabinet minister."

Chapter 13

*N*o-o-o! *It can't be!"*

Katya's screams rent the air, ripping the cozy quiet of the breakfast room to shreds. Staring at the television screen, which was now showing unrest in the Middle East, she saw only a London street and a twisted, blackened hulk of metal that had once been a car. If Nikolai had been in that car, she knew, his body would be reduced to infinitesimally small fragments of blood and bone. Handsome, capable Nikolai—the man she loved.

"Mommy! Mommy! What's the matter?" Davey dropped his fork so that spaghetti slithered across the tabletop. Her distress and horror instantly communicated to him, he flung his arms around her neck.

For her part, Midge had gone white as a sheet. "Dear God," she whispered as she unconsciously pleated a dish towel between her fingers. "It can't be true. There must be some mistake."

A moment later, she put her arms around Katya, too.

The phone rang, and Midge dealt with her shock sufficiently to answer it. Still seated at the table, Katya had begun to rock back and forth with Davey in her lap. Though she seemed to be staring at some inner vision, her eyes were still fixed sightlessly on the television set. "No...no...no..." she crooned to herself.

The caller was Will. "Has she seen the news?" he asked without preamble.

Despite her dismay and confusion, Midge recognized his voice. "We had just turned it on," she answered. "Is it..."

"True? I'm afraid so. I just spoke to our man in London. The blast was so fierce they can't find a body. But several witnesses saw Dvorov getting into the car just moments before it blew."

Midge winced as if he'd struck her. "Surely you don't want me to tell her that!"

"Good God, no. If she asks for details, just say they're sketchy yet." Will cleared his throat as if he too felt shaken by what had occurred. "This is a terrible thing," he said. "How's she taking it?"

Glancing at Katya, Midge shook her head. "Not very well, I'm afraid. I don't think she quite believes it yet. But when the truth sinks in...she should see a doctor."

"I think that's a good idea." He paused, as if making a mental checklist of what had to be done. "I'll send someone over," he added in a more normal tone. "And I'll call her parents. I'm sure they'll want to catch the first flight to Washington."

Though she seemed almost anesthetized, a thousand images were whirling through Katya's head. She imagined Nikolai getting off the plane from Russia and sitting across the table from her at the Swiss embassy. Nikolai making love to her in the firelight at her parents' farmhouse. Nikolai being blown to bits, so that even if she renounced everything to search the earth for him, she couldn't find him anywhere.

With a moan, she rested her cheek against Davey's hair. Her little boy looked so much like his father. Yet they'd only been able to meet for a moment. They should have shared a whole childhood of sledding and zoo trips and baseball games.

I'll try, Nikolai had told her with such love in his eyes. *If there's a way, I promise I'll try, my darling.* But no matter how much he'd wanted to, the man who meant more than life to her wouldn't be coming back to them.

Instead, he'd been killed—by mistake, if the news reports were to be believed. Or maybe it had only been arranged to look that way by a hit man from Nikolai's own agency. To Katya, the how and why of it didn't matter. What mattered was that her husband was gone.

I shouldn't have complained that he had to leave me, she thought. *At least he would have been alive and well. I could picture what he was doing in Russia. Imagine him happy sometimes.* In the new dimension she inhabited, Nikolai didn't exist.

With sudden, unbearable anguish, Katya gathered her child close. *A person can't be alive one minute and then vanish without a trace the next, leaving nothing but a void in the space he once occupied,* she told herself. *Can he? Nikolai was real. He loved me. He can't just disappear!*

Blinking, she looked up at Midge, her eyes hollow and her face somehow featureless, like a beach that has been swept bare by a hurricane. "I refuse to let this happen," she said.

"Oh, Kat..." Her housemate floundered, clearly unable to come up with an answer that might bring her an iota of comfort. "My dear, I'm so sorry," she quavered, enfolding them both.

Already whimpering, Davey started to cry.

When the phone rang a second time, it was Petra Dane. Getting to her feet though she moved like an automaton, Katya took the call. "If Nikolai's gone, I don't want to live, Mom," she said without intonation, suddenly realizing that was how she felt.

Petra's love and sorrow reached out to her via the network of telephone equipment, bridging the distance like an embrace.

"I know you don't, sweetheart," her mother answered helplessly. "He was a fine man, and we're very grateful to him. Right now, he'd want you to hang on and think of your son...even if he never knew Davey was his. Try to have courage for his sake, darling. Your father and I will be there just as soon as we can get reservations."

Somehow Will found a doctor who was willing to make house calls. The gray-haired physician was both professional and sympathetic. He gave Katya a shot to calm her and help her sleep. He also left a prescription for tranquilizers.

Acting as if he weren't quite sure of his welcome, Will came over, too. He volunteered to entertain Davey while Midge put Katya to bed. He was still there at sunrise, hunched over a mug of coffee with Katya's housemate, when the Danes arrived.

Katya didn't wake for a long, long time. When she finally stirred, touched by a stray beam of sunlight that had crept past her tightly closed bedroom blinds, she had a moment's respite. Then the brutal truth of what had happened hit her again, crashing like a mailed fist into the softest part of her stomach.

Nikolai was dead . . . dead . . . dead. For the first time since viewing the newscast that had announced his fate, she began to weep.

It was spring. Walking in her parents' Wisconsin apple orchard while Davey attended nursery school, Katya reviewed those terrible days. Next week, it would be three months since Nikolai had died.

She could say it now, without coming unglued or crying as if her heart must break. At least sometimes she could. Other times, the tears would flow like water from a broken faucet, and she wouldn't be able to curb them completely for hours.

There hadn't been a body or a funeral. Nothing to make what had happened seem final. Just that awful, aching emptiness where Nikolai had been. Even her desire to contact the Dvorovs and express her sorrow to them would remain forever frustrated.

It was the death card, she thought, remembering Midge's tarot reading the day Nikolai had reappeared in her life. For once it *had* signified death, not a new beginning. That night at the airport, she shouldn't have let him go.

She knew about the stages of grief, of course. Denial, guilt, anger and finally acceptance. Thinking that somehow she could have prevented the explosion that had killed him definitely fit into the guilt category. On a rational plane, she knew she could have done nothing to stop it.

Yet while she seemed to hover between guilt and impotent rage, she felt no acceptance in her heart. In the absence of any proof, save eyewitness accounts placing Nikolai in the car a few seconds before the blast, nothing about what had befallen them seemed real to her.

All of her faith in happy endings was gone. Why does the essence of life have to be sorrow, she asked herself? The greatest happiness must always be tinged with it, like a tear in the finest silk or a stain on velvet. Why must we always see the specter of loss grinning at our wedding feast?

Everywhere she looked, the natural world seemed to mock her grief. The day, balmy but cool, reminded her of a similar occasion when she'd waltzed with Nikolai in a field of flowers near his parents' dacha. If only she could have preserved that moment in amber, the way she'd wanted to then.

Yet it was difficult not to feel some kinship with the bursting life around her, heralded by the chirping of birds and buzzing of bees, the delicate scent of the apple blossoms. Today, each of the gnarled old trees in her parents' orchard wore a perfumed mantle of lacy pink. As spring lengthened into summer, small green apples would appear. In the fall, they'd be red. She and Davey would help harvest them. Alex and several of his volunteers who were also good friends would press them into cider. Supposedly there was a time for everything and a purpose under heaven. But she wasn't able to see it yet.

Three months earlier, hit by the catastrophic suddenness of Nikolai's loss, she'd given up her Washington job over Will's objections and moved back to Wisconsin to stay. By now, Davey was happily settled in a Hayward nursery school. Though he missed Midge, his grandparents made up for it. Katya was thinking of teaching international relations at a local junior college, beginning with the fall semester. Life had to go on, for her little boy's sake.

I wish he and Nikolai could have known each other, she thought. They'd have loved each other so much. But

Davey would never have any of the sometimes magnificent, sometimes trivial, memories that returned to haunt her at odd moments.

She turned at the sound of Petra's voice.

"Katya," her mother called, a note of surprise in her words. "Will Chalmers is here to see you from Washington."

What in the world was he doing here? Before Katya could return to the house, Will was striding out to meet her. She would have recognized his lanky, loose-jointed figure anywhere.

"Hello, Will," she said.

"I've missed you, Kat." He gave her a brief, hard hug and then stepped back, as if reminding himself she didn't want his affection.

"And I've missed you." But there was no real enthusiasm in her tone.

"You're looking well," he said, pretending not to notice. "How's it going, my dear?"

Katya shook back her tumble of light-brown curls. "A little better, I think. I can sleep for six hours at a crack now. And my dreams aren't as tormented as they once were."

For a moment they simply stood there, looking at each other and thinking their separate thoughts. For her part, Katya was remembering the pain of the last time they were together.

"What are you doing here, Will?" she asked. "My parents' farm is hardly on the beaten path."

"The truth is, we need your help."

Her brow furrowed in puzzlement. "I don't understand."

Will shrugged. "I can't tell you much about the situation to begin with," he said. "Just that it's a temporary assignment. A rather critical one. Would it be possible for you to come back to Washington with me for a couple of weeks?''

Stubbornly Katya shook her head at the idea of getting involved in State Department business again. ''You know I'm finished with all that,'' she said. ''The memories it would bring back are just too difficult to face.''

Will persisted in his request, and gradually, as they talked, she found herself wavering. Of late she'd become restless at her parents' house, with little to do but brood. At least a trip to Washington might provide a diversion.

Finally she agreed on a provisional basis. ''If Mom and Dad are willing to watch Davey *and* if the memories don't prove to be too much, I'll do it,'' she said.

Later seated beside Will on the plane, she realized he'd given up hope that someday they'd get together. I'm glad, she thought. Will is a fine person, and I like him very much. But he isn't Nikolai. And Nikolai is the only man I'll ever love.

The weather in Washington was even lovelier, with a high in the low seventies, clear skies and a soft southern breeze stirring the fresh, green foliage. Gathering up her things, Katya looked forward to contacting Midge as soon as she was settled in the city.

To her surprise, they didn't head into Washington directly from the airport. Instead, Will instructed their driver to take a route leading into the Virginia countryside.

''Where are we going?'' she asked finally. ''I thought . . .''

But Will was unusually closedmouthed. ''You'll see,'' he answered. ''Perhaps you'll find it familiar.''

A few minutes later they pulled into the entrance of a large country estate. To her amazement, Katya recognized the safe house where she'd stayed immediately following her return to the United States. Yes, there were the same venerable oaks and glossy magnolias lining the drive, the classic red-brick mansion she remembered.

Several members of Will's staff were waiting for them in the gatehouse.

"The party I want you to meet is waiting at the main residence," he said, giving her a benevolent look.

Everyone else was staring at her with the same odd expression.

"I don't understand what this is all about," she protested, confused and troubled. "What am I supposed to say to him? Or her?"

Still her former boss refused to explain. "I'm sure you'll think of something," he answered, giving her a little shove.

Realizing no one was going to satisfy her curiosity, Katya set off down the drive. Partially obscured by hundred-year-old plantings, the main house beckoned. Its white pillars gleamed in the sunlight that filtered through the trees.

As Katya approached, a figure moved out onto the porch, though it remained in shadow. It's a man, probably in his fifties, she thought. A bespectacled man whose reddish beard is salted with gray. He looked slightly bent at the shoulders, as if he had carried a load of troubles. The color of his hair was hidden by a baseball cap.

Then suddenly he straightened, and she realized the man she'd come so far to see was much younger than she'd guessed. An effort had been made to disguise that fact. There was something about him....

With a start, she noted broad shoulders, a compact, muscular physique. Making things easier for her, he doffed his cap to reveal thick, dark hair that was liberally streaked with gray as part of the camouflage attempt.

It can't be! she told herself, hesitating. *He's dead. I know he is, carried off by a car bomb in London.*

As if he could read her thoughts, the man Will had asked her to meet moved partially into the light. Doubting the evidence of her senses, she took one step toward him and then another. Had she gone mad as a result of too much grief, too many nights spent thinking about him? Or was she asleep in her bed at her parents' farm at that very moment and only dreaming this?

"Katya," he said, holding out his arms to her. His dark eyes—Nikolai's eyes—were overflowing with love.

She would have known those eyes, that deep, Russian-accented voice anywhere. It was Nikolai! Alive and whole—not an apparition! Uncertainty collapsed like a house of cards, and she ran to him, burrowing frantically against his chest.

"Nikolai!" she wept, giving herself over into his keeping. "It's you, really you! You're not dead! Oh, my love!"

The ferocity of his embrace had lifted her off her feet. Achingly he held her, his strong fingers digging into her flesh through the lightweight fabric of her linen skirt and silk blouse. "Yes, *drushenka*," he said hoarsely. "Alive and well, here in the United States."

"If you only knew..." Her face was wet with tears when she raised it to his. Like a blind woman, she ran her fingertips over his eyes, his cheeks, his mouth, verifying the impossible as she reclaimed him in a frenzied ritual of touch.

"I love you so much," he whispered.

"And I love you, too."

Like an avalanche, his mouth descended on hers. All the pent-up frustration he'd had to endure, all the despair and grief she'd suffered, fell away in a single kiss. So rapacious and loving she wasn't sure she could bear it, he tasted her, savored her, devoured her sweetness. The unaccustomed roughness of his beard scraped her chin as, delving inside, his tongue promised a much deeper union.

For her part, Katya clung to him as if she'd never let him go. Eagerly her tongue dueled with his as, pressing tightly against him, her breasts were flattened against hard pectoral muscles. A well of longing opening deep within her, she could feel the firm outline of his desire.

"Oh, Nikky," she gasped. "I want you so!"

From the gatehouse, she caught a flash of sunlight on what might be glass or metal. Someone was watching them through binoculars. Katya could almost hear Will remark dryly, "I see things are going well."

Nikolai had noticed it, too. "Come into the house," he said, drawing her into its seclusion. "Upstairs there's privacy and a big bed for us to wrestle in. My arms have been empty of you much too long."

Barely aware of the crystal chandelier and black-and-white marble-paved foyer she'd last seen four years earlier, Katya clung to the man she loved as they mounted one wing of a formally balanced Georgian staircase.

The room he'd been using opened off the second-floor gallery. His bed was an antique four-poster, the sort George Washington might have slept in. She saw a carafe of water on the night stand, rumpled sheets. Several unfamiliar shirts and a spare pair of trousers were draped over wooden hangers in an open closet. A few basic toilet articles lay scattered on a dresser.

However he'd managed it, Nikolai had probably come over with little more than the shirt on his back. How long had he been secreted away, undergoing a thorough grilling by Will and her former colleagues, while she'd grieved in anguish for him?

"Darling..." she began, then let the question go.

There were far more urgent priorities at the moment than extracting some answers from him. Kissing her again with a marauding sweetness that made her knees go weak, he set aside the horn-rimmed glasses that were part of his disguise. His beautiful eyes burned into hers as he unbuttoned his shirt.

"Yes," Katya breathed, imitating him. "Oh, yes, Nikolai..."

Feverishly she watched him undress as she removed her cream-colored blouse and camisole, let her nubby topaz linen skirt drop to her feet.

He took off her lace bikini panties himself. Magnificently naked, he knelt to kiss her breasts. The sensations caused by the scraping of his beard against her tender skin and the wet tugging of his mouth on her nipples nearly drove her out of her head. Deep within, her need for him was expanding and growing—so rapidly she thought it must encompass the earth.

In a wordless paean of praise, he ran his hands over the supple curves of her hips and thighs. Katya shut her eyes, unconsciously swaying at the tumult of pleasure she felt.

"Please, Nikolai," she moaned, urging him to his feet. "Come into me, darling. I want you to fill me, make me wild...."

Letting go of her briefly, he extracted a foil packet from the pocket of his discarded trousers. But she wouldn't let him use its contents.

"When I thought you were dead," she told him, "I wished desperately that we had made another baby. Davey needs a little brother or sister. And I need you . . . flooding into me with the life force that will outlast us both."

With a groan, he picked her up and carried her to the bed. The sweet preliminaries they'd do without would come later, she knew, as they made love again and again—stopping only to eat and sleep when their bodies cried out in protest. At long last, after so much denial and separation, they'd have all the time in the world.

Joining himself to her, Nikolai lit the fuse of her most passionate need. All too quickly she burned out of control, arching away from the mattress as the shudders took her. Seconds later he followed, making their union complete.

Like embers drifting down in the aftermath of a fireworks display, they lay sated in each other's arms. A light breeze stirred the curtains at an open window, cooling their brows and feathering over their heated skin. Katya could feel Nikolai's contentment as if it were her own.

For the rest of their lives, they'd be together. Yet she couldn't contain her curiosity another moment. "There are a lot of things I want to ask you," she said.

"And I have a lot to tell you."

Moving off her, he trailed one questing finger over the swell of her right breast, making its nipple stand up again. Her stomach was flat and taut, her waist incredibly slender. Yet if the spark of life were to ignite between them as urgently as it had before, she might already be pregnant. Considering the idea, Nikolai found he liked it very much.

"How did you manage to survive that car fire, make it here in one piece?" Katya asked. "You're more phoenix than fire bird, I think."

Nikolai grinned at the implied compliment. "The blast that was supposedly aimed at a British cabinet minister was staged by some friends of mine," he said. "I jumped out, and into a waiting van, just seconds before the car blew. We made it seem like a mix-up had occurred to throw the KGB off the scent. The car went up like an inferno. No one was terribly surprised when they couldn't find a body to hand over to the Soviets."

To Katya's surprise, he'd spoken as if his former allegiance didn't exist. Still finding his presence in the world—let alone her arms—difficult to believe, she snuggled against him.

"Why didn't you let me know sooner that you were all right?" she complained. "I've been through absolute hell, thinking I'd lost you for good."

"I know, dearest. But it couldn't be helped. For more than two months, I was in the hands of British intelligence. They refused to put a message through, saying it was for my own protection. Will and company got me a couple of weeks ago."

Katya's cheeks flushed with anger at the thought. "Why didn't *he* tell me at least?" she demanded. "He knows how I feel!"

"Hush, don't be angry with him. He was only doing his duty." Lovingly Nikolai drew her into the circle of his arm. "This is a pay-as-you-go world," he reminded her. "If I wanted to stay with you in the United States, I had to present Will with the price of admission, so to speak."

Suddenly the reality of Nikolai's situation hit home. "Oh, sweetheart," she mourned. "You didn't have to betray..."

Firmly he shook his head. "Don't worry about that. Though I may never see it again, I still love my country. I could never bring myself to betray it, no matter what the cost. What I ended up telling them was a favor to us both."

Loving and trusting him, Katya waited.

"I gave them the name of a master spy who's been cheating both sides," he explained. "It's Andrei Mikoyan. No doubt you remember him. I was able to offer them places and dates, describe several critical transactions. I just found out about his clandestine activities myself a few months ago."

Stunned that the husband of the woman who'd tried to prevent her escape had inadvertently paid for Nikolai's safe-conduct to the West, Katya was silent a moment.

"I feel so badly about your parents," she whispered at last. "Believing you're dead the way they do."

"You needn't," Nikolai answered. "I'm sure they miss me, just as I'll always miss them. But they know the truth. The phones of all high Soviet officials are tapped, and, long ago, my father and I adopted a secret code phrase. I was to use it if I ever had to disappear. Before my so-called death took place last January, I phoned him and inserted it into the conversation."

Absently she stroked his inverted triangle of dark chest hair, torn between sorrow for the Dvorovs and joy for Davey and herself. "Do you think they know you're with me?" she asked.

Framed by his impossible beard, Nikolai's mouth curved into a smile. "I imagine they can guess. My mother knew from the beginning how right we were for each other. And I think lately my father has realized it.

They're sufficiently in love to understand and to be glad we have each other."

The fact that Davey and any future children they might have would never know Lev or their Soviet grandparents was a sorrow they'd always share. But there was so much happiness between them, too—a whole life ahead of them to plan.

"I don't know how or where we're going to live," Nikolai mused, his thought running on the same wavelength as hers. "It's anybody's guess how I'll be able to earn our daily bread. Diplomacy is out, and I've given up spying for good. I'm getting too old to roll out of cars a few seconds before they blow, and I'd like to get a lot older with you at my side. But a book exposing KGB tactics or lectures on the evils of communism would smack too much of treachery for my taste."

He feels as if he's been cut adrift from everything that's familiar to him, she thought, beginning to understand. Except that unlike me when I was trapped in Russia, he can't hope to go home again. It'll be up to me to indoctrinate him into pizza, rock music, Fourth of July celebrations....

When it came to a job, why couldn't Nikolai teach?

As always, he was one step ahead of her. "I thought that once I got my legal alien status I might apply to lecture at a small college somewhere," he said. "After what we've been through, I have quite a lot to say about international cooperation. Maybe I could help Americans see the good in Soviet life, understand the changes that are happening there."

It was a goal worthy of his talent, energy and considerable intelligence. Together we'll make it happen, she thought. Nikolai will teach full-time, and I'll lecture part-time while I raise chickens, cows and babies. They would live on a farm in Wisconsin like her parents, of course. She didn't doubt it for a moment.

Stirring against her, Nikolai was ready to love again. That afternoon, as sunlight faded into dusk, they set a second and third seal on their reunion. Finally, ravenous from so much exertion, he phoned the gatehouse that they were ready for something to eat. As if he wished to make amends by participating in Katya's Americanization plan for the man she loved, Will sent them pizza and a cold six-pack. The aide who delivered them also brought up her bags.

The pizza—thin crust, Italian sausage, green pepper and mushroom—was stone cold. Doubtless it had been sitting around in its cardboard carton at the gatehouse for hours. After tying on a flowered robe, Katya reheated it in the upper half of the unfamiliar kitchen's double oven. It won't be the best, she thought. But it's a start.

When Nikolai got out a half-full bottle of vodka, she stayed his hand. "In the U.S.," she said uncompromisingly, "with pizza you drink beer."

They ate sitting cross-legged and seminaked on the bed. When their hunger was satisfied, Nikolai set aside the remains and stretched out beside her again.

"Tell me about our son," he requested. "I know what he looks like, but I want to discover what makes him happy. Learn how his mind works. Does he play cowboys and Indians? What did it feel like when you carried him in your body?"

As dusk blended into night and the soft chirping of crickets filtered into their room, Katya told Davey's father everything she could think of about their baby. His fondness for toy cars, his loving nature, his prowess at nursery school—all these things she shared with him.

"I love him so much already," Nikolai confessed after they'd made love again and turned out the light. "As much as I love you but in a different way. I hope that soon the three of us will be together."

Epilogue

Warm sunlight flooded the big bed where Katya still lay asleep. Lightly Nikolai touched her shoulder. Opening her eyes, she saw that he carried a tray with two steaming mugs of coffee and a bag of donuts.

"Wake up and drink this, my darling," he said. "Will just phoned from the gatehouse. We're going to have visitors in half an hour."

Rubbing the sleep from her eyes, she sat up and accepted a portion of the steaming brew. Darn Will, she thought, taking a calming sip. Can't he give us twenty-four hours? She wondered if he was bringing over the undersecretary. Or did he just want to question Nikolai again?

Whatever the case, they wouldn't be able to make love. Well, she thought, I owe it to the benign power of the universe to be gracious. Nikolai is alive, and we have each other. She gave him a lingering good-morning kiss.

Already showered and doused with a tangy-smelling cologne, he was wearing the pair of slacks she'd seen in the closet and a black polo shirt. Yet with the glasses and the beard that didn't match his hair, he still looked almost like a stranger.

I'd love him if his hair was purple and his beard a mass of polka dots, she thought as she got into the tub, pulled the curtains shut and turned on the spray. But maybe when things settle down a bit, we can get rid of some of the gray in his hair. He can go back to being his handsome self.

She had just pulled on jeans and a T-shirt, brushed her hair and added a dab of lipstick when she heard footsteps on the colonnade.

"They're here," Nikolai said.

They stepped out onto the second-floor gallery together. As they watched, the front door opened. It was Will and another man she didn't recognize.

And Davey.

"Mommy!" he shouted excitedly, catching sight of her and racing up the stairs as fast as his three-year-old legs would carry him. "Uncle Will sent for me! I came with his friend Joe on the plane!"

But it wasn't Katya who scooped him up into her arms. Instead, Nikolai's strong fingers fastened on his son as if somehow he could make up for lost years through the physical contact.

They'd met only once, briefly, and Nikolai looked very different now. It wasn't surprising that his son didn't recognize him.

"Hey!" Davey protested, trying to wriggle away. "I don't know you!"

There was such deep happiness in Nikolai's eyes that Katya could feel tears slipping down her cheeks.

"I know *you*," he told the boy, including her in the circle of his embrace. "You're David Nicholas, and you're crazy about miniature race cars. And I love you...and your mother...very much."

* * * * *

FOUR UNIQUE SERIES
FOR EVERY WOMAN YOU ARE...

Silhouette Romance

Love, at its most tender, provocative,
emotional...in stories that will make you laugh and
cry while bringing you the magic of falling in love.

6 titles
per month

Silhouette Special Edition

Sophisticated, substantial and packed with
emotion, these powerful novels of life and love will
capture your imagination and steal your heart.

6 titles
per month

SILHOUETTE *Desire*

Open the door to romance and passion. Humorous,
emotional, compelling—yet always a believable
and sensuous story—Silhouette Desire never
fails to deliver on the promise of love.

6 titles
per month

Silhouette Intimate Moments

Enter a world of excitement, of romance
heightened by suspense, adventure and the
passions every woman dreams of. Let us
sweep you away.

4 titles
per month

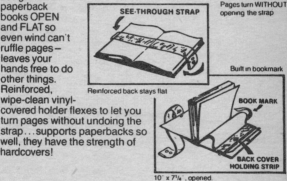